Tales
from
the
Cameron

Cam Serrom

To Liu Difen

Then, as all my souls be,
imparadised in you,
in whom alone
I understand, and grow, and see.
The rafters of my body, bone,
being still with you,
the muscle, sinew, and vein
which tile this house,
will come again.

A valediction of my name, in a window
John Donne

To unnamed friends

Contents

Tales

from

the

Cameron

Prologue

The Big Bang Theory suggests that the expansion of the universe is bell shaped and started from a point, a singularity, preceding the inflation and quantum fluctuations. That singularity, probably spherical if shape existed outside of it, contained a compressed universe. Over a long period of time, the slightly denser regions of the nearly uniformly distributed matter gravitationally attracted nearby matter and thus grew even denser, forming gas clouds, stars, galaxies, and the other astronomical structures observable today. The details of this process depend on the amount and type of matter in the universe. In physics, matter is a physical substance and is distinct from mind and spirit. It occupies space and is distinct from energy.

As a description of the origin of the universe, the Big Bang has significant bearing on religion and philosophy. As a result, it has become one of the liveliest areas in the discourse between science and religion. Some believe the Big Bang implies a creator, and some see its mention in their holy books, while others argue that Big Bang cosmology makes the notion of a creator superfluous.

At that point in time, did God grab that singularity, form it into a sphere, toss it up, and knock it out of the park with his Louisville Slugger? The movement of bodies suggests a bell-shaped path, which coincides perfectly with a well placed homerun.

If God hit that singularity out of the park, he must have done it with purpose and thought, leaving purpose to all bodies, and thought to their placement. This included synapse to some of its living matter. Before the Big Bang, that singularity existed in three dimensions. Inflation and Quantum Fluctuations required a forth dimension called time. The development and placement of galaxies, planets, and other bodies required a fifth dimension called thought.

Thought, the most generic and the most specific, is more than a superset of the other four dimensions. It has more forms than adjectives that man can be apply to it. Does thought travel like light? Can it be bundled and sent as is data in IP protocol, but with or without a receiving or sending address?

Light, with a negligible weight, is energy released from a star, but thought by itself exists without weight. Light continues after its star novas. Does thought continue after its owner dies?

Light, a form of energy, is absorbed by planets, but does it continue in space? Because it has mass, does it have a half-life? Thought will always continue if promulgated by those who absorbed it, and only if written or spoken can it be plagiarized.

God's thought, with the speed faster than light, manages the entire universe including stars, planets, and black holes. Man's visual thought is as fast as light, but his creative thought crawls, and those thoughts, good and bad, create his own black holes.

One may question the existence of God in a land without justice, and what kind of God must He be to allow the atrocities of man. How could this exist with the God of Abraham who talked to Moses and the prophets? We understand and accept by reading that original writ. God created heaven and earth, but is He, or did He create the universe?

Heaven, circumscribed by the distance man could see, did not include the entire universe, which even today remains a mystery. The heaven man could see was beyond the boundary of his solar system, and if taken as given implies that God managed those unseen solar systems as well.

That begs another question. Was man made in God's image or in the image He took on Earth? God created man to exist on a terrestrial planet composed of earth, metal, and rock. Man is not as solid as those materials, but he is well suited to the planet which they comprise. What form would life take on non-terrestrial planets composed of gases, and what form would God take? Would God be less solid on other planets composed of gases, as would be the beings he created? If true, the choice of forms is only one of God's dimensions. Man does not have that dimension, but God gave him another called thought.

That dimension does not have the magnanimity of God's. It is only partially inclusive, but thought, the fifth dimension, is the noblest and perhaps the only dimension He shares with man. Man's evaluation and application of that fifth dimension determines his salvation.

Time, the forth dimension, relates to and is involved with the first three but is not fully understood. Time is a tool, a variable, and a method of transport. It is only a constant to man. The other three are those the eye can see. The eye transmits a two dimensional image along with other information such as shadow. The brain takes this two dimensional image along with other information such as shadow and creates the third dimension as well as shades of color.

Where in God's world should one man survive and another be slowly destroyed? What dimensions existed to allow his existence and success, perhaps the seven deadly sins; and do they explain the black holes existing in man? Man's black holes, on earth, account for misery and destruction just as do the black holes in the universe, but their perception is much different. At least, that could explain man's behavior.

Black holes are a part of the universe. Are they a part of God? This could mean that God did not create the universe. God is the colossal infinite universe, maintaining many black holes and indifferent to the tragedies of man. If we can assume that the entire universe is of one God, we can be presume that He is either managing it with decentralized control, or that He can compartmentalize Himself into many forms and acts on those emergencies at hand.

The tragedies of man comprise those events occurring on the third planet from a single star in the universe. What happens on that little planet and in that galaxy is small compared to the events occurring in the Universe or during some universal continuum of time.

Comparing man to God would be a particularly difficult for a man. But comparing God to man would be a trivial matter for God. In the entire universe, our star and our galaxy must have the importance to God as a man's ingrown toenail to man, and the needs of one man the importance of a pimple on a piss ant's ball.

Nevertheless, infected toenails can cause real pain to a man, and a piss ant considerably must have great care and concern for his balls. Where then, would God ever have time or consideration to read the stories unfolded by man? Man's inhumanity to his fellow man unfolds if he realizes and records it, but it still remains unknown to God. God might concern himself with black holes that were an irritation, those black holes sucking up planets and stars, but He might not care to notice those doing little harm. Those doing little harm would go unnoticed, but those doing real harm would be satiated with the tool that He called Time.

The indifference realized by man, accounts for the exponential growth of those black holes existing on earth. Man must consider his own black holes that can be great or small. To some men black holes are a cancer but not to those who enjoy its inflection. Whether that cancer is great or small determines the number of men it destroys. If a man sucks up or destroys few other men, such as his family and friends, he would be a minor black hole on earth. To be a major black hole would require the destruction of many more men and not just a calibration of their destruction. The destruction man's spirit counts even more.

Sometime men stop men from killing other men because it's illegal, but the destruction of their spirit, always legal and far more successfully rewarding, can repeat an indefinite number of times. Those black holes, remembered as great on earth and to man, will have less significance to God than a pimple on a piss ant's ball.

What unmitigated arrogance must man have to believe that exposing and destroying those black holes on earth, sucking up other men, would stand him tall enough for God's notice? Is the universe concerned with a solar system when its star novas over some period of time?

That would require that Time be more than a tool. It would require that Time is a dimension and a tool. Only in its present tense is time a tool, but in the past and future tense time is also a dimension.

Of course, if there is no concern, Time as a tool, finds use only in the present tense, as an automatic tool. But if there is concern, Time has three dimensions and the concern for past flowing into future is the existence of God.

Man calibrates his worth on earth by the number of dimensions he sees and his response to them. The dimensions he faces are different than God's, although they number the same. God sees the past, present, and future, and if He cares uses His tool to guide them. And if God cares, man should give pause to the pimple on a piss ant's ball.

Man modified that fifth dimension originally imprinted, but over eons of time fit it to his needs on earth. During this modification, some of that dimension was lost because of atrophy and misuse.

Minds containing five dimensions do exist, but they number few. When the flag drops, they see where the last domino falls. They have a clairvoyance that can ferret what is good for man and act on it regardless its consequences to themselves or to their friends. They love truth and wisdom more than themselves or their friends. They are not Plato's philosopher kings but still number less than one in twenty five thousand. Those with less dimensional minds overrule them.

Those relatively few minds, containing four dimensions, see where the last domino falls but always ferret what benefits themselves or their cause. They manipulate truth for their purpose and gain, and some successfully rule for periods of time.

Those many more minds containing three dimensions are aware that cause and effect exists but never see where it lands. They will admit to more than one domino in the string, but are content to believe that only the first domino really exists. They are birds of a feather and have many friends. They are easy prey to the four dimensional mind and band together in distrust of those containing five.

The majority of minds contain two dimensions. Dominos do not exist, and there is no cause and effect, only simplistic platitudes. What is immediate or soon to come, is their existence and only concern. Many do well on I.Q. tests, which are aimed at the two dimensional mind.

The one dimensional mind, the congenital defect, exists in a universe of bodily function. They would deserve pity, but their mediocrity and number increases with the help and support of those with a two dimensional mind. Their goal and success is to increase their kind: the one dimensional mind.

If only history could be used to plot the outcome of a series of events that begin with the first domino. But reported history comes with the bias of the writer, and bias is all that we have. The challenge is to see both sides and look from the middle and to know where the middle lies.

Together, these dimensional minds comprise a Poisson distribution where the expected value is one. The curve is not is bell shaped, but the central limit theorem applies. The norm is mediocrity with magnetism pulling both sides to that expected value of one. When we are able to look forward and backward with a multi-dimensional mind will we see their story unfold.

Not

All

Together

Prologue

Take a fruit, any fruit; for me that would be the plum. You can buy them in the stores, stands on the side of the road, or pick them from a tree. At the end of their season, the plums you get from stores were picked green and then freshly frozen. They still have some semblance of taste but nothing in comparison to a tree-ripened plum.

If you have a tree in the back of your yard, your neighbor's yard, or find one unprotected, you can pluck that ripe plum before it drops to the ground if the birds don't first get them. The connoisseur should wait until its skin slightly softens but definitely before it wrinkles. The flavor burst forth and explodes in your mouth like a forty-five year old woman.

That's the way Jack remembered Lauren. She was too young when he first met her, but now she was a forty-five year old woman and definitely still in season. Oh God, was she ever in season! At least, that's what Jack thought. Len married her when she was too young to recognize lies and deceit, but now she was older and wiser.

Some would consider plucking young *fruit* before it was ready a talent, but in Jack's world the talent was in knowing when to pass because they needed time to develop further. Len had taken her, but Jack had tasted her first. He couldn't wait to taste her again.

Chapter One

It won't be long, he said on that long one way drive. You should have a good time with people more your own age. While I'm skateboarding with Doug, you can ride one of his bikes, swim in the ocean, or just lie on the beach. Jack's Freebord was in the cargo area along with his skateboarding clothes.

Jack didn't know Doug that well while his father was alive, but he and his father, Len, were friends since college. Doug was young and still seemed to need a father figure, and he had chosen him. It was flattering to Jack because he had never had any children of his own, and he considered himself far too old to have children with his pretty, young wife.

One of Jack's pleasant memories of Len concerned shaking hands. Len knew that Jack didn't like it. Jack thought shaking hands was proof of an open hand to avoid combat. Shaking hands was proof that one was not armed, or at least carried no weapon in that hand. Friends did not need proof of an open hand. Besides, shaking hands was an effective way to spread disease.

He remembered mentoring Doug and telling him that he should get married and start a family. You'll be sorry when you reach my age without a family. You'll get tired of this frat-house living.

Doug, left with millions when his father died, had absolutely no urge to find a wife or a job. Along with those millions, he inherited a huge house with a view of the ocean. It was a skateboarder's dream with all those winding downhill streets leading directly to it.

The house was not at the very bottom of the hill but at the end of a street twenty feet above that lowest intersection. All you had to do was to hang on, drop your knees until the end of the run, and then coast up from that lowest intersection of the street into Doug's driveway, and then step off onto his front lawn. It was a short walk across his lawn to the bottom of the stairs leading to his front porch.

Anyone looking at Doug's or his father's picture would say they were clones. They both had large heads and blue eyes that were always wet without tearing. One would think they were always up to mischief or lying. They were both well-built and, although fairly short, extremely successful with women. They had proved this to their friends without resorting financial disclosure to those girls that became their objects of proof.

Doug was dancing on the porch with two women when Jack and Debe arrived. The rest of his frat-house friends must be playing pool or pinball. Some of them could be out surfing. But if the surf was good, Doug would not be dancing on the porch even if the girls were hot. He waved as he spun around before stretching out his leg.

Glad you're here, Uncle Jack, and you won't have to share a room.

It had been years since Jack had seen Doug's father dance, but he remembered that dance-step and thought Len, the father, must have taught it to his son. He remembered Len, with his leg stretched out to his side, moving heel to toe, using the other supporting leg. You look like you're trying to drop a log without unbuttoning your pants, Jack said with a wink.

Len would laugh and say, I'll keep doing this as long as it works. Besides, maybe I am, and then he would laugh even harder. As he danced away, he would look over his shoulder and wink. It's just that I am so bitchin'.

Jack only said that a few times. He would ask himself if he was being clever or simply envious because he, himself, was such a lousy dancer. Although Jack and Len never double-dated, they separately went to the same parties. Double-dating was never a concern to either one, and they never discussed it. Instinctively, both knew that it was far less successful. Life only concerned women and school.

They rarely watched or talked about sports, unless it was part of their plan of seduction, and unlike the wannabe, the never-was, or the has-been, they never jerked-off over a game.

Doug came down the stairs, crossed the lawn, and lifted the hatchback. He set the luggage on the steps. Girls, take my uncle's and his wife's luggage up to the guest room. You know the one I showed you this morning? He turned to face Jack and his wife. Why don't you guys join me for a drink before you go to your room?

Jack and Doug sat in chairs next to each other. Got any root bear, Jack said looking at him? By the way, this is Debe, and she loves to dance. Doug immediately got up, excused himself, and laughed.

It's nice to meet you, Debe. I thought uncle Jack would never get married after living with that bitch and her kid. He was laughing with that customary leer but managed to size her up from head to toe. Just like his father, he had lost his upper right first molar.

Those wet eyes and missing tooth gave him a look of lascivity. He and his father never wanted an implant or a bridge. His father told his son that it would bring him luck. That missing tooth was his lady luck, but it wasn't the only thing missing. Those lucky ladies discovered what was missing sometime later when it was too late. Two of the luckiest of those lucky ladies were receiving spousal and child support, and the third was his widow.

Len, Doug's father, was never bitter concerning their support because there was always more than plenty left over for him. He also seemed to enjoy sharing things other than his money. He would share his time and money with friends. Perhaps it was because he got nervous when he was alone. It was sharing his and other people's wives with his friends that got him into financial trouble.

Len said he understood why they left him, but it was obvious that he never really got it. He simply looked forward to the next party. Len was great at a party, even as an adult. In fact, he never objected when they called him a party animal. He would say there was more to him than that and try to keep a straight face.

Jack hoped the apple would fall far from the tree but knew that it really had not. Perhaps having one half of a mind was genetic. Most minds have two halves. One half wants and asks what will it take to get it, and the other half asks what the alternative costs are of getting it. Whether Doug was born with the first half only, or if the second half had died from atrophy was a moot point because the apple had not fallen far from the tree. Perhaps it was genetic, or perhaps his father had taught Doug those lessons.

Len once tried to help Jack. Both were studying for the same exam. Len scoffed and said that will never be on the exam. It's too difficult because the professor can't even explain it. You're cutting your nose off to spite your face.

Jack didn't even look at Len. He kept laboring over the same pages. He finally looked at Len. You're right; I would get better grades and spend less time, but I just can't help it. I have to know it. Len just shrugged as he walked away, but he never chided Jack's study habits again. One of the foundations of their friendship was that neither one of them belabored the same thought or argument. Once was always enough.

You sure can pick 'em Uncle Jack. Doug had circled Debe and then lifted her arm by her hand and twirled her in another circle. How about we go for a ride? Why don't you get into your skateboard clothes and Debe can stay here and play pool with the guys? My driver will take us up the hill, and we can ride all the way back without skating.

Jack carried the luggage upstairs to their room. How do you like it, he asked his wife. She said that she would have preferred a room with a view of the ocean.

I think Doug put us in this room, so we would have our own private bathroom. Besides, we weren't the first to arrive. Will you be all right while Doug and I skateboard?

Debe said to go ahead, that she would be fine. I'll snoop around and maybe learn to play pool. You've talked so much about Doug and his father that I think I already know him.

Besides, I'd like to meet his friends. If I don't like them, I'll take a walk on the beach or maybe sunbathe. She was amused because she was one of those Asians that had a perfect tan without any need for sun.

Chapter Two

Doug was waiting at the bottom of the stairs, holding both boards. He, with a smirk, asked Jack how he could leave that young, totally hot wife and go skateboarding with him. How come I never got to meet her before you got married? You know she's too small for you but just perfect for me.

Since the death of his father, his long dimples had turned into thin vertical furrows making his incarnation complete. Doug was still grinning with those wet eyes and missing molar.

It was very pleasant driving up that winding, empty street. The cars were inside or in their driveways, and the phone lines were underground. It was obvious that this was a wealthy neighborhood, and the trees could flourish without phone-line protection. Pruned only for their beauty, there wasn't a power pole in sight.

They got out while the car turned around and headed back. Doug said to wait here while his driver drove down the street. When we hear the honk, we'll know that he's blocked that intersection at the bottom, and we can let it rip all the way to the bottom.

The honk was like the starting bell at some race track. They both pushed off at the same time, *S-tracking* on their way down. There could be no concern for cars leaving their driveway. All you could do was to pray and hang on. There was no delay to pushing off. If you took time to take a breath, even for a minute, the other rider would call you chicken shit all the way down. Of course, if you passed him, you could yell out and call him that same name for the rest of the way.

That simultaneous yell came from both, but Doug was the first to arrive at his house. He was laughing on his porch when Jack jumped off on his lawn. Doug had learned to jump off his board and roll, head over heels, on his lawn to the bottom of his porch and then run up the steps. Debe was brushing the grass from his back. She was wearing soft cotton, pink shorts, and a halter top.

He beat you, old man!

On his table, Jack said to his wife as he came up the steps. Debe's elbows were at her side, and her palms were outstretched.

What is that supposed to mean?

When Jack reached the porch, he took a breath before looking at her. Never play a man for money on his own table.

Well you weren't playing for money, were you!

No, but that street is his table. Would you mind getting me a glass of water?

For one brief moment, Debe looked at Jack. She smiled and flipped her long, black hair as she turned around and walked into the house. Had her hair been short she would have passed for a gymnast with her muscular butt and perfect legs. So many women had under-developed calves below their knees. Jack looked at Doug and then sat down.

How did you meet her, Doug asked?

She was born in Taiwan, and her father and I were on good terms. He had an early death because of a brain tumor. With his dying breath, he asked me to take care of her. I've known her since she was six. Her father left her well enough provided, so that she could finish college. Her visa was about to expire, and I thought this would be a sure way to take care of her.

Well, how is she in bed? Doug, like his father, was leering with his wrinkled smile, wet eyes, and missing molar. All the guys have the hots for her, he said. He had his elbow in Jack's ribs when he asked.

That's a little too personal for me, and it should be for you. Jack wasn't smiling when he answered. He looked at Doug and took a deep breath before he said, I guess you'll just have to eat your heart out because you're never going to find out.

Jack was surprised at how easily it went down. It was as if Debe and he were working as a team with one common goal and on the same common ground. But Debe would never have teamed with him voluntarily, and Jack preferred it that way. She was always suspicious of him, or perhaps it was contempt. The people she trusted were those with an agenda to diminish or to take and destroy. At least, that's how Jack saw it.

On their way up to their room, Jack saw Lauren coming down the stairs. His mind flashed back to those magic moments. She was the only one he really wanted to marry. His time in school, outside of study, he spent getting in girl's pants without proposals of marriage. Being open and honest with girls talking of marriage on the first date always complicated the issue at hand. But Lauren was different. For her, he wanted to do it the old fashion way.

Jack thought the courtship was going well until Len showed him the scratches on his back. He told Jack that Lauren wanted him but didn't know how to let Jack down gently. Jack was able to hide his tears as he looked away. She's all yours, buddy. Tell Lauren that she shouldn't give me a second thought.

That was so long ago, and here he was standing on the same landing with Lauren looking at him. I'm so glad you came, she said. I think we'll be the only adults at Doug's party. Lauren had changed so little, or perhaps Jack had thought in his mind that he had overlaid Lauren the woman with Lauren the girl. Their eyes laser pathed for that one brief moment before she kissed him. I think you should introduce me to your new wife.

While shaking hands, Jack noticed that his new wife was scrutinizing Lauren. Although shorter than Lauren, Debe faced forward. She did not lift her head but instead looked up with her eyes. He had seen that contemptuous look many times when he introduced her to others. It was probably only apparent to those who knew her well or for a long time. Jack nodded his head as he looked up the stairs. His plan was going well.

What do you think I should wear to dinner, Debe asked Jack in their room.

Why don't you wear those flats and that short, soft pink dress I bought for you last week? I know Doug likes to dance at his parties, and I don't dance at all. Debe had that familiar smirk when she took off her clothes and went into the bathroom to shower. Jack read while he waited for his turn.

Debe was already downstairs when Jack came down. Everyone except Lauren was dancing, and the partners switched from each other as if they were doing it on cue. It had the semblance of a country square dance, but the music was a soft, romantic rock.

Debe slowly moved to the music in the center of that surrounding circle. Using her hands at the back of her head, she flipped her hair forward to cover her face and then reached out to take Doug's hand. They danced so well together as if they were students from the same dancing school.

Doug was sitting at the head of the table, and Jack was at his left, facing Debe. Lauren sat on Jack's left. It was so easy for Jack to talk to Lauren. It had been so long since she and Len had married, and Jack and Lauren hadn't spoken since that point in time. They laughed and spoke of friends gone bye, while Doug showed Debe the delights of Champaign and caviar. Jack and Lauren, shoulders together, watched each other as they spread Roquefort on warm French bread.

After dinner, Jack and Lauren sat on the porch and continued talking about friends gone bye. She looked at Jack and asked why he had dumped her so abruptly.

Jack looked at the floor before facing Lauren. Len said that's what you wanted, and when possible I never intrude on my friends.

Lauren took a deep breath and then closed her eyes. Had I known him better, the way I do know now, I would have called you. I felt so rejected before I decided to give myself to him. She looked away with tears in her eyes.

Let me get this straight, Jack said. Are you telling me that those scratches on his back were not from you?

Lauren took a breath before she looked and smiled at him. I'm not a scratcher, but you should know that. However, I can be a screamer, but no one knows that except for you. Oh Jack, we did it together, and I can't blame you.

Jack's tenderness for Lauren rekindled. I should have known that those scratches were Vivian's because she did the same thing to me.

Jack remembered standing next to Len with their backs to the mirror. Look, Len said to him. He said that he had won.

Jack just smiled at Len. Your scratches are just fresher than mine. Did you eat her?

Len shook his head and winced as he looked away. Of course I didn't, he said as he pursed and tightened his lips.

Jack remembered looking at him and smiling. I think that's one I have on you. He remembered Vivian crying while she clawed his back because some girl had stolen her sweetheart, but she didn't know who. He remembered women crying while they climaxed, but Vivian had very different reasons. Those scratches on his back were not an endorsement, but rather a further association with her personal demons. She may have clawed Len for the same reasons.

Where did you go, Lauren said smiling?

Jack just shook his head before he answered, where I don't want you to go. Remember that I was almost as young as Len, he said to Lauren.

I know you're talking about Len, but you could be talking about Doug. They're so much alike. That's probably why we don't get along. I tried to put Doug on a path different from his father while he was still young, but it was always two against one. … And I always lost.

Of course you did, Jack said. You didn't want the sins of the father inherited by his son, but that father was always in charge. What are your plans for your future?

I have no plans, Lauren said, but I know Doug wants me to move out. Even though I'm only his stepmother, my presence seems to hamper or curtail his pursuits. I think Doug feels that if I were gone, he'd be far more successful with women. What and where would you be if I moved out?

Jack thought Lauren, in her quiet way, was looking at him without concern for herself. He hoped her concern was for him.

I'd be the same person I always was but with the truth on my side. I should have known that Len would dump her to get to you. I was surprised when it happened. He and Phyllis seemed to want each other so badly. Her need was essential to Len. What was essential to Phyllis was to have control over him. I guess he got tired of it. I always knew that it would.

You know Phyllis always hated me, and for Len's best man to get drunk at her wedding was all the ammunition she needed. Phyllis used that to forbid me from entering their house, but with her permission Len and I could go fishing. I decided to let the friendship go when Len said I would have to come to them if we were to stay friends.

Resa said that I could have pushed a peanut across the floor on my hands and knees using only my nose and remain unforgiven. I should have got-it-together when I saw the arrangement of the tables at their wedding. They were to be on stage while the audience watched in awe. And I got everyone to dance. For God's sake, who doesn't dance at a Jewish wedding?

Lauren took Jack's hand and placed it in her lap. We all knew, and so did Phyllis. She was always nervous around you. You were that, not to be trusted, intellectual free spirit. You opposed what she was about, the regurgitation of convention. She could never allow Len to be even near any symbol of freedom. For her, people could not be married and still think independently. She was the center of that Jewish clique majoring in Semitism and made sure it did not include *goyim* like you. What happened to you made me realize that domino effect, and how race and religion could affect it. Did you know his first wife, Terry?

I only met her a few times, said Jack. You know they had to get married. That's the conventional term for it, but I don't think Len thought it was his duty. He was happy about it, and I think she was too, at least at first. Terry was one of those blessed or cursed with a multi dimensional mind but seemed not to have any use for it. She was only amused at where the last domino fell, at least for a while. I think it was she who wanted the split.

You know she kept a stunning figure after having four more kids with Ron. I hated to see her go. I think Len did, too. Love was a path that hurt, and he never took it again. I tried to be friends with Phyllis for Len's benefit, even though she had the body of a brick and the imagination of a rock. She was proud to have a conventional mind and sought other ways to further advance it.

Lauren said she was tired and wanted to go to bed. Before I go, I want to ask you something. Do you know anything about a letter in a letter? I mean a letter in an envelope inside of another envelope. Jack looked away before he smiled. Lauren let go of his hand as she stood up. God, I really hope it was you!

Jack stood up and took her hand. He looked at the floor and said, I found that old sealed letter with your name on it. I couldn't open it, so I mailed it to you. Who wrote it and what did it say?

Lauren had that look of surprise with tears still in her eyes. Oh God, I may have made a terrible mistake. This is something I have to keep to myself, and it matters far more if it wasn't you.

Jack was sitting alone when Debe came out to see if he wanted another drink.

Doug thought you could use another drink.

No I'm fine, but I think I'll go to bed. I want to be home early because I start the installation of IBM's latest operating system next Monday, and I'd like to beat my old record. Don't wake me when you come to bed.

Chapter Three

The next morning, on his way down the hall, Jack heard Lauren call his name. Jack, did you write this letter? She handed him an envelope with her name on it and asked him to come into her room.

This was more than Jack had hoped for. Lauren was not just being polite. He couldn't help but remember other women he had met after their relationship had gone south. They would talk about their husbands and how sensitive they were, without any eye contact, and then walk quickly away.

What was wrong with reaching out to another only to discover they had made the wrong choice? Sharing their thoughts and body with another does not mean that they had lost it with him, and what is wrong for them to look again for their next soulmate? If they had lingered for only a moment and recognized that he was still the same person, he would have told them that nothing was lost but only misplaced. They could have remained good friends.

That's not the way it was with Lauren. She was not ashamed of being human. She was not afraid to reach out to correct or at least examine the possibility of a misplaced mistake even if the mistake was not hers, or if it in some way affected her.

Jack made a big mistake, and that was trusting Len. Lauren had just given him a sign or a signal, but he had to be sure of his interpretation. This was not the time to make a mistake. His plan was set in motion, and this was not the time to allow an unknown variable into his equation.

Lauren, I don't want you to misconstrue this because I'd love to come into your room, but I think we should stay in the hall.

Jack, never governed by propriety, wanted to tell Lauren how he felt, but not in a hallway of ears. That would have to wait until he had cast the players. He looked at both ends of the hallway before opening and reading the letter.

Not in this Life

Some ancient Greek said
A tear has not been shed
that has not been shed before.
Then my genes were passed
through my father
from someone passed whom
I never knew, and I
coupled with my mother's
became someone else
that no one ever knew.
With older genes than he,
I taught him like the child
who hated me.
Before he ran away,
I could say that he too taught me
even if negatively.
What was right,
I knew before I could talk.
Why didn't he?
And how many others are like me?
So when you came into my room
and saw through me,
I should have acted differently
because I did not see
the friend like me.

That son of a bitch! This reads as if written decades ago. Jack put it back into its envelope. Lauren, I wrote a lot of stuff way back when, and Len was the only one who knew where I kept the key to my shack. What was the return address?

Lauren shook her head and said there was no return address on either one.

Jack pursed his lips and rolled his eyes up at the ceiling on his way to his room. His plan was going well.

Debe turned around in her seat and waved at Doug as they drove up the street. Jack thought he could see Doug's missing molar. You slipped into bed without waking me. Did you have a good time, and what time did the party end?

Debe sat back in her seat but was looking out the window. I had a really great time, and I want a divorce.

Jack saw, in his rear view mirror, Doug's house replaced by trees on that winding road he had just skateboarded down the day before. Well this is all very abrupt, he said, but you always were, or did you just wait for me to start the next installation? How long have you been living with this?

I've been waiting for a long time, Debe said, but this was my first real opportunity. Doug said he wants me, and I want him. I don't know why you married me because I never had anything but contempt for you. The only reason I married you was to stay here, and now I can stay in this country without any need for you. To me, you're just some meddling, stupid old man.

Jack wanted to pull over and slap the shit out of her, but that benefit would only apply to a real person. Besides, she was responding so well. He always knew she held him in contempt, but he never knew why. Their only difference other than sex was race, which with anyone else time and acquaintance always erased. But race was the only difference they had ever shared. Perhaps she was leaving him because he was a white, non-minority, but Doug was the same, and he, like his father, was always proud of that. She would be leaving one house for another, except for size and comfort, just like it. But Jack learned early in life that problems concerning racial differences would always settle with money. He wasted little time with those groups belligerently standing with their palms outstretched.

Debe was a dichotomy of contradictions. When it came to clothes, friends, or anything that could personally affect her, she was resolute. But she wanted a government to grow even larger and make all other decisions for her. Government was never big enough for Debe.

I think a divorce is not what you want, Jack said. That takes time, and you should consider what time makes known to others… if you can. An annulment is as quick as the drop of a gavel, and I'm willing to sign an act of non-consummation because that's what you'll need. You'll have to do this by yourself because it will be assholes and elbows for several months for me. You couldn't have picked a better time to screw me. I think you should remain in my house during its process.

Debe placed her hands on the back of her head without looking at Jack and said that would work. I will say one good thing about you. You know how to make things easy. Her forced smile was brief before she turned to look away.

She can do a nice smile, Jack thought, even if it wasn't for him.

The installations during those next months, filled with ten-to-twelve hour days, went well. Jack was pleased with his team, and there was nothing left but to convert the catalogue of that operating system. That was his point of no return because a fall-back added more grief than going ahead.

He had signed the forms with the help of Doug's attorney within those thirty days. Jack just shook his head when he checked off incurable physical incapacity on form FL-110. His only stipulation was that Debe live with him until her wedding. She always had her own room, which Jack never entered. He wanted to make sure that his second installation went as well.

Doug called and asked Jack if he would give Debe away. Jack reply was brisk, only if Lauren attends the wedding. Jack knew her moving out of Doug's house had ended inimically. She's still your stepmother, for God's sake. Besides, I'll need someone to talk to.

Jack interrupted Doug before he could answer. Debe will be coming alone and should have someone there to help her dress for her wedding. You know you'll have to start thinking of someone other than yourself.

Chapter Four

Jack noticed that Debe had packed when he came out from his bedroom. I guess you're ready he said while putting on his coat. How do I look?

I'm glad to see you wearing a Tux. I didn't know you owned one. It was Doug's idea for you to give me away. I didn't like it at the time, but Doug doesn't need to know that. His chauffeur will be coming soon, and I'll leave the keys on the table. I'd like it if you were gone when he gets here. I didn't appreciate your stipulation that I live with you until the judge annulled our marriage.

Jack turned to face Debe on his way out. That will give you and Doug something to talk about after your wedding. You will find that I had your best interest at heart. He looked at the floor before he looked at her. There was no expression on his face when he turned an opened the door.

. . .

Where have you been for the past several months? Wow was Jack's only response when Lauren opened her door. How did your installation go?

I'm trying not to be smug, but I could never fool you. Both of those installs are going extremely well, and I am so ready to relax and spend time with you.

Lauren was standing naked, inside to that opened door. Confidence surrounded her as she smiled at Jack. We're both single, and neither one of us is in a hallway. Would you like come in and first have a drink, or would you prefer another install?

That was all Jack could stand. He picked her up and carried her into her bedroom. They were fondling and kissing while trying not to tear each other's cloths. They were touching and caressing when Lauren started to scream. Years had passed, Jack thought, but she hadn't forgotten.

27

Do you know how long it's been since I've done that?

Of course I do, Jack whispered when he rolled her on her back. Len always said how quiet you were. I didn't know if it was an intimate comment to a friend or a cunning entrapment.

Lauren, still lying on her back, was looking at the ceiling. I thought he would give you that message, or perhaps it was because I couldn't stop thinking about you. I tried to be fair to him and to be a good wife, but I could never be his party girl. He would laugh among his friends when I complained of a headache and left those raucous parties.

Lauren was moving her thigh back and forth over him, with her knee bent back, so that her toes were touching his. Would you like to have a drink before we go see a wedding?

Only if it coats my stomach, Jack said. I have to toast them at their reception, and I want you to pay attention to what I have written. There are several things that I want you to know. One of those is that my marriage to Debe was purposely unconsummated.

Lauren's hand was caressing his chest. Never be concerned, she said, with what has flown or gone before. We're going to have a wonderful time, and it will be our time.

. . .

I thought you were gallant when you gave her away, Lauren said in her apartment. Debe seemed pleased when I helped her dress for her wedding. I thought we might have a little girl-talk about you, but her only concerns were for Doug and her wedding. I was glad when you came back and sat with me.

Jack blinked his eyes while looking at the ceiling. Believe me girl, so was I. I hope you don't think it presumptuous, but I have a small travel bag in my car.

When they came to that winding road leading to Doug's house, Jack reached over and took Lauren's hand. We should be there soon, and you should have a good time with people your own age, but I can only think of one. He stared straight ahead when he said, what goes around comes around. He could see Lauren's eyes looking at him without turning her head. It reminded him of

28

those parties so long ago when she would make that cute little smirk and look away. That happy memory was cut short when he remembered the outcome of honor and trust that he had for Len.

Glad you're finally here, Uncle Jack. What took you so long?

Doug and Debe were dancing on the porch. The caterers were making last minute checks while their boss was talking to him.

Lauren, amused at what Doug just said, looked at Jack. Shall we tell him or just let him see the love-bites on my neck?

He'll know soon enough, Jack said, when you have that mother-and-son dance.

Lauren looked at Jack and said, he won't be happy when he does. After his father died, he tried to get in my pants. She blinked her eyes and looked away before she looked back and smiled at Jack.

Are those tears for Len or for Doug, Jack asked?

Not for either one, she said, but for the fact that he tried. I don't know why it bothered me, because if Len could possibly be looking down, he would probably laugh and think his son was just a chip off the old block. But it did bother me.

Jack looked at Lauren. Take my arm, ... and it also bothers me.

The tables, arranged to be parallel and three feet from the walls, formed a large disconnected horseshoe. In front of each place setting was a name card except for the center table, which had room for four but place settings for two. That table, separated from the rest, stood by itself allowing easy access for their guests. There was plenty of room to dance. The guests sat with their backs to the walls without any need to turn and face the happy couple.

Jack had saved his oysters and Roquefort for dessert. Lauren's head was on his shoulder.

You smell like pheromones.

He laughed as he spread that wonderfully smelling cheese on the warm bread. Let us eat from the same loaf.

He held up his and Lauren's glass for more campaign while whispering in her ear. Life's never a single edged sword, and it's too bad they'll never see the other side. He waited until he had caught the server's attention. Is there anyone here without a full glass? He waited while the servers made their rounds before he stood.

It may seem ironic to those watching me give Debe away. However, as some will agree, I am the most qualified. Jack turned to wink at Lauren while Debe, Doug, and their friends could not stop laughing.

May the dimensions of your minds add to each other's. To question actions when they are not obvious with why, leads to indecision, and perhaps forgiveness, and then to sympathy, which can lead to trust. Why, should not be a resting place for indecision when action is required. Jack smiled at Lauren as he picked up the book. He made eye contact with everyone before he turned to face the happy couple

I'd like to read from *The Prophet* written by *Kahlil Gibran*.

> *You were born together and together you will be*
> *forevermore.*
> *You shall be together when the white wings of death*
> *scatter your days. ...*
> *But let there be spaces in your togetherness, and let*
> *the winds*
> *of the heavens dance between you.*
> *Love one another but make not a bond of love:*
> *Let it rather be a moving sea between the shores of*
> *your souls.*
> *Fill each other's cup but drink not from one cup.*
> *Give one another of your bread but eat not from the*
> *same loaf.*
> *Sing and dance together and be joyous but let each*
> *of you be alone. ...*
> *Give your hearts but not into each other's keeping.*
> *For only the hand of Life can contain your hearts.*
> *And stand together yet not too near together:*
> *For the pillars of the temple stand apart, And the oak*
> *tree and the cypress grow not in each other's shadow.*

Let us raise our glasses and all together drink to this altogether adorable, happy couple, who are now all together.

Every one stood and raised their glass and drank to the adorable couple. Lauren reached over, sliding her hand under Jack's coat, and grabbed his ass with an unseen hand. You big phony, she whispered with a smirk. She knew it would turn him on.

No, I really do wish them well in spite of my concerns. Would you care to dance?

The servers moved the chairs and pushed the tables against the walls. Lauren excused herself and went to the ladies room. Debe and Doug had finished their dance and were circulating and thanking their guests.

Doug had that knowing look when he faced Jack. I didn't have to dance with Lauren to get a good look at that hickey on her neck. How was she? Jack was looking at Doug's wet eyes, furrows, and missing molar.

That's a little too personal for me, and it should also be for you. Jack wasn't smiling when he answered. He looked at Doug and took a deep breath, and said I guess you'll just have to eat your heart out because you're never going to find out. But you won't have to ask me about Debe after tonight.

Doug stood closer to Jack and continued his grinning. Well tell me about my wife. Is she hot? My dad said you could always tell how good a woman was in bed by kissing her lips.

Jack laughed at Doug and said his father was a flatterer. No one can tell that, but there is a similarity among sphincters and their skin tissue. The mouth and vagina are both sphincters, and– by the way– I never kissed your wife. You'll know how good she is after tonight. Besides, even if I knew, I wouldn't tell you because it would spoil the surprise. Just remember this will be your first time together, and it can impact your marriage for several years. Think of her as an *ingénue,* who is letting you lead the way.

Jack looked at Doug and thought of his father. Lauren is hot but you'll just have to take my word. Jack turned Doug around to face Debe. I think she wants to dance. You should go to her. As

31

Doug nodded and walked away, Lauren returned and said she wanted to cool off on the patio with a little champagne. What were you two talking about?

Lauren burst into laughter when Jack said that Doug wanted to know if his wife was a good lay. I think it's a little too late to seek an endorsement. I hope that's not what it was. I hope, for their sake, that he steps away from his father. I think we're both ready for more champagne, she said as she took Jack's hand.

They were sitting outside when Jack filled their flutes. I want to have faith and trust at my age, but skepticism always seems to find its way. We both knew Len, and I know Debe. She is an *ingénue* in more ways than one. Although a good paper I.Q., she has a two dimensional mind and forever relies on what she heard said the first time.

How often have we seen memory and intelligence used as synonyms for each other when we're really speaking of regurgitation. I think thought without the aid of memory can exist, but we should, whenever possible, test it with history. However, it is truest of thought that arrives without the aid of history.

That could work well for Doug because Debe's mind will not process newer information. She's thinks that if she listens to a second point of view, her first point of view, which is better, will be lost or erased. For her, the act of listening to a second point of view would surrender the first. She never thought for herself and is afraid she can't recover what was lost. Debe has never learned to surrender and remain true to herself.

Debe went to liberal schools where her only exposure was to limited views. She heard those promulgated views from those playing the race card. So fervently believed by others, she thought they must be true. While she never played the race card herself, she became a product of those that did. She never learned the right way to listen or to think with another view. When no previous ideas exist in her mind, she swallows the new without consideration or surrender.

Actually, I don't think she would be a good lay because that takes surrender, a surrendering that is something traded back and forth. It's to let go. It's to give yourself to someone else, but I don't think she can. She's too self absorbed to let go, and surrender would be her shame. Ejaculation can be conquest or surrender to a man or to a woman. She doesn't know that it's just part of the game. May I serve you more, or have you had enough champagne?

Are we speaking about champagne? Lauren laughed when Jack said he would get her coat.

Jack thought he would not drive that winding street for a long time on their way home. He knew he would soon be unwelcome at their house. Debe may not know why, but her contempt for him would increase. She was happy to get away but will soon realize that so did he.

She'll work on Doug, Jack said, because that's how her mind works. He turned to face Lauren. Now that you're on your own, will you go back to nursing or live on Len's trust?

Even though Len didn't like it, Lauren said, I renewed my license every two years. I knew before it first expired that I wanted to keep it, and I'm so glad I did. Being a CRNA offers more benefits than just having a job. Besides, after taking up a seat in the program, I thought I should give back, deliver the goods, but still live on his trust. Certified registered nurse anesthetists are still hard to find. Lauren reached over to put her hand on his leg before she looked at him. Jack, you never did say if you wrote that poem or not. Did you?

Before I answer that, would you tell me how he died? I only remember that there was some sort of inquest.

Lauren was not looking at him or straight ahead into the glare of the headlights. She was looking out the side window.

All they could find, she said, were signs of asphyxiation and a higher lever of metabolites than normal. He must have died in agony. The only puncture mark found was from that day when he had donated blood. All three of us went the hospital together. I thought it would be a nice thing for a family to do— and to think

33

that I was lying next to him when he died. That's all I remember. And now it's your turn, she said looking at Jack.

Saved by the bell, Jack said. May I park my car next to yours? I noticed an empty parking slot next to your car in the garage.

You don't need to ask, she said looking at him.

. . .

I'm on my way Jack said when Lauren told him the water was already warm. She soaped him down and said, and now it's your turn. Jack! Did you, or did you not write that poem?

It's funny that you brought that up. It seems I found a letter in an envelope inside another envelope. It was on my chair at the reception. I can't say how it got there, but your name was on the envelope. I just put it on your dresser.

Lauren looked at him and said this will not get you out of your turn. She had her back to him when he soaped her down.

Who's in a hurry? Jack said. There's a get-well card in the envelope.

Lauren had the envelope in her hand. She was resting on her shins while facing him before she lifted her leg and slowly straddled him. When she slowly sat down, Jack heard that deep breath through her nose. She smiled at him when she opened the card. You know you may think that you're very clever, and many do, but in all these years your handwriting and printing has never changed.

Jack was lying on his back and held her face in his hands. He smiled before looking up at the ceiling. Well, what does it say?

Lauren was still straddling Jack, using her left hand on his chest as support and to push her shoulders back. She held the letter in her right. She was laughing with that skeptical look on her face. She stopped when she started to read the letter.

Something Else

And through your rhyme,
or perhaps in time,
I saw the friend like me.

What went wrong?
I awoke, and you were gone.
Look behind and see,
that what was lost
was only in your mind.
Nothing is ever really gone.

Lauren leaned down with her face next to his. Thank you for
giving me another reason.

And I thought you had lost your reason when you married him.

I suppose I did, Lauren said, but reason and reasons return
when you least expect them. Lauren still had her face next to his.
I want to know that it was you who wrote those poems.

He pressed her shoulders back, so that she sat upright. He was
admiring her face and breasts, in turn. He rolled his eyes up and
smiled at the ceiling before letting her go.

Not in this life.

Listen you bastard; I think you had too many *all togethers* in
your speech. Her face again was next to his.

Neither one of them is altogether, and I was just having fun.
Love is letting someone in your head that you want to be in your
head, to keep them there and in return to be in theirs. They will
have to learn to delight in and support their differences. They will
have to be altogether to accomplish that.

Lauren, you weren't there when Doug asked me how I met
Debe. I could have told him about her father, but confiding in
Doug would have brought regret. Perhaps it was her father's
academic environment, because he always enjoyed messing with
people's minds. Perhaps it was the tumor because he was always
competitive and was a consummate politician.

But he did not need an audience when he messed with people.
He did it for his personal reasons, which was part of his disguise;
and those who could not see through him enhanced his pleasure.
He did not pass this to his daughter, who prefers the frontal
attack.

35

I have other concerns not only for them. Those concerns are for the mental state of their children because each child will have something missing that their parents could not provide. Where is the man or woman who recognizes that the future of mankind may lie between her legs? Unlike the mama dog inspecting her litter, they will not have the simplicity of recognizing an abnormality and stopping its procreation. Besides, how can anyone with that same thing missing identify it in others? Jack wondered why Lauren was laughing.

Oh Jack, admit it. You do not love what lies between our loins because it may spawn the future of mankind. She did not wait for his answer. I want to take you to Tahoe. It will be a good use of Len's money. Lauren was back on her side lying next to him with the inside of her thigh resting across his stomach. Her toes were caressing his knee. I wonder if Len is still at rest on his back in his coffin, because he, like his son, enjoyed taking your love away.

Len had it right, and it did hurt, Jack said, but I used what I learned from him to play it against his son.

Jack, just in case you have any concerns, you should know that no sane person kills what they killed for, and I never understood why Jesus turned the other cheek, and I don't bend over twice.

Jack thought to himself. For all those years Len thought he had won, but Lauren had never loved him. Phyllis' revenge after Len left her was that he had lost Terry. Len's revenge on Phyllis was that he had gotten away, and she would have to live with it. Len died before Jack could take his revenge, but then he could take it on his son. The only revenge for Jack on Doug was giving him Debe. Doug and Debe could take revenge on each other, perhaps altogether, or would that be all together?

Jack closed his eyes, fondly holding his reclaimed prize. She had everything he needed in life: the splendor and the quiet. There should never be any revenge for people like Lauren, but to love, avenge, and then love again had its moment. Some win at the start, and some win at the finish, but there are those who win every day. At least, that's what Jack thought.

A

Physician's

Footprint

Prologue

The house of Hapsburg was one of the most influential royal houses of Europe. The Habsburgs, between the years 1438 and 1740, continuously occupied the throne of Spain. The Kingdom of France, under the Valois and Bourbon dynasties, rivaled the House of Hapsburg, whose two branches ruled the Holy Roman Empire and Spain

For much of the sixteenth and seventeenth centuries, France faced Habsburg territory on three sides: the Spanish Netherlands to the north, the Franche-Comté on its eastern border, and Spain to the south. The Spanish king, Philip IV, was the head of the house of Hapsburg and commanded all three territories.

The house of Habsburg stood in the way of French territorial expansion, and France faced the possibility of invasion from multiple sides. France therefore sought to weaken Habsburg control over its possessions.

Cardinal Richelieu, appointed the first chief minister of France by King Louis XIII in 1624, seeking to ensure that its major ally, Sweden, remained in the war and to ensure an outcome favorable to France, decided in 1635 to involve his kingdom in the active fighting and declared war on Spain.

Because fighting was mainly on France's northern borders, most of the citizens of Spain and southern France led a relatively undisturbed life.

Life continued, and as customary to the times affluent families planned their sons' future. The more popular studies included law, medicine, and the priesthood. Other than affluence, students enrolling had little in common. However, a commonality did prevail regardless of study or interest. Education was for the privileged, and all students were male.

Mendoza, freshly graduated from medical school and now Dr. Fernando Mendoza, was proud to feel his father's arms all around him. He knew his father, Dr. Don Francisco Mendoza, was disappointed with his eldest son, Roberto, who did not want to become a doctor. His father said *the sins of the father will be visited upon the son,* but he would not force them on his firstborn. It would be years before Mendoza realized his father's words. The sins of the father, if he is a doctor, occur when he buries his mistakes. Besides, Mendoza's father lost respect for Roberto when he heard him say that war provided an opportunity for profit. This was not the legacy his father wanted to leave to his family name or to the practice of medicine.

Don Francisco's only chance of leaving that legacy or of having the family name reinstated at the Spanish Court was with his second son, Fernando. His father tried a different approach with him. While visiting his patients, he would take little Fernando with him. He tried not to show it, but it was his second son, Fernando, who won his respect. The boy marveled at the science of solving the mysteries of life and death.

His father realized his dreams when Fernando graduated at the head of his class. Because of Mendoza's placement and of the school's recommendation, the king rescinded his banishment of the name Mendoza at court. The king's physicians opposed this. Their concern was that the young doctor, like his father, would believe and practice the Hippocratic Oath.

Mendoza did not accept a position as one of the king's physicians but offered his services to the king's soldiers fighting in the Hapsburg territories bordering northern France. He remembered the tears and pride in his father's eyes when they waved goodbye to each other. His father's words slipped in and out of Mendoza's thoughts on his way to the front.

No more than three years, my son. You must return home and take over my practice.

Mendoza stayed more than five years at the front. His general understood when Mendoza told him his father was dying.

Thanks to you, his general said, we have well-trained replacements. Fortunately for them, they show more caution than you. Behind and on these battlefields, doctors need to be fearful for their own protection. You have lost your fear and no longer flinch at the sound of cannon shot. You and your patient, that wounded soldier, become one while you operate. You try too hard to save their limbs while other doctors move on after they amputate.

Life exists beyond the battlefield, and those lives will, too, need doctors. This may sound callous, but I will not trade a gallant surgeon's life for that of a soldier's. You won't last another year if you remain here. I'll miss my warrior surgeon, but I'm sending you home, he said as he hugged Mendoza.

Mendoza, heading home, could not shake the memory he had grown accustomed to in those flame-lit hospital tents. He felt a presence next to him while operating on wounded soldiers. That presence remained at his side until their deaths, but it left during his surgery on those who would recover. He thought it was a sign that he could save them. It pained him to watch wounded soldiers piled into carts and treated like cattle. Some showed relief, and some showed resignation for those not going home. It was a time when horse-drawn carts served as beds for the quick but not the dead.

Mendoza wondered if that presence escorted their souls in groups or individually. He decided to leave his bitterness behind him and to respect his adversary. There were many names for her. He did not understand or agree with the English name, Grim Reaper, but in his country they called her, *La Muerte, La Parca, La Huesuda,* or *La Señora Muerte.*

Mendoza was not comfortable with any of these names. He thought they were misleading. During surgery, when he witnessed that agony and atrocity of amputation, he created his own special name. It must be broad enough but not too specialized to capture her true identity. It must not be a limiting factor or undermine her personality … if she had one. It must be personal as well as a sign of respect. He thought of a befitting name, one more meaningful to him that would not offend her.

Although Mendoza had never laid eyes on his adversary, he would at times reflect on her face and call her *Aquella Señora …* for the rest of his life.

Part One

No man is an island entire of itself.
Every man is a piece of the continent,
a part of the main, and
if a clod be washed away by the sea,
Europe is the less,
as well as if a promontory were,
as well as any manner of thy friends
or of thine own were.
Any man's death diminishes me,
for I am involved in mankind.
And therefore never send to know
for whom the bell tolls.
It tolls for thee.

John Donne

Chapter One

It would be another beautiful day. The sun was starting its journey, and shop keeper's wives stood in the middle of the road, spanking their floor rugs. Two were having their usual discussion.

It's beyond all reason to me why Barcelona, the capitol of Catalonia, is not also the capitol of Spain. It's so much more pleasant here than in Madrid. She shrugged her shoulders and waited for her friend's answer.

I think Madrid is easier to defend and safer for the king, especially when we are at war with France. Of course, he has other castles at his disposal that are not in Madrid.

They walked back to their husband's shops when they saw the approaching carriage. What was about to happen would become less than a distant memory.

Just look at that. It's disgraceful! You would think they should show more decorum.

After watching the man and woman snuggling on the carriage seat, they walked into their husband's shops with tears in their eyes. They both knew what was happening and were glad it could never happen to them.

Juana's mother was teaching her the alphabet and wishing her daughter could go to school when she heard a knock on the door. She smiled at *Juana* but knew the knock was not her husband's. She had not seen him in weeks, and they were never married. He let her call him husband for his daughter's sake. She left *Juana* outside to practice drawing those alphabet letters in the dirt while she answered the door.

She was not surprised to see their landlord. He always seemed to know when her husband was out of town and choose those times to visit. She had to invite him in this time, because their rent was due. Before he could speak, she said she knew it was that time of the month, but her husband was out of town.

You made your mistake, he said, when you chose that *Inglés*. You should have chosen me when you had the chance. Your husband, he snickered, left town with a Catalan woman. My friends who saw them leaving town told me it looked as if they had packed for a long trip. Did he leave you my rent money? He did not wait for an answer. If he did not, I'll have to evict you.

Because you were never legally his wife, I cannot hold you responsible for his debts. You can leave now, or you and your daughter can stay for one month. For one brief moment, he looked at her, lasciviously. But during that month, you and your daughter will attend to my pleasures. We haven't had debtors prisons for nearly a hundred years, but some of us think we still should.

Juana entered the room with her pet snake before the landlord could approach her mother. He won't bite you if I tell him not to. They watched him back his way to the front door in haste.

I'll be back with the magistrate!

Juana wondered why her mother was crying.

Her mother sat *Juana* on her lap and hugged her. *Juana*, this is no longer our home, and we must leave before the landlord returns with the magistrate. I should have known your father was leaving us when I noticed his clothes were disappearing. I never knew that he was such a coward. Take as much food and clothes as you can carry, and free your pet snake. He will have a better chance than you and I will have together.

Standing on the porch, she shut the door to what had been their home for years. Leaving town, some of her neighbors came out to say goodbye. They seemed to know her husband was leaving before she did. *Juana* did not understand when two of their neighbors yelled at them. We'll stone your place after you leave town.

Juana's mother was apprehensive when she saw the magistrate. He smiled at *Juana* and offered them a ride out of town. Thanks for making my job easy, he said. We're here to enforce the law even if doing that brings no justice. He drove them to the outskirts of town. When *Juana* and her mother got out of the magistrate's carriage, he handed her a fistful of *reales*.

. . .

Juana, you have to walk ahead of me and stay on this side of the road. It's a long way before we get to the tavern. Don't tell anyone that I have a handful of *reales*. I'll try to get food and lodging by working as a scullery maid. We will work our way, tavern to tavern, until we reach Sant Sadurní d'Anoia. I am good friends with the family who owns that small hotel, and we will be safe there.

Juana and her mother were exhausted when they reached the first tavern. The tavern keeper was sympathetic when her mother told him of their plight. He told her a scullery maid's wages would not pay for one night's lodging, but he would let them sleep in his stables and feed them if she cleaned his tavern. He knew his wife would not allow any favors to any woman of that beauty.

The next day when they left the tavern keeper and his cleaned tavern, he wondered if the woman knew that the family had officially sold their hotel and moved back to Barcelona. Of course, it was not his business, but he was glad he had fed and given them a few *reales*.

Juana's mother was pleased. The tavern keeper fed them and gave them a knapsack of food. She would carry it incase they had to eat before they reached the hotel. She was pleased that her luck had changed. She had started their journey with nothing, but now she had a whole handful of *reales*. She waved at the oncoming carriage. Perhaps they, too, were on their way to Sant Sadurní d'Anoia.

Juana was looking for wildflowers before it got too dark. She hoped they will put a smile back on her mother's face. From her side of the road, she watched the carriage stop. She froze in fear behind the trees when she saw her mother grabbed and pulled into the carriage. She cupped her ears with her hands to block the sounds of her mother's screams as the carriage drove out of sight.

45

She thought she could follow the sound of leather that cracked on the horse's back.

Tears filled her eyes, and in terror struck she ran after her mother. She did not know how many times she fell or how much time had passed before she found her mother lying on the side of the road. Her mother's clothes were torn and her *reales* were gone. *Juana* was glad that she carried their blanket, but she had neglected to pick up their food that she passed lying on the road. The worst part was not *Juana's* or her mother's fault. They could not drink or clean themselves because the carriage had taken their water.

. . .

Juana was grateful for the full moon. She could follow the road and could see if the blanket slipped from her mother's back. They had fallen many times before *Juana* saw those candle lights.

Her mother asked the tavern keeper where she could find the hotel. He laughed and pointed her to the brothel. It looks as if you're already dressed for that hotel, he said, but you should take a bath first.

He shook his head and laughed as he stepped inside. He wondered why whores always called it a hotel instead of a brothel. He could not remember when the madam converted the hotel, but just the same, those whores had money to spend, and his business had definitely improved.

With all the strength she had, *Juana* helped her mother climb the steps to see her collapse on the porch. She knocked on the door until she saw the light flickering behind it. When the woman looked out, *Juana* took the woman's hand and pointed to her mother. She knew the woman, her mother's good friend, would take them in when she, with mime and body language, tried to explain.

Juana did not understand why she could make no sounds from her mouth and collapsed on the porch when the woman spoke.

I've never seen either of you in my entire life. Who are you, and what do you want?

Chapter Two

Normally, the ride from Barcelona to the brothel in Sant
Sadurní didn't seem that long, but Mendoza dreaded the thought
of seeing another dead body, especially that of a woman. If only
more of his patients were children. He was far more successful
with them. He examined the woman lying in bed ten days ago
and told the madam the problem. It wasn't the French disease but
rather consumption. He also told the madam to keep the child
away from her mother.

On other occasions, he would play chess with his friend, the
padre, but would surely lose this time if he did. Losing at chess,
although he hadn't lost in years, was so much more preferable
than losing at that never ending game called life and death. At
chess you could manage to smile at the victor. But how could
anyone smile at life's rejection except his adversary.

Mendoza finally reached the village. They had been there so
many times before. When his horse neighed, he let go of the
reins. He would soon rest his horse behind the madam's brothel.

He regularly checked her girls hoping to avoid spreading the
disease and more smiles from his adversary. Mendoza would
always struggle to keep her girls from that ominous smile, but
here and concerning consumption, no one could say the doctor
had won.

He rode through the village remembering its beginning. Only
three businesses brought in new money. If it were not for the two
wineries and the brothel, money would merely change hands. The
other businesses survived by servicing them.

The wineries were there because of the soil, the sunny days, the
cold nights, and the small river between them. The brothel was in
Sant Sadurní because it was the perfect distance from Barcelona.
If two friends came together, they could trade places and lookout
for each other and never be caught in a brothel. Whether it was
strategy or whether it was a game, they could laugh and discuss it

in the local tavern with each other or perhaps with others who had done the same. The brothel was at the end of that well traveled road to the village.

The local tavern sprang to life because of its symbiotic relationship with the brothel. The blacksmith survived by cleaning carriages and coaches of visitors and tending to their horses. The general store served those businesses, and because of the new money brought in by the wineries and the brothel the town had quadrupled in size. Even a small barbershop managed to survive. Not big enough to be called a town, Sant Sadurní remained a village.

Mendoza's horse took his carriage behind the brothel and into the stable. The madam took him into that ill-omened room. He felt the head of the woman lying in bed and wondered how many days had she been cold. He had lost again. A doctor's solace was only in temporary delays. He closed the dead woman's eyes and said that his adversary had won. She waits for only the souls she takes, he said shaking his head. Cover her in a pauper's grave with a sufficient quantity of lime.

She had won, or perhaps she was kind. Whether she won or whether she was kind depended on who smiled first. Mendoza had closed the eyes on many dead faces, and some were almost smiling. Those were the ones worn down by life and waiting for their pain to be over. He wondered if she smiled back, or if she smiled only at those taken in terror. There would be no way for any to know because during that final transition, they would see only one side of that fatal coin and take the knowledge with them. He turned to face the madam.

Where is the motherless child?

I'm surprised you didn't see the child running out while calling to her mother. And I didn't understand her mother's last words.

I will be there where you will find me, and I will always be waiting. It's better to die behind my skirts than to live as a slave or a whore.

I remember the day when I first saw her dirty mother and that even dirtier child. They looked as if both had walked from

Barcelona. I knew they would be rejected by anyone in town. In my profession I have learned to recognize injustice and deceit, but I was looking at two gaunt faces begging for food on the steps of my brothel.

I gave her food and a place to sleep if her mother performed the duties that my girls refused. She was only a scullery maid, but that led to other problems. In order to respond to my girl's complaints, I had to tell the child to sleep in my stable.

Oh doctor, I should never have taken them in, but I feel sorry for any child who is born a bastard. The child's father told her mother that he would return, but of course he never did. He left her mother his dirty curse. The only course that lying bastard left her was destitution. And now the town calls the innocent child who believed him the brothel's bastard.

At first, the children in the village called her *bastarda de burdel,* but they soon came up with a more demeaning term, garbage bastard. They would snicker, laugh, and feel superior to the *basura bastarda.* The child also foolishly thought her father would return. I'll tell you more in my parlor.

Mendoza remembered when he first met the madam. She had been successful in Barcelona. She saved her money and purchased the small hotel in Sant Sadurní. When she first enlisted the services of the doctor, she told him the French disease was not the only downside to being a whore. A woman of the streets was at the mercy of her clients. There was always a chance that sadistic behavior to whores would go unpunished or even be encouraged by those watching in the streets.

It only happened once in the madam's brothel, and the small village of Sant Sadurní discovered that she was an excellent shot. The villagers who testified to the magistrate only saw a man about to slit a whore's throat in the street. The only evidence was a hole in the back of his head and the dagger in his hand.

The madam reminded the magistrate, and a frequent client, that Mary Magdalene also had a soul. He ruled it a justifiable homicide and gave the madam the dead man's horse. She remained a champion to her girls and enjoyed some civility from the village. To this day, she shops in Sant Sadurní without verbal scorn.

Oh doctor, I couldn't let the child live in my brothel. My girls said they couldn't perform because she made them feel nervous. She would sneak in to get food and to see her mother. Then she would take it back into the forest. That was her only refuge because the children would stone her if she stayed in the village. Even in my brothel, my girls called her *basura bastarda*. I would not recognize her if she had a clean face.

The madam poured wine for the doctor. Don't consider taking her with you. You would never be able to find her. Besides, you wouldn't want her. She examines every thing, but she never speaks. She looks and then runs away. She is surely retarded. I will leave food for her in the back, near the stables. The madam used her handkerchief to wipe her eyes. As you ride back to Barcelona, I will be begging our padre to hear my confession.

The doctor finished his wine. Your problem is that you are a good person and had only one choice. Go to confession, and I'll consider the child on my way back to Barcelona. I'll leave one of my pigeons, and you must let me know if you find her. Although I have never laid eyes on her face, I think I might, from what you have just told me, know her.

Mendoza stretched out in his carriage. Of course, his horse also knew his way back to Barcelona. He was thinking of the ragged, dirty little child. He considered what the madam told him. The child would look and then quickly turn away. He was not sure of the madam's description, but it reminded him of someone he had seen before. He had delivered a kindred spirit that was a generation apart from him, but now ... there may be another.

The madam was on her knees before the priest. Oh Padre, please hear my confession.

I will listen to you, my child, inside the confessional.

Padre, perdóneme ya que he pecado. No sé cuando era mi última confesión. She told him what she told the doctor. I have turned away an innocent child to save my business because my obligation to my girls is larger. I didn't know what I should do.

The madam was surprised when she heard the padre laughing and waited for his answer.

I think Jesus would have created one of his unknown miracles. I don't know what I would have done if I had to choose between the child and the sisters. Do one hundred hail Marys, and pray for her soul. Pray that she does not become prey to the forest. And leaving food is an excellent idea.

In nomine Patris et Filii et Spiritus Sancti. Amen.

The *basura bastarda* felt safest in the forest. She arrived with a loaf of bread and a knife stolen from the brothel. Her mother had taught her to pick mushrooms and greens that did not make her sick. She made her camp near the pond created from a waterfall, and on warm nights she could sleep behind it and feel safe from the humans. She preferred the safety behind that waterfall, but on cold nights she would sleep at the foot of her favorite tree and cover herself with leaves.

She could venture out at night and steal grapes from the vines. They had become her friends and did not seem to mind. The dangerous mission was to leave the safety of the forest in daylight and to get food from the humans' outside table after they had returned to work. On her luckiest days, she could grab bones from the plates that still had meat. She would do this every day except when the church bells rang because that outside table would be empty.

She never knew what day it was. She only knew when the church bells rang. Just before that ringing sunrise, she would carve a notch into her favorite tree, but she did not know why. Perhaps if there were enough notches, her mother would come forth from that flowing waterfall and smile. Time passed slowly, and there were more notches than fingers. She would have to include her toes.

She would climb the tallest tree and look down at the buildings. This was the most important part of the day. She would look for that big brown and white horse. If he and his mounted rider came into the forest with his dog, the *Pachón Navarro,* she would climb down to the ground and hide behind the waterfall.

She would watch carefully because if that *Pachón Navarro* was with him she could leave no tracks. If the human carried his crossbow, she would have to jump into the river downstream and wade, and even sometimes swim upstream to reach that big rock and climb up to hide behind the safety of her mother's skirts, that flowing waterfall.

Hiding in the forest was different than hiding in the village. She had learned to wait until after sundown before sneaking into the brothel. The humans' children would be enjoying their dinner without any thought of chasing or laughing at her while throwing their stones. Her mother would be there with some food, and she could take it back into the forest and eat it next to her favorite tree, where she and her mother had picnicked, near that waterfall.

She no longer could hide or sneak into the village. Her mother was no longer there. She would have to hide in the forest. But in the forest, she would be more realistic prey. In the village, the stones might draw blood, but they would bounce off, and she could still run away. In the forest, the human's arrow would draw blood. It would not bounce off— and she could not run away.

His hunt, with the help of his *Pachón Navarro,* would be over, and he would at last have his triumph. He would take her mounted head into his house after hanging and flaying her body in the barn like the deer he killed in the forest. Whether those bones left on that outside table still had meat would no longer matter. She hoped her head would not hear him laughing, but she did not know what would happen to her skin.

She disliked that *Pachón Navarro* because if it came with the human and his crossbow and it was near the end of the day, she would be wet until the sun came up the following day. She knew it was unsafe to have the comfort of a fire.

If they came in the morning, she would be wet from hiding behind the waterfall, but she could take off her clothes and dry them in the sun at the south edge of the forest.

While her clothes were drying, she could sneak between the vines and gather the ripest grapes. She could also look for good mushrooms and greens. She would take her greens, her mushrooms, and her grapes back to the pond below the waterfall and eat them at the foot of her favorite tree.

She had learned that the human and his *Pachón Navarro* usually came into the forest on the same day as the church bells rang. But because she could never be sure, she would, except for eating and sleeping, spend her life in the tops of trees, watching and waiting.

Chapter Three

Mendoza was sitting in his most comfortable chair and smoking a *cañuela*, but something was missing. Just like the pipes made of clay, it would burn your fingers if you held it the wrong way. You had to remember to keep your fingers an extra distance below that glowing end. The reed held so much heat without showing. That would never have happened with a pipe made of clay. You just had to remember to set it down without touching the bowl and hold it only by its stem. It was more than once that he had found himself guilty of that same mistake, and his fingers had justly paid for it.

Another problem with clay was that those long stemmed pipes broke so easily. He preferred the long stem because it allowed the smoke to cool, but he had forgotten more than once when he would turn his head and slap it against his bookshelf or some corner wall. That would never happen with a *cañuela*, but the reed always flavored the tobacco and gave it that rank taste of weed. There must be a better way.

He had tried several woods, but the ones that carved easily could not stand any heat. He had several blocks of cherry, acquired from an artisan friend. His friend had drilled the bowl so that its bottom ended, barely touching the intruding draft hole. All Mendoza had to do was carve it into the shape of a pipe, perhaps the shape of a straight billiard, smooth it out, and make it pretty. He would make two pipes, giving the best one to his friend, the Padre of Saint Sadurní, and keep the other for himself.

They had been friends since childhood. The padre had chosen to treat the soul, but Mendoza had chosen to treat the body. Both found frustration with their professions. Mendoza would find relief and possibly satisfaction with carving pipes into various shapes and enjoying those results, but the only solace for the padre was in playing chess.

They would play whenever Mendoza traveled to the village where he would buy wine and inspect the madam's girls. The padre said that if he ever won, he would record it as a historical event by writing it down.

The pipes were finished, and the artisan supplied stems were a perfect fit to his handcrafted bowls. He was shining the wood with the oil from the side of his nose when he heard the sound of a horse, a solid dismount, and a knock on his door. The young lad burst in before Mendoza could answer.

Doctor Mendoza, you have to come to the winery. I think Count Miguel may be dead. There's no time to waste. The condesa gave me her favorite horse. You will have to come at once, he said after taking a deep breath.

Relax lad, there's no reason to hurry if he's already dead. Mendoza walked the young boy out to look at his horse and then soundly chide him. This is no way to treat any horse, especially one as fine as this. Did you gallop him all the way to Barcelona? Mendoza did not wait for an answer. Water him down while I get my carriage.

Mendoza noticed the young lad's hands as they rode out of town. As a physician, he always examined his deliveries, and that included their extremities. He had not delivered many before he became aware of their hands and their fingers proportions. They were different for boys than girls. The most recognizable difference in infants was the relationship or length between their index and ring finger. He then realized that this small, young lassie was wearing the clothes of a boy. What is your name, girl?

She looked embarrassed and said it was *Juana*, but he could call her Jane. Her mother called her *Juana*, but the Englishman who fathered her, as told by her mother, called her Jane. She was sitting next to Mendoza and watching their passing surroundings.

Don't you ever ride a horse that hard again! Mendoza maintained the stern look on his face and waited for her answer.

I'm sorry sir, but I want to please the condesa. Would you like some of my water? Mendoza's anger softened because the child offered all that she had.

55

He remembered when the count married. He said he had found the perfect wife if she were not so thin. Although fat women were a sign of wealth, it actually did not bother him. He learned to let her have her way because he knew she was faithful to him. Whenever she rode into the village, she carried a dueling pistol in her saddle bags and a sword in a sheath attached to her saddle. She also carried a dagger attached to her belt.

Even though she was the count's wife, the men in the village wantonly looked at her. The count wanted her to have the company of one of his hands. She would look at him and twitch her nose.

Do you want me to have protection or him?

Of course, he would say and laugh. Not only was she a beauty with raven black hair and blue eyes, but she had a palate possessed of only one in ten thousand men. Although lean, her perfect skin stretched over her muscled body, but she always wore clothes into town that would hide it.

Her mother, considered a fine cook, had no taste at all. Her secret was her dearest daughter, who would taste the ingredients in every meal when not fighting with her brothers. The condesa had learned to bite and to kick or even grab a stick in order to win. Although only a girl, her brothers treated her with respect. When her father died, her mother gave her daughter to the count. Anna was her youngest and favorite child.

Her mother and brothers were at her wedding. The count hoped he would get the family winery as a dowry but would settle for her and some family silver because he needed her gift of taste. Because her father had died, her eldest brother, Cesaré, gave her away. But it was obvious that the count was not pleased with the now fulfilled marriage contract.

The count taught her every step he knew in making wine. What he could not do himself, Anna already knew. With tears running down her face, she could smell and know if the first stage fermentation was going well. During this time, she would taste the acid in the grapes. She knew when to add stems and when to remove them. But most of all, with her nose, her taste, and her gifted hands, she knew when to get off of the skins. She had a large map of their vineyard and on it had drawn lines indicating various sections. Because of the vineyard's topography, the grapes matured at slightly different times.

Anna would spend the summer in the vineyard feeling the sun. In some years the sun on sections would change, and she would redraw the lines. Besides, the vineyard had two types of grapes.

They always picked in October, but the question was ... which days. The men would come to her with a labeled bunch of grapes from each section and handwritten notes. She had taught some to read and to write.

The count would watch her in the fields and pace back and forth on his covered veranda. He would stop from time to time and silently pray to his god. And then he would listen for that sound of birds in circled flight. He thought he could hear his wife's laughter when she banged on that triangular bell. He would drop to his knees and give the sign of the cross before he yelled. *Este es el tiempo para picotear las uvas.*

The count would see his wife crushing a bunch of grapes in each hand. Her clothes spread over the vines, and her sheathed sword rested against them. Her arms, outstretched to the sun, glistened as the juice ran down her arms and dripped from her breast. They too glowed in the sun with refractions and reflections of light, giving them that rainbow of colors: red, yellow, and green. She would grab more grapes, squeeze, and then rub them all over her body. She would arch her back, resting on her knees, and then roll in the furrows between the vines. Mud covered her skin, including her face. Clutching her clothes and sword in her left hand, she would walk back to the house passing the field hands, who were running to start with the picking.

What began as an opportune marriage became suspicion and loathing. The count at first hoped he would learn to love her. That hope had turned into suspicion before turning into hate. If only he could be granted a divorce, but the winery would return to its original state. She was a far better vintner than he, and she prayed to different gods. He had no proof, but the harvest had almost doubled over those years. He wanted to slay her, but she was a better swordsman than he. He was content to despise those that she loved.

Mendoza looked at the young child. We should pick up the padre on our way through the village if the condesa wants me to come straight to the winery, and the count will need his last rites if he's still alive.

Sir, I think the padre is already there.

Mendoza rode through the village and was now on the road leading to the winery. He was looking forward to seeing his old friend. He was startled at the sight of a barking dog running straight towards his carriage. The liver colored dog, evenly ticked with white, would at the withers measure almost seven hands. He had a solid liver patch as if a saddle on a horse had slipped to its side and a solid liver head. Mendoza grabbed his whip and snapped the reins.

The young girl grabbed Mendoza's hand holding the reins. She pulled it back, causing his horse to slow down. Oh please, Doctor Mendoza, can we let him ride with us? Jane patted her leg when the carriage stopped. Come here boy. Mendoza was surprised to see the dog jump from the ground onto the carriage seat.

Keep him on your side. I don't want him licking my face. Mendoza snapped the reins while the dog licked Jane's. I've never seen a dog like that before. If he were fat, he'd look like a speckled clown. What kind of dog is he?

Jane smiled at Mendoza as she patted the dog's head. He's a bastard just like me. A mixed-blood hound sired him, but his mother was a *Pachón Navarro*: a Spanish pointer. The count was culling the litter when the condesa grabbed his hand and pleaded for his life. She said it was prophesized that she would have a saddled dog, and, like the prophet, his name would be Ezekiel. The count was so mad that he killed his *Pachón Navarro*.

The condesa lets me call him Zeke, and he sleeps with me in the stables. The condesa also pleaded for me when she found me sleeping in the woods. The count knew someone was stealing scraps from the field hand's table, and he would come with his crossbow and *Pachón Navarro*, looking for me.

Mendoza smiled at the young girl, who was smiling, petting the dog, and looking ahead. There seemed to be a conflict in her story, but that was often the case with children. He listened while she continued to speak.

And now, I get to serve the food and clean the field hand's table. Take that road to the left where the sign reads *La Casa*.

Mendoza showed surprise when he looked at the girl, who was still petting the bastard dog's head. Girl, can you read?

Jane covered her mouth, making a cry as she drew in her breath. Oh please, Sir, don't tell the count. He'll send me away and kill Zeke. The condesa teaches me when he's away. Please don't tell anyone that I'm a girl or that I can read. The condesa said we should keep it a secret because it would enrage the count.

Mendoza put his arm around the girl to comfort her. Well, little lassie, I think everyone should learn to read and to write. Your secret is safe with me. He paused before smiling and looking at the young child. And ... are you learning your numbers as well? There's much more to numbers than just counting. Do you know how to add and to subtract? He listened as he steered his horse to the left of the sign.

The girl smiled without looking at him or turning her head. She was looking straight ahead and had her arms were around her bastard dog. Mendoza watched her little hands stroking that bastard dog's slipped saddle to the rhythm his horse's four hoofbeats dampened by that dusty road. She turned to smile at Mendoza and had to look up to face him.

Sir, I can also multiply and divide.

Field hands were waiting when Mendoza and Jane arrived. They told him to follow the torches into the woods, and that the padre was already there. It was starting to get dark, and the torches helped Mendoza find his way. He drove as far into the woods as he could. When he set the break, Jane and the dog jumped from his carriage.

It's this way Doctor Mendoza. Don't forget your case.

Mendoza was happy to follow the girl. Besides, it was starting to get dark, and he stepped with caution on the uneven ground. Jane waited to hold his hand, but the dog ran ahead. He saw two torches blazing on each side of the count's body. He saw the condesa slap her hands and point at the dog, who was fiercely growling. Pointing her finger as if holding a musket, she ordered the dog to back away.

Mendoza was surprised to see the dog growl because he had been so friendly in his carriage. He heard the condesa call to the child.

Jane! Don't let him near the count. Keep Zeke over there while the doctor examines his body. Mendoza watched the condesa waving the torch. The padre was still bending over the count as Mendoza approached, walking on the uneven ground.

After a brief examination, Mendoza stood up slowly and shook his head at the padre. He was brief with his questions to the condesa. Why did you call me, and how long has this man been dead? The count has been gored or possibly impaled and then trampled to death. He has fang punctures on his left arm, and, judging by the look on his face, he died in terror. You must have known he was dead. Condesa, can you tell me what happened?

I found him lying on the ground near that felled tree with the projected rotted limb. His horse must have thrown him and then trampled him to death. I didn't see the horse because it was gone before I arrived. Perhaps the smell of blood frightened the horse, but I was able to whistle him in. She took a deep breath before looking and smiling at Jane.

Of course, I thought the count could be dead, but … as his loving, obedient wife, I did what I had to. I guess I'm still in shock. I mean to say that I did whatever I could to save him and his immortal soul. That's why I called the padre and sent Jane to fetch you. Would you two take charge of his body?

Mendoza was looking at the condesa's expressionless face as she faced her dead husband.

My men are at your disposal. The family crypt is in Barcelona.

Mendoza felt that he was looking at the condesa for the first time. She was calm and remained expressionless as she looked into his eyes. He watched her turn to face Jane and then smile.

Jane, take the count's horse and ride back to the house with Zeke. Choose a couple of men to come here with a wine cart. Wait for us at the house, and tell my cook to set a table for four.

Doctor, I don't know your horse but most become disturbed around a dead body, and you will need to follow me back to the house in the dark. I'll tell Roberto to stay with the count and to leave two of the lanterns. All three watched Jane mount the count's horse with the condesa's help and then call the dog.

Thank you both for coming.

After Jane was out of sight, the condesa faced the padre. Padre, would you stay with the count? Roberto is a little superstitious.

The padre just nodded his head, held his cross, and walked to the felled tree. Roberto was sitting on it but as far away from the count's body as he could be. He seemed to get nervous when they could no longer hear the condesa's horse or the doctor's carriage. He tried to compose himself as he faced the padre.

Relax, my son, death is a normal part of life, and you are in the company of a priest. Do you know anything about the way the count died?

No Padre, the condesa brought me here, and the only thing I found were two arrows in that tree over there, the one with all those notches, and the count's crossbow laying on the ground. I used my knife to get the arrows out and put them back into the count's quiver. I think there are more arrows in the forest, but I was afraid to look.

The padre picked up a lantern and examined the rotted tree limb. It was still wet from the count's blood. He told Roberto to hold the lantern while he examined the count's body. It was obvious that this limb impaled the count. He held Roberto's hand and received his confession until they heard the men coming with the wine cart.

Roberto was happy to help load the count, now that he felt no longer alone. The three men laid his body onto the bed of the cart. The padre turned his head and back away from the men when he saw the driver spit on the count's face.

. . .

Jane was waiting when they arrived. The condesa told the men to put the count's body into an empty shed, and she told Jane that the padre and Doctor Mendoza would be spending the night.

Jane walked over and stood next to Mendoza. She looked down and drew her lips between her teeth before she looked up at him. She could not stop the tears in her eyes as she tried to wipe her cheeks.

The condesa said, I get to eat with you tonight … and at the same table!

The cook was serving the table and looking down her nose in contempt at Jane. Mendoza and the padre were embarrassed when she called Jane a *basura bastarda*. They watched the little girl cringe as she lowered her head over her plate and whisper that it was not her fault.

Gentlemen, the condesa said as she followed the cook back into the kitchen.

Jane was standing and listening to the condesa as were the men. She was looking down at the floor.

Yes, she is a bastard, they heard, and left on the side of the road like garbage, but you will leave this house if you ever say it again. We are all God's children. They could hear the cook crying as the condesa entered the dining room.

Gentlemen, thank you, and please sit down. I want you to try my new wine. It's the most troublesome *Vitis vinifera* I've ever faced, but the results, I think, are astounding.

As they clicked goblets, perhaps in relief, the condesa started to laugh. Please presume after what you have heard that you are now part of our family. Your rooms are being prepared, and Jane will be sleeping with me tonight. She turned her head to face the frightened child. Jane, ladies do not stand when another leaves the room. Sit down and hold up your head.

Mendoza smiled at the padre as the condesa, while looking at Jane, continued to speak.

Jane! Hold this in your left hand. It's called a fork.

They were in the living room, sitting and facing the fire. Jane was sitting on the floor next to the condesa. Mendoza and the padre were lighting their new pipes. The condesa looked down at her newly acquired ward. Jane, fetch me the count's pipe on that mantel, and then serve us brandy. Doctor, may I try some of your tobacco?

After serving brandy, Jane sat in front of the fire, and she was crying.

Girl, what is wrong with you, demanded the condesa.

Jane looked at the condesa with tears running down her face. I've never had this much honor before, but I can't help but worry about Zeke. He will be alone in that cold stable with all those big horses.

We've always had each other to keep warm. Condesa, it would be a great honor to sleep in a bed, but may I be allowed to sleep with Zeke, in the stables?

It's time to call me Anna, she said smiling at Jane and then at the men. You will clean Zeke, especially his feet, every time he enters this house. The condesa was lighting the late count's pipe as all three watched the young girl run from the house.

It will be interesting to discover what I have to put up with. Jane has to learn to excuse herself when she leaves the table, the condesa said still laughing. Have either of you ever seen this type of pipe? The count bought figurines of this material on his last trip to Turkey and found this same white mineral floating in *El Mar Negro*. He had an artisan friend carve it into a pipe. After lighting her dead husband's pipe, she warmed her brandy snifter with her hands.

The condesa, the padre, and Mendoza were talking about the count's disposal when Jane and Zeke entered the room. Two of her men would follow Mendoza to Barcelona with the count's body using that same wine cart. Jane and Zeke lay down in front of the fire.

Jane was sleeping when Zeke lifted his head and looked at the condesa. He turned back to face the fire and then rest his head on Jane's neck. Except for Jane, they could all hear the sounds of his contented breathing.

Mendoza was smiling when he fixed his eyes on the sleeping child. Months had passed, but he remembered the madam's words. Was this was the brothel's dirty, little bastard that ran from the brothel calling for her dead mother. Was this the child that reminded him of another, and is it possible that they could be in the very same room together. The cook had scrubbed her clean, and she was wearing the outgrown clothes of another. He thought he should tell the condesa it was he who closed her dead mother's eyes but realized it might not be appropriate. Besides, the dead woman might not be Jane's mother.

On their way to their rooms, Mendoza was talking to the padre. I never really knew the condesa. Her company is a delight and an absolute pleasure. She speaks as an educated man. I knew she had gifted hands and a mind, concerning the grapes, but I just had the

63

pleasure of speaking with an intelligent, desirable woman with the heart and reasoning ability of a man.

The padre smiled when he placed his hand on the doctor's shoulder. Fernando, I've known this since she was a child.

Chapter Four

Jane was lying in the condesa's bed, and Zeke was sleeping on the floor. I don't think I've ever slept in a bed, and this is the second time in my life I've ever been in a room with a fireplace. She watched the condesa take off her clothes and stand next to the bed. She had never seen breasts before, at least not like those. She could not remember. Her own breasts were just starting to form, and hair was beginning to grow in three new places.

Perhaps it was her season because there was no rhyme or reason to believe that Jane was her soulmate. There was no rationalization, but somehow in that miracle, and in a separate dimension of time, the condesa knew that she and Jane had been split apart.

From a terrified dumb creature to become a lover of its offspring was something she had never seen in a child. Jane did not blame the *Pachón Navarro* for doing its job. The girl's mind snapped and took a picture of every event and then decided whether it was new or part of an old paradigm. The condesa continued to ponder and question those never before felt sensations.

My love for Jane is more than that of a mother, a sister, or a friend. My mother touched me all over when I was borne from her womb. Over time, I became her sister and her best friend. I want even more than that for Jane. I want to touch her all over as if she came from my womb. I want to feel her every joy and share it with my daughter, sister, and best friend. I will keep my lust in abeyance and protect this *ingénue* that came out immaculately clean from dirty rags and as prey to the forest. But I will continue to touch her, to be her mother, sister and love her.

The condesa still stood naked at the side of the bed. She was staring and smiling at Jane when she drew back the covers. Jane felt a sensation in her groin as if she had to pee but couldn't.

65

When the condesa rolled her over, she pressed Jane's face between her breasts and wrapped her arms around her. Jane, with the help of the condesa's feet and loving hands, felt her legs and cheeks spread apart. She felt air simultaneously and in syncopation circulating between them.

Her eyes closed and her mouth obediently opened when she felt the condesa's gentle fingers. Her body, covered with known hands, was helplessly floating in a smooth current of air. She knew she was going to die on her way into heaven, but she did not know why she had to scream. It was the surrender of a daughter, a sister, and a friend to a woman and a mother who would never have a child of her own.

Jane felt safe in the arms of the condesa. They were lying face to face on Anna's pillow, and there was no place on her body that Anna's hands and lips had not touched. Each touch in itself was a shape of silence that held no words. These were sensations that Jane had never felt. She turned her eyes, looking away from the condesa.

Please love me back because I think you just made me want to become a woman.

You're not a woman yet, but you will become one. Anna rolled the child across and over her. She penetrated Jane's ear with her whispers. Together, their toes faced the ceiling. Jane, her legs spread by the condesa's feet, could feel the condesa's hands holding her waist. The condesa, without objection, spread Jane's legs apart and reached their destination. Jane gasped with outstretched hands and closed her eyes as her face rested next to the condesa's.

And now, Jane, you have a second secret that you must never tell. The first was terrifying, but the second will always hold you warm. I could be hanged if the first secret were known and be burned alive were the second shown.

Jane put her hands on top of the condesa's to guide them. I would gladly give my life to stay with you, to be owned and to become your slave. I am no longer afraid because you have lifted me from terror and darkness.

They awoke the next morning, and Zeke was lying at the foot of their bed. Call me condesa in front of others but Anna only when we are alone or with family. As you grow up, if you are to grow up, you'll need to learn to use your own mind. It's so easy to let others or another think for you, especially when your thoughts have been dictated to you as a child. Never swallow or react to what you first hear until you have heard the other side even if you have to build and advocate it. Never forget that life is a two edged sword. Your mind will then be your own, but be prepared to stand alone.

I don't want to stand alone. I will always want to be with you.

The condesa took Jane's face in her hands. We will not be separate, but we will separately be our own persons. I will teach you all that I can, but the time will come when I have to send you off to school. Don't worry, that will come only after a few more years.

Jane held the condesa's hand as they sat on the bed. Last night I almost died twice. When the count's arrows hit that tree instead of me, he took out his dagger. Zeke bit his right hand as he raised it to stab me. I think the count kicked Zeke, because he ran from me. When the count switched his dagger to his left hand, I heard the thundering sound of your horse's hoofbeats.

You grabbed his left hand with your right and galloped toward that felled tree. I heard the count scream when you dragged him against that rotted tree limb and said those frightening words. *Vaya al diablo, usted el hijo de una hembra.* The second time I almost died was in your arms last night. I thought I had died and gone to heaven.

I'm not sure where heaven is, the condesa said. I think it can be anywhere, and that is also true for hell. Let's get dressed, and you can run outside and play with Zeke. Come back to the house after he finishes his ... walk.

Zeke did not run from the count. He knows my horse and got out of his way. Go help my cook serve breakfast. The doctor will have a long ride back to Barcelona. Let's make sure that he is well fed.

. . .

Jane ran to Mendoza's carriage. The cook helped me make this sandwich for you, and the condesa is giving you this firkin of her

67

new wine. She wants the cask back when it's empty. She wants you to create a compound that will kill vinegar spores but not harm wine. She's been trying sulfur and saltpeter separately because she thinks gunpowder is too dangerous.

Jane was smiling, and her eyes were looking around in that childlike mischievous way. She grabbed Mendoza's flask and ran back into the house. When she returned, she handed him his flask. Treat this like brandy. It'll really get you drunk. The condesa makes it with apples and plums but only in winter.

Mendoza watched Jane run back into the house. There was something about the way she ran. He had seen a girl run like that before, and now he could remember. He would stop to see the madam and tell her that she had no reason to worry. God had intervened. The two, one of which he had touched at birth, would now be joined together, even though only God can ignore time. Mendoza snapped the reins and was still laughing when he saw that the condesa's men were ready.

. . .

After their breakfast, Anna and the padre were smoking. Jane and Zeke were outside, playing. The padre was blinking his eyes while looking at his emptied plate.

I don't know how we are to survive. The cardinal took all of our funds. He told me he had the greater need, and his authority could not be questioned. I wanted to beg, not for myself, but for our parishioners and the sisters. Condesa, can you spare any food?

The condesa took the padre's hand and dropped to her knees. *Perdóneme el padre, ya que he pecado. Este es mi primera confesión.* I took a life to save one, and my only regret is … that I have none. The count wanted to kill a dog because it was a bastard, and a small child for stealing scraps from the table, or perhaps it was just for the sport. Our first years were happy. I don't know what changed him.

Padre, you must hear the events leading to my confession. I found a child sleeping in the woods and took her home and fed her. It took weeks for her to trust me, but she never lost her fear

68

of the count. She was always apprehensive and even nervous around men, but she shook with fear whenever she saw the count. She would try to hide behind me. I thought she was dumb until I overheard her talking to the dog. Until then, I thought she could only respond to hand signals. I used the dog to bring her out and to turn a frightened creature back into a person. Perhaps it was my protective instincts, but I soon began to love her.

The count would only let her sleep in his stable. I don't know why, but I think he already or soon despised her. Perhaps it was because I loved her. I let her take food and play in the woods with the bastard dog. I saw the count watching and waiting and then follow her, riding his horse, into the woods with his crossbow.

My child, I forgive you for having no regret because I heard all of the count's confessions. I can only pray for his soul. His confessions, which have the seal of the sacrament, will remain with me, and so will yours. There is no need for forgiveness when saving a life. You did what a good person had to.

And now, Condesa, you must hear my confession. I feel closer to God because He must have listened to me when I prayed for the soul and the strength of a young child. I watched you grow, but I still remember that little child. Your confession to me, when you were a child, is proof that He answered me. The padre smiled before placing his hands on Anna's head. The Lord, He will surely provide. *In nomine Patris et Filii et Spiritus Sancti. Amen.*

This is not your first confession. I remember some of yours as a child. Your brothers had thrown you into the water to teach you to swim. When you climbed out from that pond, you attacked your brothers and slapped Cesaré's butt with his sword. That was your first confession, and it came in two parts.

You said you wanted forgiveness because you enjoyed it, but a part of you had remained in the water. That's when I knew there was something special about you because you returned alone to that pond, jumped into the water, and tried to get it back. I prayed God to give me the wisdom to answer your questions. It was the first time I felt lacking, because I couldn't explain them. I prayed that someday He would answer them for you.

The padre laughed and said he remembered another confession. Cesaré wanted forgiveness because he wanted to marry you after you spanked his ass with his own sword. Oh, my God, I've broken the seal of his confession.

Padre, I already know Cesare's love for me goes beyond that of a brother. But even if incest were allowed, I could never be the property of a womanizer. We will give you food and wine, and you and the sisters will dine with me until the church has funds.

You and the sisters must go into our village and pray in the streets for money. You will have to get money from the village because this is the time of our harvest, and the winery is at its lowest funds. I'll have our cook pack some food, and two of my men will follow you back to the church. The condesa smiled at the padre. There will be plenty of food for you and the sisters.

When the padre stepped out, he saw Jane struggling with his saddle. She had removed his horse's saddle to groom him, but she was too small to put it back.

Padre, would you help me with this saddle? It's not very well behaving.

It was amusing to watch her try pushing the saddle onto the horse's back, but it was even more amusing to see it fall on the other side before she could catch it. Let me help you with that, the padre said. How did you know that it was I who was standing behind you when your back was turned to me?

Jane was smiling while the padre was saddling his horse. Padre, it had to be you because it wasn't the condesa.

Then how did you know that it wasn't the condesa, or do you have eyes in the back of your head? He saw the child smile as she looked back at the house while shrugging her shoulders before she turned to face him.

I'll bet your horse really likes apples.

Two of the condesa's men followed the padre. The winery's cart carried food and a firkin of wine. They thought it funny because the padre was talking to himself, and thought it even funnier that while riding the padre looked at the sky and gave the sign of the cross.

He remembered his time in the seminary, studying Plato as a young man. He never believed that beings originally had four arms and four legs, or that Zeus had split them apart. God created man in His own image with two arms and two legs. But, just the same, what he had just seen troubled him. He prayed to God for an answer.

¿Mi Dios, es esta su respuesta?

Chapter Five

Mendoza parked his carriage and carried his flask containing apple-plum brandy. He checked the fireplace for glowing embers before informing his cook of his arrival and then waited until he heard the approaching wine cart. After lighting his pipe, he stepped out and handed the men the letter.

Take this letter and the count's body to the mortuary. Come back and dine with me before you return. I'm by far too tired to examine the count's body. That will have to wait until tomorrow morning.

We can't come back, they said. The condesa said there can be no delay.

Then come back and pick up some food to eat along your way. I have to shelter my horse and carriage. As they drove away, Mendoza smiled and shut the door to his horse's stall. I hope you don't mind, but if it's any consolation, we'll both be dinning alone. He laughed all the way to his front door.

The padre was having breakfast with the sisters. The condesa will feed us, but we have to get money from the village. While you sisters beg in the village for money, I will talk to our local madam. She knows how to run a business and could provide me with a solution that hasn't occurred to me.

The sisters looked at him in shock. Padre, you can't go into that brothel. What would people think? And ... you should never speak with that evil woman.

The padre opened his hands and examined his palms. Our Savior walked alone in the streets, and He saved many more Marys than one. If you had not been taken in by our church, you might be working for the madam. She has taken good care of her girls and, with the doctor's help, has not spread the French disease.

You will receive what I am about to say as a sanctity of a confession. She and the condesa are our most generous

72

benefactors. The condesa had to secretly provide us with money without the count's knowledge, and the madam wanted it kept secret for the sake of our church.

Oh Padre, please forgive us. Let our false pride be our only sin.

Sisters, prepare for the journey into town. We will dine with the condesa tonight and store any money we receive in her vault. We will have to keep this secret from the cardinal … if we are to ever survive.

. . .

Mendoza was at the mortuary examining the count's body. His torn shirt concealed a left hand within that same left sleeve. Just like a rope, his sleeve was twisted and ended in a knot. He examined the punctures on the count's right arm before looking at that damaged hand.

The mortician was more indignant than surprised when he heard Mendoza laughing. How could he look and laugh at that mangled body… and all at the same time. As the doctor changed coats, he smiled realizing the mortician's frustration.

I never knew the condesa was such a fine horseman.

. . .

Mendoza saw a coach in front of his house when he arrived. What does the king want now. He already has many surgeons at his disposal, and I have to be here for my own patients. He tied his horse to the hitching post.

The king ordered us to bring you to his castle. Don't worry Doctor; he wants you there to attend him, and your safety is our biggest concern. You will find comfort in his coach, and one of us will follow you, driving in your carriage.

There is no time to argue, Doctor. The king is certainly failing. Doctor Mendoza, you are the only physician he trusts.

Mendoza packed his bag and spoke to his cook. The king will decide when I may return. He balanced an ember on his pipe as he got into the coach. He remembered the king's words when he returned home from the front.

Not only are you the finest surgeon, my general said that you are a magnificent healer. The king wanted the doctor to join his staff of physicians, but Mendoza reminded him that he would be one of many men serving one man. He would be one man serving many men in Barcelona.

Sire, I'll always be at your beck and call, but my call is to be one serving many rather than to be one of many serving one. It was then the king extended his hand and reinstated the name Mendoza at the Spanish Court.

The padre was enjoying wine with the madam while the sisters were begging for money in the streets. She kept a clean, comfortable house, probably because of the doctor's instructions. Over the years, the padre and the madam became good friends.

Madam, I know you can keep our secret. Our cardinal took all of our funds. We have to think of new ways to earn more money, other than donations.

The madam stopped sipping her wine and smiled at her padre. I'm very good at making money. I will give what little we can, but the fastest way I know to earn money is to gamble and sin. I could auction my girls in a lottery, but a man will not gamble for what he can easily afford with money.

I could action my girls at half of their price, but it would only be appealing to the poor, and how would my regular clients respond when I charged them more? Padre, you know nothing about running a business. You assume that your parishioners give an honest tithing and do not bargain or rationalize with their Lord, but I run my business without discounts. It would be demeaning to my girls.

I don't think you know this, the madam said as she poured him another glass of wine. The padre watched her get up and then slowly sit next to him. She took his hand before she spoke. My clients, she said in amusement, would give a week's wages, perhaps a month's, for one night with the condesa. She let go of his hand and moved back to her chair.

I know this will be difficult for you to understand, but in my profession success comes from knowing the ways to promotion and pay. Padre, did this not occur to you?

She smiled before she continued speaking. Here is something you may not know because lust is not the main subject of men when they are unburdening their souls. They are afraid of her. They have seen what she can do with a sword, and they know how well she stands with her brothers. She's the flame to the mouth and the spider's parlor to the fly. I know you have loved her since she was a child, but consider her now as a woman.

. . .

Mendoza awoke to the sounds of the city. It was much noisier and larger than Barcelona. He was able to sleep along the way in the comfortable coach built for his king. He hoped this Philip would be stronger than his father, Philip III. The doctor remembered his father, Don Francisco, openly telling Philip II, the king's grandfather, that this was the wrong season and the wrong reason to invade England. Spain should have invaded the Dutch.

After the remainder of Spain's armada sailed home, Philip II banished the doctor's father, Don Francisco, from court. Before Mendoza got out of the king's coach, he purposely lifted his leg and let a fart.

The king was lying in bed, and he was as pale as a ghost. The doctor was glaring at the court's physicians. When will you stop reading old texts and pay attention to your patients? Blood is red when it's going away and blue when it returns to the heart. Whatever was lost or taken from blood, when red turns into blue, is needed by our bodies. And you are wasting those messengers! Have you never treated men on the field of battle? He could see their contempt for him, but that encouraged his further scolding.

Seal his wounds from your wasteful bloodletting and boil a cleaned chicken, cut into small pieces. Boil in a clean pot. The doctor took out his stethoscope and listened to the king's heart. Get those candles away, and give him fresh air.

Two soldiers entered the room while Mendoza was tending to the king. Doctor, we brought your travel bag and this firkin of wine.

Mendoza had forgotten to take it into his house. Get me a clean goblet. Don't worry. I will drink from the same glass. He took a drink from the goblet and passed it to the king's mouth. He saw the king's feeble smile.

You bastard, even though your father humiliated my grand farther, he still loved him. He said he still loved yours even if he, too, was a bastard. I'll do whatever his son tells me.

Mendoza smiled at his king. Your father, Philip III, was an OK guy, and I liked him, too. My problem was with his father, Philip II. I never forgave him for what he did to my father, Don Francisco. You should sleep warmly to break that fever even if it takes two women.

He turned to look at the court's physicians. Give him freshly squeezed orange juice in the morning, as much as he can drink. Mendoza then turned to face his king. Now, I want to be fed and have one of your courtesans for company this night. This *consideration* will not be part of my payment.

The king managed another feeble smile. You always were a bastard, but I always trusted you. I could have your head for what you just said, but … I know what's good for me. Physicians, get me that broth the doctor ordered and two warm women. Fernando, I hope to see you in the morning.

. . .

The padre and the sisters sat at the condesa's table. Jane sat on her left, and Zeke's head was resting on the young girl's lap.

Condesa, we have several handfuls of *reales*, but we want you to keep the money for our church. The villagers have already given what they could. More begging tomorrow will annoy them and be a waste of our time.

The condesa was coaching Jane on the use of a fork while talking to the padre. Was that your only hope?

No, Condesa, I spoke with a mutual friend, who told me to pass on her salutations. I hesitate to tell you, but if you are willing to listen, we will have to speak alone. Condesa, I would keep this discovery to myself if I were a better man.

The condesa had her arm around Jane. Each of her hands held one of Jane's during that knife and fork exercise. Are you speaking of our town recruiter? She let go of Jane's hands when the padre nodded his head. Jane, you and Zeke stay with the sisters while the padre and I have our brandy and enjoy a smoke in my study.

While Jane was cutting meat, all by herself, the sisters watched the condesa and the padre leave the dinning room. It was only a matter of seconds before the sound of footsteps faded on their journey down the hall and vanished behind that now shut door.

The condesa was smiling and shaking her head. It just warms my heart when I see Jane eat. She's so happy to have a full tummy. She has this big smile and her eyes glaze before she lies on the floor with Zeke. She smiled at the padre. The most realistic, practical, and intelligent person I know in the village is the madam. Padre, are you speaking of her?

Yes I am, Condesa, and you must be aware of the manner and solutions in which the madam has succeeded in life. She related the conversations to me from what she heard from most of her clients. They would pay dearly for one night with you, but I must consider the worth of my soul and what it would do to you. If you agreed, I could be dammed for just asking you.

Padre, let me correct you. If I volunteered, you would not lose your soul, and I think the madam's girls will keep theirs because they never had a choice in life except for slitting their throats. God would have to ask himself … what other choices they had. But I do have a choice and must consider what effects volunteering to become a *puta* would have on my own soul. You and I must each consider our own souls and what could happen to our friendship. At this point, I'm not volunteering, and my answer is, No.

Chapter Six

Mendoza awoke the next morning to see the courtesan still sleeping beside him. He slid his arm under her head and pulled her face next to his. Thank you for staying. He could feel her breath on his chest and her leg across his. Her toes were caressing his.

I hope you will ask for me the next time you come. In you, I saw a wonderful person who has made me feel clean again.

Mary, you'll probably be gone before I return.

No, Doctor, I'll still be here. You must know that I'm damaged goods, and no one would want me. She smiled at the doctor. Thank you for being so kind.

Mendoza smiled back at the young woman. Never had he seen such beauty encapsulated in quiet humility. Besides, she had blue eyes, just like Jane's and the four Barcíníu children he delivered so many years ago. Just looking at her made him feel younger.

Mary, you're so young to see past the first domino. You will have breakfast with me before I see the king. He, calmed by her helpless trusting, held her in his arms.

Sire, how do you feel? I see that you slept warmly. Mendoza put his hand on the king's forehead and listened to his heart. You chose the right two women. They would keep any man warm. Sire, I think your fever has broken. He ignored the two fat women as they climbed out of the king's bed.

Stay on this diet, which includes boiled water and wine, and don't ever let yourself be bled again. The stern look on his face then turned into a smile. I have to get back to my patients, who actually need me. Sire, you're going to be fine.

The king smiled at Mendoza while adjusting himself on his pillow. You old bastard; you did it again. I'm happy to pay your exorbitant fee, but I want you to leave that firkin. It's the finest wine I've ever tasted, and I know it has healing powers. I want to know the name of that winery. You will consider this a demand from your king.

Mendoza continued to smile at his king. Then I'll take the courtesan. Before I give you its name and leave you that firkin, I have to remind you what happened to the last winery your father confiscated and what happened to its wine.

The king raised his hand as a signal to quiet Mendoza. My father did not confiscate that winery. It was confiscated by one of the pope's cardinals after his Inquisition, who said the family had to leave Spain and had donated it to the church. We lost tribute and taxes. The cardinal, no longer well received at court, still had the Pope's protection. I think it was the first lesson I learned from my father. *Si esto no está roto, no lo repares.*

The cardinal said my father was vengeful because he would no longer buy the new wine. Now tell me the name of that vineyard and its location.

Is the courtesan mine? Mendoza continued to speak after the king nodded his head. The Barciníu vineyard lies between Manresa and Barcelona. It now bares the family name of the condesa, who has three brothers. I think you may be familiar with their family name. It is a well guarded secret that she, while not as strong, can wield a sword as well as her brothers. I speak of Cesaré and his two younger brothers. He saw the king smile and waited for him to speak.

You may have identified the source of another problem. I have received more than one bitter complaint from the French king concerning a marauding Spanish regiment. He has accused us of using spics in this war, but he has no proof.

Their only proofs are dead French soldiers. My response was that France could not blame Spain for spirits coming from Italy or Portugal. France would have to provide verified evidence. Listen to me, my friend. *Esta conversación nunca ocurrió.*

The condesa will be respected at court. Besides, I would never waste a regiment over three men and a woman. I will return that empty firkin and replace what I traded it for with another courtesan. Loan me three of your pigeons, and I will lend you three of mine. I would speak to you of other matters, but first, let's have more of this wonderful, healing wine.

As you already know, the Inquisition has become part of our heritage. I'm not comfortable around the inquisitors, and their power is increasing. Lands have been deeded over to them while those owners were on the rack. They say that power corrupts, and there is no power to compare with he who controls the rack.

Sire, don't call your servant. Let me pour your wine. Your grandfather learned an invaluable lesson from Sir Francis Drake's raid at Cadiz. England had a full year to build their warships. The delay was not his choice, but the lesson is clear. Don't ever give your opponent time to get stronger. The other lesson your grandfather learned was what can happen when ignoring my father. Mendoza smiled at his king. I think we're done here. Sire, may I have your permission to leave?

Before you go, I have to tell you about my grandfather, Philip II. His armada's defeat was not his only regret. He asked my father to reinstate the name Mendoza after he was dead. It was his pride that stopped him from reinstating your father. I removed that banishment when you graduated and waited until I could reinstate it. I knew the apple would not fall far from the tree. My general's letter was less than I needed. The king reached for Mendoza's hand.

. . .

The condesa had placed the padre at one end of the table, but he sat next to her while Jane and the cook served the sisters. Sitting so closely, next to each other, they could speak together as if they were the only ones in the room.

Condesa, I can only thank you for your kindness. God has surely abandoned me because I have sinned against you and our Lord when I told you of our troubles. It was arrogant and almost spiteful to bite the hand of my host, who is now feeding me. Thank you for not letting us go hungry.

Padre, the condesa interrupted, you could ask the good sisters to offer themselves instead of me, but would Jesus feel that He had been cheated and consider it adultery?

The padre laughed and shook his head. You always were a rascal. There are only two sisters who would bring money. They would lose all respect for me if I asked them, and their minds would collapse if they obliged me. There are many reasons for joining the order, and the church must embrace them all. We must always ask ourselves if we are truly serving the lord, or are we self-serving. I am, of course, speaking of hypocrisy and conceit.

Padre, when I gave you no as my answer to becoming a *puta*, it was not solely to protect my reputation. To myself, I am not in any way a stranger after I found that abandoned, frightened child. Padre, I found that day what I lost in the pond. What I lost was shivering at the foot of a tree. It has striped away all hypocrisy and conceit to know that I was completed by a *basura bastarda*.

I would consider that any man who had me would be violating Jane. I would, the next day, ride in the village analyzing those who knowingly smiled at me and then slay them. But I will still consider your proposal, and Padre, you must surely have known this.

Jane entered the dining room and set the padre's plate at the other end of the table. She was looking directly at him and pursing her lips from side to side. He stood up when he saw her pull back his chair and stand, waiting for him, behind it.

The condesa grabbed his hand after he was standing. Padre, I'm still rejecting your proposal, but I ask instead that you consider mine. I am offering my onetime service to the church, but there are several conditions. We will discuss them after dinner in my study. Now it's time, she laughingly said, for you to relinquish the *basura bastarda's* place.

Chapter Seven

Mendoza was sitting next to the courtesan. Her trunk was following in the doctor's carriage. You will not have the luxury of the king's court, but you will not be cast aside when you grow old. You will be my mistress but have the reputation of my housekeeper and my assistant. You can only have this reputation if you actually do both. I want you to have a second chance, one better than that of a wife to this old man.

The courtesan held the doctor's hand and smiled at him with tears in her eyes. This is a second chance for me, but I would be honored to be the wife of this middle-aged man. Everyone at court is a politician, even the ladies in waiting. I will never be a politician … against you. I will always be your politician … with and for you. I will never forget what you did for me.

The king was kind to me because he let me keep most of my clothes and a few pieces of jewelry. That's why my trunk is so heavy. I've never had a profession that could be accomplished while standing. But my greatest treasure he gave me. This long box with a handle holds my vihuela. The king said no one could play it and sing like me, and he allowed me to keep it.

Mendoza smiled and patted the courtesan's hand. From this day on, I will call you Mary. You will be my late brother's daughter. You are my niece, Mary Mendoza, and you will play it and sing for me. You will assist me with patients. You will learn to heal wounds and to deliver children.

The words that just passed from his mouth brought him feelings of guilt, but he could not take them back. Were his reasons selfish, or were they for her. The only relationship he had known, other than with his mother, was a dance with death, but during that dance, his oath *do no harm to others* was always with him. He must remember and apply it to that sunshine sitting at his side.

82

Mary and Mendoza sat and slept next to each other on that long winding road back to Barcelona.

. . .

The condesa and the padre were smoking their pipes and enjoying apple-plum brandy. Anna was warming the snifter in her hands while looking into the fire. I don't want be known as the village *puta*, but I could bear that shame if I knew it was untrue. Padre, I just had an excellent idea that could satisfy us both. You preach the joys of simple pleasures, but you should know that their combination and juxtaposition is a compelling titillation. The men in town are afraid of me and what my reprisal would be.

Anna jumped up and pressed her dagger against the padre's throat. Padre, behold and think of this. They would be buying a chance to face danger and pleasure in the presence of their comrades and friends. It would add to their excitement by paying more. Each man who bought that chance would be considered bold as well as brave. He would brag and stand tall among his comrades and friends.

She sheathed her dagger as she sat down. A blindfold would allay some of that danger, but the chance remains that it might slip off. We must find a *puta,* who is built like me, and tie a cloth around her face. We could sell positions where *voyeurs* could watch this play. This could work, and I would, the next day, smile back at those smiling at me.

The padre laughed while he spoke. I would be part of the conspiracy of this lie, but I will not feel shame for doing it. I will pass your suggestion to the madam. She never imagined reselling positions to *voyeurs*. She will, I think, enjoy knowing new ways to promotion and pay.

You don't need to feel shame, Padre. It may not be a lie. I could still change my mind, but you would never know it. That chance of innocence will still be yours— that chance to avoid His wrath, *Oh ye of little faith.* Work this out with the madam. Tell her, I will be there that night listening and watching or even perhaps performing in her house of ill repute.

After they returned to her living room, the condesa poured the padre a second glass of brandy. Jane was playing with Zeke, and the sisters were on their knees thanking God for a very fine meal. Both burst out laughing after the condesa sat down and winked at the padre.

After Jane and the sisters shrugged their shoulders, the smiling young girl stood in front of the padre.

Zeke wants to know what you're laughing about. He wants to know your little secret.

The condesa smiled before she knelt next to Zeke. She patted his head and whispered in his ear before returning to her seat.

And now, my little friend, Zeke knows our little secret. They laughed even louder when Jane twitched nose and mouth and glared at both.

Chapter Eight

After the king's men put Mendoza's horse and carriage into his stable, they carried the courtesan's trunk into his house. They had many days to ride but would stop first at the local tavern. The doctor introduced his niece to his cook, who was delighted with the news. She could go home in the evenings to be with her grandchildren, and the gossip about her and the doctor would end.

Mary and Mendoza's cook cleaned the cook's old bedroom and hung the gowns in Mary's new closet. Mary set the thin box with a handle on its end in the corner of her room during that transition. From now on, the cook's old bedroom would belong to Mary. At least, that's what the cook thought.

. . .

The padre and the madam were sipping wine in her parlor while the sisters begged in the streets for money. The madam said the condesa has given her a new idea. I have a peephole in the hallway doors to each room to see and make sure that my girls are well treated. I could put many peepholes in its adjacent room's walls and rent out those rooms.

There will be only one room in its intended use for that night, but I would be renting three. Tell the condesa she has broadened my ... entrepreneurial skills. My girls will sell those chances in saloons and to their clients. Tell the condesa I'll need one of her coopers to drill the holes, and that I am still on good terms with a woman who could act as her replacement.

Padre, I don't wish to offend your delicate nature, but the woman I speak of is the wife of a nobleman. He is old and thinks he'll grow older only if he does not share his bed with his wife. He allows her a minimal amount of freedom outside of his house because she has an appetite that would satisfy ten men. She and the condesa, until the condesa married, were very good friends.

85

The condesa may not know it, but she may have been thinking about her old friend.

I'll send her a letter, and it will be in our own code. She will choose the date to give herself away as the prize because I have forgotten the time of her flood. What a wonderful choice I have made because this nobleman's lusty wife would do it for free. Padre, I see your glass is almost empty. May I refill it?

Jane and the condesa rode to the edge of the vineyard. Jane had her own horse and named it Charlie. It was too small for a large man, but the condesa liked its spirit, and Jane could mount it by herself. They were waiting with Zeke at the edge of that small forest, dividing the two wineries. The condesa was holding one of her pigeons.

She laughed when she saw her brothers riding out and at the cart trailing behind them. And why would I need two cannons? The condesa watched Jane's eyes growing bigger with excitement.

Cesaré rode next to Jane and pulled her from her saddle and then sat her on his lap. I will exchange this little damsel for these two cannons. He held the reins of Jane's horse and rode next to the condesa to kiss his sister.

Jane was kicking Cesaré's shins with her heels and trying to strike his chest with her fists. He, without delay, grabbed her wrists and held them in one of his hands. Do you want to get spanked? He was laughing while looking at his sister. I will trade with you for this fine damsel if you will cook for us tonight.

They were all laughing at Jane while Cesaré put her back on her saddle. Jane pulled her shortened wooden sword from its sheath only to see it taken from her hand. When Cesaré put it back in its sheath, he smiled at his sister's returned prize. You should show more respect for your uncle. Jane looked at the condesa for her approval before she grabbed and kissed him.

The condesa was smiling at her brother. Where did you get these cannons? She had a smirk instead of a smile before Cesaré could answer.

These are smaller prototypes of the French king's cannons. They're more portable and only one third of the metal, and so is the shot. You can chain the shot and fire them precisely together like twins, or you can, without chain, allow them to be savage individuals.

The condesa was not smiling. Does the French king know?

He knows only that he's missing four cannons and twenty men. Rodrigo followed and cleared the tracks from their wheels. We have already mounted ours. You should camouflage yours, and keep them out of sight. We left their bodies but kept their swords, muskets, powder, coin, and cannon shot. Of course we kept their horses, so they would not spread the alarm. Little sister, why is Jane following our cart?

That *chica poco femenina* is fascinated by your cannon and wants to keep Zeke a safe distance from our horses. She'll probably want to fire it when we get to the house. Oh Cesaré, she was such a frightened, dirty, little creature when I first found her. But look at her now. With a washed body, food in her tummy, and my clean, old clothes, she has sprung fourth like the goddess Minerva. She has the love and safety of our family, and I'm grateful to you, Mama, and our brothers for that. I never thought you or your brothers would be that patient. That wonderful spirit must have arrived inside her at birth. All I had to do was to release it.

Cesaré steered his horse to be next to his sister, to look into her eyes, and to hold her hand. Not one of us would not want her, were she not already taken. What you think is our patience is our most pleasant memory. Our hope is that we have erased some of hers.

Anna leaned over to kiss her brother. We're having pork medallions soaked in a cranberry, orange, lemon, and onion sauce with green beans and, of course, my new wine. We will also be serving *Arros Negro*, compliments of Jane. Do you want to keep my pigeon?

When Cesaré casts his eyes to the sky and said he still had three, Anna released it. Come on, she said, I'll race you back to the house, or should I spank your butt with my sword?

. . .

Mendoza and Mary finished the dinner prepared by his cook. Mary had cleaned the dishes, and Mendoza was smoking his pipe. He was sitting on his couch with his feet on his ottoman. Mary sat next to him.

Do you wish to teach me more about chess, or would you prefer a different game?

Mendoza took Mary's hand. Let's play chess while we digest and then consider another game.

Mary studied the board after the black rook's move. Fernando is a wonderful name, but it's difficult to associate it with you. Were you always called Fernando, or do you have another name?

It's funny that you should ask. My father called me Fernando, but my mother and older brother called me Nando. I haven't thought about it in years. You can call me either when we're alone. But right now, I believe it's your move.

You're right, it is my move. As exciting as this game is, and as complicated as these moves are, I have other moves in mind that by far are less complicated than on this simple checkered board lying flat on this table and in this room. The other board I have in mind is found in another room, usually the bedroom.

Mendoza was laughing when he said, you're right, and that board serves little use when lying flat. Even when it's in place, it serves little use. I don't think they've ever been considered effective. I never had the occasion to use one, and it's time to prove that I don't own one. We'll finish our chess game tomorrow by keeping our priorities in their proper order.

. . .

Padre, how can we choose the winning lottery card, and how can we deliver the prize? These men may wish to flaunt their lust in saloons with bragging and lies but will want to remain unknown to their prize.

Dear Sisters, each of these men has wagered more than a week's wages for one night with the condesa. Each will want proof that he had a fair chance, and we must handle this lottery properly. Selecting the winning card must be done using the virtues of honesty and fairness. Perhaps ... a public drawing where all can see? Have any of you sisters experienced games of chance?

Padre, I used to watch one played when I was a little girl. My mother would take me to church on Saturday nights. She called it *Lo Giuoco del Lotto D'Italia.* It's played on cards showing twenty five numbers, five columns, and five rows. There's a large basket of numbered balls. They number more than fifty but less than a hundred.

Sister, that sounds like an honest game, one that could provide amusement for all, but we don't have any balls. We need to think of a game we can play with dice, and where we can play it. The question is ... how can we select a winner of a lottery prize ... without any balls? The padre looked at the ceiling while the sisters were laughing, but the idea came to him in a flash.

. . .

Mary was sitting next to Mendoza as they rode into town. He wanted the merchants to know she had his permission to purchase, but that was not all. He wanted to showoff his new prize. He was surprised to find himself surrounded by Cesaré and his smiling brothers. Mendoza was laughing before they could introduce themselves.

Don't even think about it. She's far too good for any of you. But please pass on my regards to Mama, Jane, and the condesa.

After introductions, Mendoza and Mary waved to the brothers as they rode out of town.

Nando, why did we not invite them to dinner?

Mendoza smiled at Mary, and then he whispered. I did not want to put them in a position to decline. Their business does not include drinking wine. They are here to take orders for their wine, and to make a withdrawal from the bank. It's a long

89

dangerous ride back to their winery, and their numbers help ensure their safety.

Last year, Cesaré came alone into town Three highwaymen attacked him. He reported it to the magistrate, but it delayed his return. The town cheered at the sight of three dead highwaymen, but the condesa ordered that the winery could not mix business with sport or pleasure. Since that day, they conduct their business together.

Mary questioned Mendoza on their way out of town. Fernando, why are you so looking all around?

Mendoza's face was solemn when he faced her. For one brief moment, he felt a long forgotten presence. What we see only once, he said to Mary, I have felt many times. I thought I had forgotten her. Don't worry your pretty head because she's no longer here. He knew Mary would not understand and offered her no explanation. I still want you safe at home, he said while snapping the horse's reins.

Chapter Nine

I've got it, the padre said, looking at the sister's lottery card. It was her keepsake from the days she spent with her mother. He drew five columns and five rows.

Number of Dice Used and
Lowest Value

2	3	4	5	6
6	5	9	15	24
10	13	7	21	35
3	18	23	28	25
8	16	4	12	27
11	14	22	29	33

Highest Value
12	18	24	30	36

The sisters watched as their padre drew the box and wrote the numbers. We'll roll two dice for the first column, three dice for the second column, four dice the third column, etc. I wrote the lowest possible value on the top and the highest on the bottom. Sisters, create one hundred twenty cards, and fill in the values as I have almost randomly done.

There can be no duplicate numbers on any card. Is that correct, Sister? I think I know where we can play this game, he said when the sister nodded her head. Oh, by the way, don't use my headings. I wrote them down as rules for you to choose the numbers. Decide among yourselves on an enticing heading. While you ladies are having fun, I'll ride over and talk of our business with the saloon keeper.

. . .

The padre, the wife of a nobleman, and the madam were sipping wine in her parlor. The sisters were not begging for money in the streets because they were happily buying food and provisions in the village. They had sold all their lottery cards. The remaining money, almost down to the last *reales,* had been stored in the condesa's vault, and her coopers had finished their job to the madam's satisfaction.

It was the condesa's decision to supply the material and the labor from her men as a gift to the madam's brothel, but it was the madam's decision that those laborers would have their payment-in-kind. She had a wistful smile after each of the condesa's men bought a lottery card and tore it in half. She told them their combined chance together was exactly one in ten. She kept the torn cards as a sentimental souvenir. Reaching back in her memory, she realized that no one had ever done it for her.

The cardinal was in the Cathedral of Saint Mary, sharing wine with the spies he had sent to the village. He was furious because the padre was stealing his money with the help of the condesa. He told his spies to seek out each man who bought a lottery card and buy it back even if they had to triple the price.

I'll have her and prove she's a witch and a *puta.* After her Inquisition, I'll have her winery, her land, and all the money in her vault. I'll replace that padre with a monsignor who will report directly to me. The padre's death will go unnoticed, and the sisters will serve the monsignor and me, to his pleasure and to my satisfaction.

The condesa, Jane, and Zeke were sharing the condesa's bed, and all were lying on their right sides. They were, except for Zeke, looking into the fire. Jane had snuggled herself into the curve of the condesa's body. She was using Anna's right arm as her pillow.

Condesa, I loved reading about Ruth and Naomi. They remind me of us. I didn't even know there was a Bible, but I'm reading it, thanks to you. Was Jesus really the son of God?

The condesa laughed when she leaned away and rolled Jane on her back. Only a child, she thought, could span both Testaments in a single breath. She slid her hand under Jane's gown, and Jane stretched her arms and legs to facilitate the condesa's caressing.

Jane, no one knows if Jesus was divine except Mary, his mother. What we do know is that his words are divine, and we can worship them as we worship Him. Our minds have the right of free choice, to follow and seek for ourselves what we call the divine. I think I found the divine in dirty rags hiding and shivering under a tree. You don't even know where you were born, but I think it was in a manger.

Zeke awoke when he heard Jane scream. He crawled up to the head of the bed to find them sleeping. They were still lying on their right sides, and Jane's head was still using the condesa's right arm, using it as her pillow. The condesa's left arm was still wrapped around Jane. That's the way they were lying when he first fell asleep. Zeke crawled back to the foot of the bed. His place was still pleasantly warm he thought as rested his head. There was not a sound from Jane or the condesa. That scream must have been part of his dream.

Mary and Mendoza were settled in his home. They secretly lived as man and wife, but to the town she was his niece and medical assistant. Mendoza waited until their cook was in the kitchen, storing their provisions.

Mary, because we are together, you are in my confidence. You will know most of my secrets, but there are those you may not know … for your own protection. The secrets you do know must be kept to yourself … for our own protection. Cesaré told me of the cardinal's plan. The cardinal has spies of his own. The cook will take care of our house while we ride to see the king. We should hurry, but don't forget to bring your vihuela.

Mary was resting against Mendoza on their way to see the king. Cesaré and his brothers are handsome, she said, and they seem to be fond of you.

Mendoza laughed as he slapped the reins. I delivered all four, and each is worth more than ten men. I love them all, but you must keep this our secret. Anna has always been my favorite. I think you will learn to love her as I do, and, by the way, none of those brothers are married.

Cesaré, the padre, and the condesa were making plans in her study, behind a shut door. The sisters were playing ball with Zeke, and Jane was sword fighting outside with her other two uncles. Jane had improved enough to be given her own dagger, but the ones they practiced with were made of wood.

Dear sister, Cesaré said showing his concern, there were only eight men who would not sell their cards to the cardinal's men because they are under my protection and spy for me. By my calculations, the cardinal has one hundred twelve lottery cards. His chances of winning are more than nine in ten. My spies gave me their cards. They know what could happen if they didn't. Little sister, methinks you have made a terrible mistake.

Anna and the padre were laughing at Cesaré's expense. Big brother, politics, and survival make strange bedfellows. The madam has a friend who resembles me, and you may even have known her. The padre knows of my plan. You and your brothers should have a very good time.

Anna grabbed her brother by his ass as she laughed and kissed him. Sit down and listen to the madam's and my plan. She gave me twelve, torn lottery cards. The cardinal's chances are exactly ten in twelve. Cesaré, I want that jackal to win.

The doors to the condesa's study suddenly burst open, and Jane ran in, followed by Zeke. She was carrying her wooden sword.

Jane, the condesa said, before you ever enter this room, you will knock whenever its doors are shut. I will excuse you this first time only because our business is done. Why are you here, and what do you want?

I'm here to slay my Uncle Cesaré. Jane held her wooden sword by its handle and put it to her chest. Apparently, she had seen his brothers do that before they practiced.

Prepare to meet thy doom at the hands of a fellow soldier. The padre and the condesa smiled at Cesaré as he slowly stood to face his opponent.

Prepare to meet thy maker at the hands of your fellow paddler. When Cesaré clapped his hands and made a lunge for Jane, she squealed and ran from the room, with Zeke following behind her. Cesaré placed his hand over his mouth to keep from laughing. Oh little sister, behold what you have found. He winked at his sister before he left the room.

Padre, may I offer you some of my new wine?

They could hear Cesaré still laughing outside with the sisters. Come here, you wicked, little damsel, and see what will happen to you.

By the time they walked out, they found Jane stretched out over Cesaré's knee. He had pulled down her pants and was spanking her bare bottom. Jane was kicking and squealing but made no attempt to escape. Everyone was pleased when the condesa invited them to lunch, and Zeke was wagging his tail.

Jane was helping the cook, who was preparing lunch. She wanted to ignore the sister's and her uncle's laughter. She waited until she heard the condesa laugh and call her name.

Jane! Come here at once and sit on your pink bottom.

Jane entered the room with her shoulders back and her head held high. She quietly sat in her place next to the condesa. She kept her eyes closed while the padre led them in prayer. Hers had been finally answered because they had all stopped laughing.

Oh Lord, thank you for this food and for
your wondrous bounty. Bless this house and
our associations within it. Lead us in the
paths of righteousness. Be with us as we
journey fourth and forgive us and remove us
from our sins.
In nomine Patris et Filii et Spiritus Sancti.
Amen.

Jane was happy and at peace in her new life. She was looking at
twelve just people, who were all her friends. Love seemed to be
traded back and fourth across the table. She still thought of her
life among the trees. They had sheltered her and would always
remain her friends.

. . .

Doctor Mendoza and his niece, Mary, received an audience
with the king. The king poured a glass of wine. I would offer you
the wine I traded for your new niece, but that firkin is empty.
What do you think of this wine from the cardinal's vineyard and
of his supervision? I want your honest opinion.

Mendoza took a second sip and looked at his niece. What do
you think, my dear?

Mary held her hand over her mouth and discharged the wine
back into her glass. Well, it's wet and alcoholic. I think it should
be used to clean wounds for those inflicted in battle.

The king could not stop from laughing. You would never have
said that to me when you were in my court, but I'm glad you did.
The cardinal said I needed a more sophisticated palate. He wants
me to buy all of his wine, and at a very high price. Doctor
Mendoza, I'm glad to see you and your now new niece, but why
are you here?

The winery that supplied you with that firkin of wine has
doubled its production and has kept the same quality and price.
I'm here to talk about saving what may be the finest winery in
Spain. I think the cardinal is about to seize the condesa's winery
by way of his Inquisition. He is trying to fabricate evidence that

she is a witch and a whore. I stand here to protect that winery and my friend. Sire, don't let him do it.

You shall not give orders to your king.

Sire, I never give orders to my king, but sometimes, from time to time, I'm known to prophesy. Mendoza looked out from the castle window. If the condesa should perish, or lose her winery, you will drink that bilge in your hand for the rest of your life without this doctor and friend.

The king was serious when he looked at Mendoza and Mary. I shudder at that thought, but my decision was made without your presence. What matters is that Spain is poor, almost bankrupt. What I need are businesses paying taxes and tribute. Every time a cardinal requisitions lands and property during his Inquisition, I lose taxes and tribute. I have only recently considered this a problem. Stay and dine with me, and we will play chess tonight. Perhaps Mary would play her vihuela and sing for us, perhaps one of her Irish songs?

The cardinal was alone in his study, waiting for his dinner. He was drinking last year's Barciníu wine. I'll have her and all of her secrets for making wine, but even if she dies on the rack before letting them be known to me, the king and all of his subjects will have no choice but to buy wine from me. Her skill is the proof that her hands perform witchcraft, but it will be God's divine guidance in mine. I will dispatch a message tonight and seek an audience with the king.

. . .

Sire, we greatly appreciate your hospitality. Mary has not had a meal this fine since she came to live with me. This fine meal and a game of chess with you, my friend, will help me to calm down because we have pressing business in Barcelona. May I have your leave after Mary has rested?

Doctor, you must be preoccupied because this is the first time I have ever beaten you at chess. Relax my friend; you have my leave as a king and my word as a man. The king smiled at his queen before looking at Mendoza. But before you leave, I will have another of Mary's Irish songs.

Mendoza and his king closed their eyes and listened to Mary. Mary sat next to her queen while she sang and strummed her vihuela. The king was at peace with himself because he was with a friend who was not self-serving. He was constantly surrounded by those who never tired from reaching with outstretched palms.

But the best part was that he had an unpaid ally who irritated the French king. France was missing twenty soldiers and four cannons. He was at peace in the company of friends. Before they left, Mary curtsied to the queen and respectfully kissed the king in front of his wife.

The queen was smiling when they left. It's such a pity, she thought. They're perfect together, except that he is too old for Mary. But there is honesty, almost a glow around them when they stand together. I couldn't help but like her when I first saw her, but I will keep my thoughts to myself because of my husband's history with Mary.

. . .

A coach coming into the city passed them after they left the castle. Mary held a small cage containing three pigeons. That's one of the king's coaches, she said.

Mendoza patted her hand. I suspected as much. It is often that one first needs to hear the truth before he can dispel the lies, and the king first heard the truth from a trusted friend. How often the truth by itself has less credibility than the messenger. Be comfortable, if you can, because we have a very long ride to Sant Sadurní. Mary slid her hand to gently rest under Mendoza's arm as he slapped the house's reins.

The cardinal kissed the king's ring. Your Majesty, thank you for this audience. My business concerns the Inquisition. I have proof of a witch, who is also a whore, making and selling wine near Barcelona. As you can see, Your Majesty, the woman is a whore, and I can prove she is a witch. If you will lend me twelve soldiers, I will ride to her winery and destroy her brothel. She, on the rack, will confess to being a heretic, a witch, and a whore.

I must remind Your Majesty that I have sworn to spill my blood to protect our holy church and carry out its holy Inquisition. May

I have your leave to select the soldiers? It is important that I make haste. The cardinal showed the king his lottery card.

Loteria para una noche maravillosa con La Condesa

8	16	7	29	27
11	13	9	28	25
3	14	23	21	35
6	5	22	12	24
10	18	4	15	33

Buena Suerta

Chapter Ten

Before the king answered, he first looked at his queen. No, Cardinal, you will wait outside while I select the soldiers. I know who is the most qualified among my men. Remember to take some of my wine, that wine you sold to me.

The king rarely lunched alone with the queen, but this was a special occasion. The queen had always shown contempt for his courtesans, but now she actually knew one. He thought this would be a good time to teach her another lesson. She had enjoyed the company of a former courtesan and, in her, had discovered a very good person. He was pleased that his wife had also voiced her concern for the doctor and his friend, the condesa.

Yes, my dear wife, I will lend the cardinal twelve soldiers and the use of a royal coach for his evil quest. But the king, as in chess, has restricted limits to his single moves. He must rely on other pieces to carry forward his plans, and there are times when he will sacrifice his pawns. The cardinal will have twelve men for his protection only, and their sergeant holds me in regard. The king must trust the more maneuverable pieces. That is the biggest frustration of being a king.

Mary wondered if Mendoza had appreciated all of the king's kindness. With the carriage's axles freshly greased and his horse well groomed, they rode out of town. The king had supplied them with food and water. This man at her side provided her a security and calmness, but she did not fully understand why. She was content to be at his side and decided to choose another subject.

Nando, tell me about the condesa and her handsome brothers. Are they all fearsome warriors?

They may not all be there when we arrive, but you will surely meet the condesa. I think the condesa holds a place in her heart for me, perhaps because my hands were the first to touch her. I held her in my arms, before her mother. She had a look in her eyes that I have seen in the fewest number of men. Of course, I paid no attention because she was a newborn child. Most infants, if not all, are born with their eyes open but not like hers. Mendoza laughed when he said he did not know if they were glaring or staring.

The child turned her head to see every object in the room, and that included me. Her eyes scanned everyone, giving them equal time before resting them on mine. She recognized objects in life and the life in objects. After nodding her head, she reached out to touch my face before she smiled and rested her eyes on mine.

When I placed her in her mother's arms, she looked at her mother, her father, and then at her brothers. Tears were already in her eyes, but when she looked back at me she began to cry. It was an unsaid sadness of abandonment after so soon belonging. She, among six other people, had recognized me as a soulmate, and I as a doctor, while riding back home, knew he was the savior who had delivered another Madonna. I have loved her from that very first moment.

On retrospect, Cesaré had more fire than his brothers, but I didn't realize it then. They're all fine men and fearsome as is the condesa. This is a secret I have shared with you that you must protect, and there will be many others. We are about to start a game that will, as in chess, have many moves. Consider that chess game you saw me purposely lose last night with the king as an opening move … in our larger game of life.

Mendoza smiled at Mary when he saw the approaching rider, who was followed by a dog. Don't encourage him. He might jump onto your lap. While the rider was still in the distance, Mary smiled at the doctor.

Nando, I hope you found some of those qualities in me because I saw them in you. I hope that's why you traded that firkin of wine for me. She laughed out loud from his answer.

My dear Mary, you must be aware of the great value and joy found from that firkin.

Zeke had stopped twenty paces short of Mendoza's carriage. He did not want to be near Charlie when Jane turned him around.

Sir, if you'll just follow me back to the house, my mistress, the condesa, said she wants you to rest before we consume. She said that we're all going to play chess while we dine, but you would have to explain your opening move.

Zeke watched his little friend riding ahead of Mendoza's carriage. He wondered why she was shaking her head and shrugging her shoulders because nothing was puzzling to him.

The condesa was waiting on the veranda when Mendoza and Mary arrived. She was smoking the late count's pipe. Doctor, I first want to meet Mary before you rest and refresh. Jane, our cook, and I have planned our first move, or is it the second? I think you will enjoy it. She was smiling at Jane, who was again shaking her head and shrugging her shoulders.

The condesa, the sisters, Jane, and the cook had prepared five courses for twelve people, and the wine was already airing on the table. Because the war had taken its toll on the population of men, their placement at the dining table was an automatic consideration. The condesa sat at the head of the table. Jane and her brothers sat on her left with a sister between each brother. The doctor, Mary, and the padre sat on her right. One sister sat on the padre's right, and the fat nun sat at the other end of the table.

The fifth course was apple-plum brandy and tobacco. The sisters asked if they could be excused and sit on the veranda. They were happy to leave seven people under that billowing cloud. Six of the seven were smoking.

Jane had that distant, dreamy look as she smiled at the ceiling while passing leftover food under the table. She was waiting for the condesa, who was holding her hand, to speak.

Thanks to the observations of Mary and the good doctor, we know the cardinal's second move, which is in a predictable order. We know his first move was to buy all of the lottery cards. The condesa was addressing those at her table, but she paid particular attention to Jane.

We have your uncle's spies to thank for that. The cardinal's second move was to gain favor with the king. We can only speculate at its success. We will consider his third move while we dine. As in the game of chess, we consider our opponent's moves, matched by ours, and their total, probable, domino effect. Those moves are traded back and forth in chronological order, but the moves in this game, while they may seem random, are in logical but not always in chronological order.

So you see, little one, in this game our second move follows the third. Doctor Mendoza's opening move was to set the stage for the actors, and my second move, which is usually the first, was to fill the players' tummies. Cesaré has made his third move to be the first. He has twenty lottery cards. Anna had tears in her eyes when she said that Cesaré had supplied eight, but the madam had supplied twelve torn lottery cards.

Jane, call in the sisters. They must know their collective roles. Mary, with the doctor's permission, you will become a nun for that night. The condesa looked down at her empty snifter and pointed at the ceiling with her index finger. She smiled, pointing it at Mary before laying her hand down on the table. She waited while Jane and the sisters returned to their seats.

The cardinal has one hundred lottery cards. He will demand the eyes of his soldiers, who are familiar with dice, to check for a winning number. He will need the sisters' help to verify the numbers as they are called out. Most will be holding eight cards. With the help of our five volunteer sisters, if Mary wears your habit, each could be examining those cards to mark the card holder's winning numbers. The sisters are the only people the cardinal will trust, but his trust will be limited by his suspicion and deceit. He may not trust the soldiers' ability to read, but he will trust the sisters.

The cardinal will in some way mark his cards. That will be his third move. His first move was in stacking the deck, ... a deck assembled by buying one hundred lottery cards. His second move was his visit to the king, another way to stack the deck. All his moves will begin and end with suspicion and deceit.

The condesa smiled as she looked at the ceiling. I will want the doctor to examine him and look for the French disease. The condesa was still smiling while everyone's eyes rested on Mary.

Mary lifted her glass. She felt as if she were part of a family and sharing its love and its concerns. It will be my honor to play this role if the good sisters will have me, and if the good doctor allows it. The only role I've ever played was of a lady in waiting at the pleasure of her king. If allowed, I will sleep with the sisters and pray they remember me, known this night until the next, as their friend and sister, Sister Mary. With the applause of eleven, Sister Mary picked up her vihuela and started to sing her beloved Irish songs.

Mendoza was quiet, sitting across from the brothers. Mary can play many roles, a courtesan, a niece, and a wife, or a queen. But wherever she goes, she brings joy to those surrounding her. He stood up and bowed his head while listening to the voice of his sweet Mary.

> Lord, bless this house and our associations
> within it. Forgive us of our sins and deliver
> us from evil. Be with us, and let us find
> justice as we journey forth.
> Amen.

Chapter Eleven

After a large breakfast, the padre and three sisters followed Mendoza, Sister Mary, and the fat nun into the village. Mendoza slowed his carriage before they passed the livery stable. He turned back, waved, and signaled the padre. The padre stopped in front of the stable to bless the blacksmith.

You seem to be in good spirits, my son. May I wish you good fortune?

Padre, I do have good fortune for this day. You can save your blessing for another day. I have sixteen fine horses to feed and to groom as well as a coach to clean. The blacksmith burst into laughter. Padre, had I known I would find fortune today, I would not have sold my lottery card yesterday. Will you be at the tavern tonight to bless our lottery?

I will, my son, and you will meet another. She has taken her vows and will be known as Sister Mary. She is truly one of God's beauties, and you will mind your manners. The padre smiled at the blacksmith and slapped the reins. In spite of the neighs of his horse, he thought he could hear the blacksmith still laughing.

The padre was not surprised to find Mendoza and the sisters, but he was surprised to find the madam and the wife of a nobleman inside his church. Madam, it's pleasant to see you and your friend, but I think it's time for me to know her name because there will be much to discuss.

Padre, only the madam and the condesa know my true name, but in this village I will be remembered as Musetta because, as a muse, I have been considered a goddess, a source of inspiration to creative artists and have mastered my trade as well as my art. Padre, I truly enjoy it, and, were you not a priest, I would bring forth the artist in you.

The padre smiled before he put his arms around Musetta. *Get thee behind me, Satan! You are a stumbling block to me; you do*

105

not have in mind the things of God, but the things of men. He kept his arm around Musetta's shoulder as they faced the rest.

All the world's a stage, and we must play many parts. This day we will learn our parts, parts designed to seek justice. This play opens and closes in one single night. Musetta knows *the things of men,* and our heroine is perfectly cast. Our villain must be prompted in his scene because he does not know his true part. This night we seek justice for our church ... and for the condesa.

Musetta left the padre's side. He did not understand why until he saw her hug and kiss Mary.

Oh Mary, how I envied you with your role to roll only with the king. I was passed and rolled with many until I was thought to carry the French disease. With the assurance of the king to my husband, I became the wife of a nobleman. But it wasn't long until I realized that I missed the role of many rolls. I have always remembered you. How have you faired, my sweet Mary?

Before Mary could answer, the padre asked for their attention. Musetta, you know your role; the sisters and Mary know theirs, but Mary must face her habit and be introduced to ... but not into ... our order. He smiled when the fat nun volunteered her old habit. She had not been able to wear it for years.

Mendoza, the padre, and the madam drank tea while the other men smoked. Are your viewing rooms ready they inquired.

The madam nodded her head. Padre, you, and the sisters will be viewing from one room. The doctor, the family, and I will be viewing from another. Doctor, will that be sufficient?

Mendoza tamped and then kindled his pipe. Jane will not be here to watch. The condesa would never allow it. She wants Jane's horrible memories erased and replaced with things wonderful and nice. She will be playing and sleeping with Zeke inside the church. Besides, she's too young to suffice. May the family tie their horses behind your house?

The madam said she had a small stable where she kept her coach and carriage, and the family would, of course, be welcome. She turned to directly face the doctor. Will I be accommodating eleven?

106

Mendoza relit his pipe and smiled at the madam before he answered. I will ask Cesaré to bring another.

. . .

The madam, Musetta, and Mendoza were sipping wine in her parlor. The padre was preparing his tomorrow's Sunday sermon, and the sisters were singing and praying in the chapel. Sister Mary, as she sang with them, was strumming her vihuela.

Mendoza thought it was unusually quiet outside as he rekindled his pipe. He stepped out onto the porch to see five armed swordsmen, followed by a dog, riding abreast through a soundless town. They followed him behind the brothel where he showed them the stables.

They unbuckled their swords as they came inside. Jane's scabbard and wooden sword were shorter, so they did not drag on the ground. The madam's cook was preparing their dinner as they discussed their plans. Jane was upset because she could not be with them. The condesa told Jane that the cook at the church would be alone and need her protection. They all smiled except for Jane.

. . .

During dinner with twelve soldiers, the cardinal was marking one hundred lottery cards. He did not like eating at the same table with commoners, but time was getting precious, and he had to explain their task. Each man would carry eight cards, and if it won give him that winning ticket. He was upset to learn that only nine could barely read.

Those of you who can … read … will carry ten lottery cards. I, too, will be carrying ten. I will wear a plain, hooded frock, and you will not be known to me. The winner will compare his card to mine, and we, with sleight of hand, will exchange cards. You will enter the tavern before me and each of you will secure a table to spread out his cards. My identity, the cardinal said, you will keep secret.

The condesa was discussing her plan while the madam's cook was preparing dinner. Madam, I want you and the doctor in the tavern with us. You will verify that I am the prize, and the doctor will make his announcement. He will examine the winner for the French disease. My brothers and I will each carry five cards. The padre and sisters will offer themselves to those needing help in reading the numbers on their cards.

We will signal you by rubbing our nose if my brothers or I have the winning card, but that combined chance is only two in twelve. If that should happen, one of you will search the soldiers for a near winning card, and show it to me. I will demand the right of verification, and one of us will secretly exchange that winning card with yours. In order of expectations, it ranks in second place.

The most likely expectation is the combined chance of one of the soldiers holding the winning card. That chance is nine in twelve and in order of ranking is our first expectation. Judging by the cardinal's suspicion and fondness for deceit, he will not let go of his cards, but his chance is only one in twelve. The order of his winning expectation is in last place. Our chance of winning by replacing a card is eleven times his.

Do not concern yourselves with ordered expectations. My only reason for telling you was so that you would know which outcome is most likely to occur. The order of expectations matters not when the outcome is always the same. What matters is that the cardinal will eventually hold the winning lottery card.

Jane, you do not know the name of this game, often played in life. Expectations of treachery and deceit are always afoot and around us.

Jane, looking at Zeke, lying on the floor next to her, pursed her lips from side to side but said nothing. She wondered why the others were laughing, but what upset her mostly was that she could not remain among them.

. . .

The tavern proprietor was pleased to have a full house. Soldiers spreading their cards took most of his tables. Men from the town and clients of the brothel packed the rest of his tables. They had money to spend and wanted to know if they, having not resold their lottery cards, might have won.

The madam, well known to the town, introduced the condesa, who smiled at the men. For one brief moment the condesa's eyes rested on a stranger wearing a plain, hooded frock. The doctor delivered his brief but emphatic message.

The padre said he was here to bless the lottery and its prize. The money would be used for his most charitable cause. The sisters were there to help those who had difficulty reading their cards. They would tell that man if he was the winner.

Cesaré stood in front of his table. We are here for our little sister and the good sisters. You men will keep your hands to yourselves and respect the sisters if you want to keep them. Enjoy yourselves with wine and ale, but remember what I told you. It would be a shame if any man did not live to claim his prize.

The youngest soldier stood with his hand on the hilt of his sword. You speak bravely for one of three.

One particular soldier stood before and faced him. Soldier, you are very much mistaken. I have battled with those brothers at my side. With their sister, they number four. I've seen Cesaré and each brother slay more than five men without resting his sword. I would not slight him even if I had eight more men. Besides, he and his brothers are my friends. Sit down, soldier, and read your cards.

The madam stood at the back of the tavern. Gentlemen, you all know that I run a clean house. The doctor helps me keep it that way. He will roll the dice, and the padre will call out the rolled numbers. We have six dice. We will use two dice on the first roll and add one for the next until we have rolled all six. If no one wins, we will start all over again with only two.

The winner will have five called numbers that are in adjacent slots, and the corners definitely count. When one of you wins, the proper word to call out is *Buena*. She looked at the padre and Mendoza, who were in the middle of the tavern, facing each other at that centered, empty table.

All eyes were on the leather cup surrounded by six dice. The doctor put two dice into the cup and moved the other four aside. He did this so all could see. He shook the cup in both hands and

109

slammed it mouth down on the table. He lifted the empty cup over his head and turned his back while the padre called out the dice rolled number.

The sisters walked among the men, and when called showed them who had a dice selected number. As each sister bent over to examine a card, the holder of that card watched her pointing her finger but kept his palms down, flat against the table. The fat nun appeared to be disappointed. She was looking forward to the titillation of their disrespect.

Are you ready, the doctor yelled?

The proprietor suggested that Mendoza wait while the men got another round. Everyone paid for an additional round except for the stranger in the plain, hooded frock. His pint remained untouched.

The doctor put three dice into the leather cup, setting aside the other three. He shook it, slammed it mouth down, and the padre called out the number. Remember, he said, this time the called number must be in the second column. The column number is always one less than the number of dice rolled.

The sisters walked among the men and pointed to the number in that dice selected column. The sisters told each man if his card contained a called out number while all the men's palms remained flat down on the tables.

The condesa gasped after six dice were thrown. She waited until the game started again. Cesaré, his brothers, the doctor, the sisters, and especially the padre secretly gave the sign of the cross when they saw the condesa slide her finger across her nose. She looked at the ceiling and smiled as if thanking the heavens.

They had proceeded to four. Wine and ale were *on the house* for Mendoza, the padre, and the sisters. Cesaré was laughing and shaking his finger at the sisters. He smiled at the proprietor. No more wine for the sisters. One of the soldiers raised his hand and called for help from one of the sisters. Sister Mary came over to check his card.

Sister, I don't know if this is an eight, a nine, or a three. His hands lay flat against the table. Sister Mary did not know if he was being respectful or if he used them to keep his balance. His speech was slurred, and he looked around trying to focus. She took his card and brought it to the condesa for her inspection.

The condesa lifted a candle and cupped her hand over the soldier's card before smiling at Sister Mary. Only the doctor could have perfectly repaired this card, she whispered while blinking her eyes. She copied the cardinal's mark on the back of her card.

Sister Mary returned to the smiling man. Sir! You hold the winning lottery card. The condesa and her brothers watched the smiling soldier stagger to the stranger wearing the plain, hooded frock's table. The stranger rubbed his eyes as he studied the card, checked his mark, and compared its numbers to the ones he had written down. He had drawn a blank lottery card and had written down the winning numbers.

He stood up with his pint of ale and without stopping drank it down. Everyone in the tavern, including the condesa and her brothers, laughed when they heard the stranger wearing the plain, hooded frock's clarion voice crack while screaming out *Bingo*. This soldier, he said to the crowd, holds my lottery card as a favor to me. He regained his composure and tightened his hood to conceal his face when he saw the brothers and the condesa approach his table.

The condesa and her brothers sat at the plain, hooded frock's table. They remained quiet while their sister spoke.

Sir, the last event to winning the prize is to trade your card for a particular coin allowing you special, brothel favors. Here is that gold doubloon worth many times more than the money spent on this lottery. You may keep it or surrender it to the madam. You have our word that the madam will honor it. The condesa said she would wait there for more than one hour.

The plain, hooded frock took the gold doubloon and put it into his pocket before surrendering his winning card. During all that time the condesa was speaking, he kept his head down and clenched his hood to conceal his face.

I will be there when the clock strikes twelve, he said. It will be less than one hour.

Cesaré wanted to thank the soldiers for their courtesy. He said he wanted to say goodbye to an old friend.

The stranger wearing the plain hooded frock watched Cesaré turn and wave at the soldiers before he followed his sister and brothers into the street. His plan could not fail, he thought, but it would require the help of the soldiers. Normally, he would not share his table with such low caste people, but with his disguise no one would notice. He called them to his table and ordered additional rounds of ale.

Except for Jane, the family and friends gathered in the madam's parlor. They listened while she spoke.

Musetta, our leading lady, knows her role, and she knows how to roll. Every one laughed including those sisters who were shocked. The madam suggested the sisters occupy the room to the right of tonight's *centered stage* with the padre, and the family, the doctor, and she would gather on its left.

Mendoza suggested that he and the padre switch places. I think the sisters will enjoy the play more if they're in a different room than the padre. The sisters looked at each other and tried not to smile, pretending they had not heard the doctor's suggestion.

I want everyone to watch him disrobe and get a good look at his face while I will examine him because after that you might only see his back.

Cesaré and his brothers will go to the tavern. The cardinal will feel more comfortable and safer if he thinks they will remain there. They will tell him their sister does not want them to watch her first time performance. Musetta will be *center stage,* with her head flagged and hands tied to the bed. The condesa and the padre will be in this room with the sisters until curtain time, and you will all have to be quiet.

Cesaré and his brothers walked to the tavern. They found the stranger wearing the plain, hooded frock drinking ale with the king's soldiers. They stood at the stranger's table.

My sister said we could not see her performance and ordered us to remain here. My own reason for being here is to suggest that you might keep your gold doubloon and leave. It will by far outlast the memory of this night.

The stranger wearing the plain, hooded frock stood but kept his face from sight. I have more gold doubloons than sweet memories. This memory tonight will be worth more to me than their total sum. He took the gold doubloon from his pocket. I will trade this gold doubloon, which bears a mark, for the memory and the delight that I will have this night. He forced a loud laugh as he walked into the street.

Cesaré and his brothers sat at that table. Cesaré sat next to that one particular soldier he had campaigned with and told him to stop drinking. You will have many nights to drink that you will not even remember. You will have a memory from this night that you will always remember. I secured a place where you will see a play that you will never forget. And this, my friend, you will always remember.

The madam answered the knock on her door. Her clock had just struck twelve. Standing before her was a stranger, wearing a plain, hooded frock. Sir, we are closed to all patrons but one this night. However, we are open to the lucky winner of tonight's lottery, who will have a gold doubloon that I have especially marked. If that person is you, step inside and be examined by our doctor.

The stranger wearing the plain, hooded frock was furious and demanded to be allowed in unchecked. He wanted to brush her aside, but the madam's retort startled him.

Sir, you did not win a night with the condesa. You won a chance for a room in my brothel where the condesa is a guest in my house this night. My rules concern the French disease as well as others. Those are my rules, and they are inviolate. You will be examined by our doctor, or you may keep your coin and leave.

After snorting through his nose, the stranger wearing the plain, hooded frock consented and handed her his gold doubloon. The madam and the doctor led him into a well-lighted room. He stood facing a ravishing creature whose eyes were flagged and hands tied to the bed. He paid no attention during his inspection, but he was happy to maintain his own erection while the madam knelt on her knees and lifted his frock during her examination.

The doctor stood behind her. Check his scrotum and testicles and make him cough. Pull back his foreskin and check the urethral opening. Stranger, I see that you were not delivered by a medical doctor. I always circumcise my male deliveries. Check his face, lips, and anus. Look for any sores.

The madam looked at the stranger as she stood next to the doctor. Sir, you have passed my examination which was … small and slight. You and the condesa will be my guests tonight. I will be in my parlor if you have any needs. The doctor has pressing business, and he must leave. Surely, you will not be disturbed.

The stranger wearing the plain, hooded frock waited for the doctor and the madam to leave. He listened for their footsteps sounding up and down the hall. He waited for the sound of an opened and then shut door. He heard footsteps up and down the hall and then heard the door open and shut again. He thought the doctor must have forgotten his medical bag.

Mendoza and the five sisters stood in the room left of *center stage*. The condesa, her brothers, the padre, and a soldier, stood in the room on its right. In each room, six people shared four well disguised peepholes to watch the cardinal disrobe and claim his expensive but masterfully won prize.

The cardinal, now on top of Musetta, wanted to put a distinct mark on her neck. She spread her legs and lifted her feet over his shoulders and forced his head down between them. Her hands easily came loose and they, too, held his face in place.

Sir, you will lick first before satisfying your thirst. Musetta knew the others were watching. Didn't your mother teach you how? She drew him up, so that his neck was against her mouth. I am well prepared to deal with your small member. If my house is too large for your little furniture, it will find cozy comfort with my navel.

The sisters were wide-eyed from shock, but that did not stop them from smiling. The condesa was biting her lips and blinking her eyes while tears from contained laughter ran down her face. Cesaré held his sister against him tightly, and each felt the other's belly shake. They stood back and shared their peephole while wiping their eyes.

Musetta placed her feet between his legs and spread them apart while sucking his neck and practicing her favorite art. The stranger without his plain, hooded frock heard the door open before he felt the bite from her teeth and the shock of a small branch inserted up his ass.

He broke free from Musetta's clutches only to see that surrounding jury and the flag withdrawn from her face. He put on his plain, hooded frock while they were laughing and ran from the brothel with the small branch still hanging from his ass. All the way from the brothel to the tavern he heard the sounds of their raucous laughter.

The condesa had an announcement to make. The first torn lottery card she had received from the madam had won. They all, except for the soldier, gave the sign of the cross.

The padre held the condesa's face in his hands. I always knew that He held you special.

Inside the tavern, the stranger was shaking and screaming at eleven drunken, too-drunk-to-stand, soldiers. He had purchased one hundred lottery cards for three times their price but had not realized the real prize. He would have to revise his plan to make it work. He was humiliated, but his exhaustion would require that his body have slept first.

The biggest thing in his favor was that the soldiers could barely read. He would write a proclamation from the king and give the soldiers their orders. He would have the condesa dead, or she could be alive for his Inquisition. He would own her land and her winery. But his first move, if his plan was to succeed, would be to remove the branch protruding from his ass.

Chapter Twelve

Plates and goblets of wine filled the madam's dining room table. They would have a very late supper. Musetta, looking at Cesaré and his brothers, said she had not yet been paid. She wanted tribute from each and would begin with Cesaré's youngest brother.

The madam said there was no reason to watch, and they should all relax in her parlor. She let the condesa borrow her carriage because her own girls had taken her coach to conduct their business in Barcelona.

After searching several rooms, including the cook's, the condesa found Jane sleeping with Zeke in the fat nun's bedroom. Zeke awoke first and licked the condesa's face. Her smile flashed across it. She uncovered and rolled Jane on her back. Wake up, you sleepy head. I think you were having a bad dream. Little one, I hope you are still hungry.

Jane threw her arms around the condesa's neck. I was dreaming that I was alone … and without you or Zeke. The cook fed me some broth and put me to bed. It reminded me of the times I slept hungry … and under a tree. I never thought that I deserved to be this happy. And then Jane began to cry.

Anna took off her clothes and climbed into bed. She held Jane's bare body against hers and stroked her head. She could feel her breasts rubbing against Jane's flat chest. She slid her hands all over Jane's back and gently rubbed her shoulders. With the aid of the condesa's gentle touch, Jane stopped crying and then began to purr. Her eyes would partially open and then completely and rhythmically close.

The purring continued in harmony and sometimes in syncopation to the skill of the condesa's gentle touch. The condesa's face was easily and exactly guided by Jane's small fingers to that favorite place. Jane was completely and all over outstretched. Her eyes were almost closed while the condesa refreshed that mark on her neck.

Cesaré's two brothers were sitting together and ignoring the laughter and the smiles of others. Listening to the continued moans and groans from *center stage* they finally joined in with the laughter. Mary was sitting with the doctor. She was wearing her own clothes, having returned the fat nun's old habit. Everyone stopped laughing upon hearing a knock from the front door. Mary stood up and answered it.

Jane and Zeke were the first to enter the madam's parlor. Zeke was sniffing the air and, followed by Jane, ran into the dining room. Her eyes and face were beaming when she returned. Mary and the condesa, already seated, watched with others while Jane, with Zeke's paws on her shoulders, began to dance around the room. Everyone started laughing again when they heard that final scream from *center stage*.

Where is Uncle Cesaré? Jane demanded to know.

The condesa smiled before she started laughing. Your uncle is having a conversation with the nobleman's wife.

Where is my sword? Even if he is my uncle, I have to protect the nobleman's wife. I heard that poor woman scream. Jane was confused by unconcerned smiles and laughter, especially from the condesa.

Jane, come here and sit with me. Your uncle is … auditioning for a part in a play with Musetta, who is the leading lady. She fired her former partner because he could not perform his part. Cesaré and the nobleman's wife were merely rehearsing. Anna smiled at her two brothers when Cesaré and Musetta entered the room. Musetta was more than smiling when she rolled her eyes and said she could eat but was no longer hungry.

Jane stood before Cesaré. She gallantly bowed. You are most fortunate, kind Sir. Your sister's words have spared your life. She was holding her wooden sword, but she dropped it and squealed when Cesaré grabbed and threw her into the air.

Musetta was laughing as she sat down and looked at the exhilarated child. You're not a woman until you can scream like me, but you're off to a very good beginning. That was truly an excellent squeal. She smiled at the sisters before fixing her eyes on Jane.

As the leading lady, I was able to audition your uncles, the condesa's three brothers. This part demands a man with a real sword and who knows how to wield it. Your uncles have performed their parts well. In fact, I have never found complete satisfaction from only three stage members. To fairly choose the right man for this part will demand further auditions from all three because the cardinal left such a poor impression as a member in this play. I can't even remember such a worthless little member.

Jane was looking at Zeke. Both appeared to be confused when the others started to laugh. Jane with careful deliberation scrutinized the nobleman's wife. She jumped from her uncle's lap and stood in front of Musetta before examining her neck.

I like you even if you are not a Barciníu. Jane was pointing at hers and at Musetta's neck. You can see that the condesa, my uncles, and I have the same birthmark. I can tell that you're not a Barciníu because you have exactly three. Musetta and the condesa simply smiled at each other.

Jane! Come here and sit on my lap.

Jane strutted on her way over to climb on the condesa's lap. Anna was holding and kissing Jane before she let her stretch across her lap. Jane had tilted her head and shoulders back and was looking at her friends, who were now upside down. Her eyes scanned the room while her condesa continued to speak.

Those are not birthmarks. They will fade after some time.

Jane jumped from the condesa's lap and stood before the nobleman's wife. Will your birthmarks, too, fade away?

The nobleman's wife slowly smiled at the questioning child. Yes mine, too, will fade away.

Well, I can't speak for my uncles, Jane said, but the condesa's and mine always grow back.

Musetta smiled at Jane before looking at the rest. Those coming back after fading away are the only ones we should remember.

118

She gently placed Jane on her lap. And those never coming back, we sometimes remember. I had a love of my own, a love like yours, but it, too, faded away. She smiled at the condesa while Jane rested her head against the breast of the nobleman's wife.

The madam's cook entered the room and said that dinner was served. Jane and Zeke were the first to enter the dining room. Jane did not know the soldier and thought he should sit at the other end of the table. She was telling him where to sit when the condesa interrupted and told her to mind her manners.

Jane! The madam tells us where we sit at her table. Jane just nodded her head, and with her big eyes smiled, admiring all the fine food on the table.

The madam had a slight consideration. She had ten women but only six men. She put the condesa at one end and the fat nun at the other. Jane sat on the condesa's left, facing Cesaré. The madam had mixed them as best she could. Each woman sat between a man except for Jane and the fat nun, who had a woman on her right. In Jane's case, it was the condesa on her right instead of a nun, but she preferred it that way. Zeke did not have a seat. He would stand between two people. His eyes would track each bite during its journey while resting his head on top of the table. However, he could not watch them eat while accepting treats from under the table, but Zeke preferred it that way.

Everyone including the sisters was in the madam's parlor. They were— except for Jane, Zeke, and the sisters— smoking and sipping brandy. Mary was sharing brandy with the doctor, while Jane, with her arms around Zeke, slept on the floor next to the condesa. The condesa smiled before resting her eyes on Jane.

I would like to say, while Jane is sleeping, that life is never a coincidence. With the help of the madam and my brothers, the cardinal had three chances to keep his gold coin and leave, the same number of chances that Peter had before rejecting his Savior. I created that coincidence for the cardinal's sake, but I knew he would reject it.

The sisters went into the kitchen to help the cook wash the dishes.

The soldier said he should get back to his men. Cesaré walked him to the door. They could all hear Cesaré's last word to the soldier which was … remember.

The padre wanted to get back to church, finish his sermon for Sunday morning's mass, and write an account of various performances for this night. Musetta would spend the night with the madam. Mary and the doctor would follow the condesa and her brothers in his carriage. Jane and Zeke would sleep in the doctor's carriage on their way to the condesa's winery, and the three brothers would sleep in their own beds.

On their way to the winery, Mary, sitting next to Mendoza, was holding Jane and Zeke. The three brothers had turned to ride on the private road to their winery. Mary asked him if this meant the game was over.

Mendoza snapped the reins as he puffed on his pipe. We have only sixteen people sworn to the truth, to counteract the lies of one cardinal hat, and four of those votes the king would never count. The cardinal has his title and eleven drunken soldiers who could do and say what he tells them. That's why we have to be there. I hope the king will listen to me. Our country is still poor because of our destroyed armada. Let us hope our king has enough sense and knows when and when not to follow the money. Mary rested her head on Mendoza's shoulder until they reached the winery.

Chapter Thirteen

Jane was snuggled against and in the arms of the condesa. Zeke was snuggled against and in the arms of Jane. Zeke was the first to awake, but he waited quietly until he heard the condesa.

Get up, you sleepy head. What happened last night does not mean it's over. Corruption, deceit, and avarice will always surround us. We must be watchful of friends and others wherever we are, even when we are in our own homes. She kissed the back of Jane's head. Little one, you're so young to learn this lesson, but you should always be ready, and … always keep your powder dry. This may be the chance to fire your cannon.

Zeke licked Jane's face before he bolted for the door. He was looking at Jane while at the same time whining.

Oh, condesa, I have to let him out. He really needs to pee. Jane left the door open and then came back to climb into bed with the condesa. Do you really think I'll get a chance to fire my cannon?

The condesa was laughing while holding her little prize. I don't know if you'll have that chance, but I'm definitely ready to fire mine.

The cook was upset because Jane was late. She had grown used to the help of those quick, little hands. But they were not that quick today. It was probably just as well because Jane was still groggy from lack of sleep. At least, that's what the cook thought.

The cook told Jane to fetch Mary and the doctor, who were walking outside in the vineyard. The condesa told her to prepare extra food because she had a feeling that the padre and sisters would be there for breakfast. This actually pleased the cook. The sisters sometimes helped serve and prepare the food, and they always cleaned the dishes.

The condesa was right. Not only were the padre and the sisters there for breakfast, but they asked if they could stay for dinner. The cook had no problem with that. She could retire to her room and read her precious old love letters. But before she did, she would walk into the condesa's chambers and look out to see if there were any passersby.

The condesa's chambers, and now Jane's, had windows facing north, south, and west. Paintings hung on the east wall with some of the condesa's personal sketches. The south windows faced the small forest that divided her land from her brother's. Their house also faced south.

The cook's favorite view was from the west windows. It looked down on the fork in the road. She could see passersby on their way from Manresa to Barcelona. She could also see if any of those passersby had taken the forked road leading to their winery. This could be a clue to determine how many place settings she would set for dinner. Of course, she would always check first with the condesa.

The area bounded by the fork and the west end of the house measured just under three thousand *varas*. Although fairly flat, there were no vines. The count had tried to grow them, but the dust from the roads caused the vines to produce poor grapes. At least, that's what the count thought. That area, for games such as *bocce* and horseshoes, was also used for breaking horses. After checking both views, the cook would retire to her room and read her precious old love letters.

After breakfast, Jane, the padre, and the sisters were playing *bocce* just west of the house. The condesa left with Zeke and walked to talk with her field hands. She told them they would not have to stay. There could be danger. She had taken Zeke because he did not know how to play. He thought the *bocce* was his personal toy.

Tears were in her eyes when the condesa returned. She told the padre that her field hands wanted to stay. In fact, they were sharpening their sickles and pitch forks, and they all had their vine cutting knives.

It was the condesa's turn to throw the *bocce*. She dropped it when she saw a cloud of dust coming from the road. She waited until she saw a coach and a dozen soldiers riding toward the winery.

Jane! Run to the house and release my brother's pigeon. Bring my sword and my shield, and make sure the cannons are ready. If you find me slain, my little Jane, fire your cannons and seek out my brothers. They are your godfathers.

The condesa watched Zeke running after Jane. She ordered the padre and sisters to return to the house. She told them to call Mary and the doctor if they were still walking outside in the vineyard.

She turned to face the king's coach and the oncoming soldiers. When the coach stopped, the mounted soldiers immediately surrounded her. Her only weapon was her dagger. She stood and watched the cardinal step to the ground before she turned to face the surrounding soldiers. There was only one she remembered.

Before the condesa could speak, the cardinal held his crucifix above his head and started to scream. Behold the Celestina, a former prostitute, and now an active pimp, witch, and virgin-mender. Bind her, for she is to face the Inquisition.

Two of the soldiers' horses reared and neighed when Jane and Zeke ran between them and into the center of that surrounding circle of soldiers. The condesa grabbed her shield and held her sword before she yelled.

Are you here to slay children, or do you kill only women? She was looking at one particular soldier.

Our only order from the king, he yelled, is to protect the cardinal.

Does my child have your leave to safely return to her home?

Of course, Condesa, we do not slay women or children …
unless ordered by the king.

The condesa forced a smile at Jane and her wooden sword. You must go home and wait for my brothers … and remember me.

Jane held her wooden sword as she faced the condesa and made no attempt to hide the tears rivering down her checks.

Entreat me not to leave thee, or to return from following after thee: for whither thou goest, I will go; and where thou lodgest, I will lodge. Thy people shall be my people and thy God my God.

Where thou deist, will I die, and there will I be buried: the Lord do so unto me,... if ought but death part thee and me.

The condesa held Jane's face in her hands, and then she looked at Zeke. You must take him with you, and be there to point the way for my brothers. Go now! Go before you make me cry in front of these soldiers. She watched Jane run, followed by Zeke, before she turned to face them and stand alone in that center of surrounding and mounted soldiers.

The cardinal was even more determined as he yelled with his clarion voice. Even the child is a witch. Behold, she can read and quote from the Bible. Only a priest may read the Bible. Bind those whores. Both will face the Inquisition. Soldiers, you have your orders.

Cesaré and his brothers had finished their breakfast. Their mother was sitting on the porch. They were laughing at what Musetta told them because each thought he had the largest member. They stopped laughing when Cesaré raised his hand and listened to their mother's discussion.

Homer, didn't Anna feed you? Let me put you into your cage where there's plenty of feed and water. I don't know why she let you go, because there is no message. She was startled by her son, Cesaré, who stood behind her. He examined the pigeon's feet before turning to face his brothers.

Hermonos! We ride to save our little sister.

Their mother watched her sons run from the house and mount their horses. The horses reared as their reins steered their heads north.

Mis hijos, why do you hurry? There was no message. There was no note.

Mama, we ride because there was no note. *Porque no había ninguna nota.* There was no time for Anna to write a note. *Ella no tenía el tiempo.* She didn't have time to write a note. *¿No entiendes?* Don't you understand?

She watched her sons vanish from sight as they rode into the forest. She shrugged her shoulders as she examined Homer's feet, and then she began to cry. Without a note, there could be no words. This was the first time she considered that terror could come without any words. This terror had no time for words. She dropped to her knees and prayed for her beloved Anna.

They rode through the trees, the overhead branches shedding patches of black and light, the sun shining through leaves where red touches green and then becomes bright yellow. They rode through the stream below the pond and its waterfall, with the mist rising, reflecting, and refracting the sun's reds on top of green with yellow in between. Deer and rabbits were running, birds were flying, and squirrels were climbing in trees to escape the sounds of horses' thunder.

Jane was waiting on her small horse with her wooden sword and the reins in her hand. She held the reins of the condesa's horse in the other. She listened to the sound of their quiet rumble growing louder until it became a mighty thunder. She watched limbs and leaves bursting fourth and rabbits bounding that birds followed at first and then flew past as if shot from cannons. She watched three mounted soldiers armed with sword and musket exploding from the forest.

The forest grew silent as their dust slowly settled below that thin current of air. *Entonces montó a los hermanos valientes, nobles.* So rode three valiant brothers, like brave, galloping *comancheros*.

When Jane saw them approach, she pointed her wooden sword and said, follow me to her condesa's, united in arms, three determined brothers-in-arms, soldiers.

The sergeant rode into the center of the circle, next to the condesa and yelled at his men. Our only orders from the king are to protect the cardinal. It does not include kidnapping or killing women and children. Besides, we are outnumbered. He smiled when he saw Jane, followed by Zeke, Cesaré, and his brothers, ride between the surrounding twelve mounted soldiers.

The cardinal was standing next to the king's coach. Whenever he traveled, he always carried a sword and a hidden dagger. With his clarion voice, he yelled at the soldiers. Slay them and that bitch and witch. You will not even spare her dog. You have your orders. Be brave, oh you king's soldiers. You outnumber them by eight. Counting that bitch of a witch, it will be three against one.

The condesa recognized that one particular soldier, who had shared the madam's table. That same particular soldier rode into the middle of that circumscribed circle and yelled to his comrades.

It will be eleven against five.

Except for the cardinal, they all laughed when they heard Jane yell. It will be eleven against six. Zeke and I together make one, and five plus one adds us to six. Jane instantly realized her mistake and covered her mouth with her hand. They all knew she could read, but now they also knew that she could add.

That one particular soldier addressed his men. You have all, except for one, followed me in battle. Will you still follow me now? He smiled when he saw their sword hilts rest against their chests and rode his horse to be among them.

The cardinal grabbed his sword and ran toward Jane, pulling her from her saddle. This witch knows numbers; she can add, and I am only obeying the Lord's commandments. He lifted his sword when Jane hit the ground, but her wooden sword, now shattered, misdirected his stroke. Jane was bleeding from his kick in her groin as she crawled toward her house, screaming in pain.

The cardinal laughed as he yelled, bishop takes pawn. He raised his sword to cut off Jane's head and swung down with all of his might. He heard the clash of steel and felt his elbows unlock. He saw the fire in the condesa's eyes and heard her cacophonous words.

Queen to bishop's three!

He saw his sword flung from his hand and felt a foot kick the back his knee and a hand throwing him to the ground. He felt the condesa's sword pressed against his throat.

Sir, you smell of sweat and shit— more shit than sweat.

She withdrew her sword from his neck and replaced it with her boot. Her boot pressed the right side of his face against the ground. He could barely breathe. The soldiers witnessed in awe and silence the face and torso of a Venus, one foot standing on the head of a cardinal with her hand on the dagger at her side and in her other a sword. Her brothers, in unison, triumphantly called out— Checkmate!

The cardinal was spitting dirt and screaming with his head pressed against the ground. I humped this whore in the village brothel, only so that I would have the proof of her crimes.

Anna stood with her boot still on his head. You tried to hump Musetta, a nobleman's wife, and former courtesan from Madrid, who now lives in Barcelona. She is truly a lady. The condesa stood tall as she faced the men and mocked the cardinal.

The nobleman's wife said she is possibly this cardinal's mother or perhaps his big sister, who can not remember him because of his small member. She forced a laugh at the cardinal. You didn't hump a whore. You confused her with your mother or your big sister when you penetrated her naval with your small member, you incestuous bastard and son of whore. *Usted hijo de una puta.*

The condesa took a deep breath before she looked at her brothers, and then she looked at the soldiers. A woman is merely the earth, the soil to bring forth fruit, and then to be trodden upon by men. I stand here before you having given myself to God and to the church. We have minds and souls as important as yours. This is my winery and is legally my land. I am more than this land, and this land is more I am. I will defend it with my blood and my last breath. She removed her boot from the cardinal's head and, with her shoulders squared, faced the surrounding soldiers.

This will be the greatest winery in Spain, and … it will bear my name.

That one particular soldier rode, leading her horse, and smiled before handing her its reins.

Escort the cardinal to the king's carriage. We will have a long ride back to the castle. He leaned down to receive a kiss from the condesa and then told her his name.

Victorio, you will always be welcome in my home. Come with me. I have a letter written by our padre. I want it delivered to the king. I want you to sign it as a witness. Your signature will add to twelve, but I must see about Jane. Before she mounted her horse, the condesa smiled and picked up the cardinal's hat and his beautiful sword.

The doctor, Mary, the padre, and the sisters were waiting when five rode to the house. Jane and Zeke were wrapped in a blanket and sitting in the most comfortable chair. She said the doctor and the condesa were the only ones who could examine her wounds.

Look at my wounds, Condesa. I almost died in battle. And I am still bleeding!

Zeke was licking her face while the doctor, the padre, and the sisters muffled their laughter. Mendoza patted Jane's head, and then turned to face the rest. I have managed to attend to her near fatal and almost mortal wound. The cardinal's sword missed her body, but it cut her *pantalones*. She managed to crawl to the house to find me waiting. He bit his lips to keep from smiling.

After a thorough examination, which revealed ... to me ... that this near mortal wound is actually her ... first-time flood. Jane covered her face while the others were openly laughing.

Anna knelt next to Jane and wrapped her arms around her. Don't be sad to leave the child who is now becoming a woman. She handed Jane the cardinal's sword. This is now your beautiful sword ... after we exchange its hilt with one that fits your hand. The jewels from its original hilt will go to the church and to the winery. And Zeke will wear the cardinal's hat.

When Jane started to laugh, Anna continued speaking but more softly. With the use of a *godemichet,* your flood will be less than one week. I'll show you how when we go to bed.

After Cesaré said farewell to Victorio, he returned to the house and simply smiled at his sister. We will sleep here, even though Victorio promised he would not return. He then turned to face Jane.

You are our niece, but we will think of you as our precious little and smallest sister. We will be your uncles and your big brothers. Regardless, you are our goddaughter, and I must console you ... to find comfort with your future floods. All women are ... on the rag ... for one week in every month. To explain their moods, we men sometimes say ... O.T.R. Consider it a blessing because it keeps your blood clean.

After diner, to calm Jane, the sisters talked about their first-time floods. The fat nun said she thought it was a sign from God to lose weight but continued to enjoy food when it stopped.

The youngest sister thought it was a sign of the stigmata. I was so sorry when it went away, but I thought it would return when I became a nun. The padre was kind when he explained it to me.

Zeke was sniffing the table, and Jane was snuggled in Anna's lap while the condesa was smoking. Jane was considering her uncle's words before she responded.

We pure bloods do not sit on rags. During our periods of time, we sit on a rainbow. O.T.R. really means ... over the rainbow or ...on the rainbow, but which one doesn't really matter. What really matters is that you can't ever say ... on the rag.

Jane was sprawled on the condesa's lap. She liked to lie across it, spread her arms out, and look at her friends, who were upside down. She was proud of her birthmark and did nothing to hide it.

The condesa was looking into the fire, smoking and holding her pipe in one hand while her other was resting and rubbing Jane's tummy, just under her shirt. Zeke was contentedly breathing with his legs outstretched, lying on his back on the floor next to the condesa's feet. Mary was singing and strumming her vihuela.

The sisters sat amongst the smoking brothers and silently watched the padre and Mendoza play chess. The doors and windows were open, a gentle breeze carried their smoke from the house, and the cook was silently reading her precious old love letters.

Chapter Fourteen

The cardinal stepped from the carriage and demanded an immediate audience with the king. He wanted to report Victorio's actions, which had been completely unsatisfactory. He ordered Victorio to wait with his men while he met with the king. The cardinal, further irritated by Victorio's response, did not find it surprising.

Victorio, having safely returned the cardinal, offered his escort. He was not surprised at the cardinal's anticipated rejection and impressed on him that he also had business with the king. He thought it prudent not mention his letters from the condesa and the padre. They waited outside in the hallway.

The cardinal was furious that the king would speak first with his soldier. He sat outside and waited for his turn while planning his strategy for further revenge. He was there to investigate prostitution, illegal gambling, and to exorcise demons from a witch. He was only there as a holy messenger sent from God.

The king was smiling when Victorio entered the room. He was holding a small piece of paper. I received this note this morning from my friend, Doctor Mendoza. One of my best pigeons delivered it. There are only four words to read. They read … wait for my letter. I believe you have a letter for me. The king was not surprised when Victorio presented him with two.

When Victorio came out and shut the door behind him, the cardinal studied his face. He did not like the words he heard from a common soldier.

The king commands you wait while he reads two letters.

The cardinal studied the back of the soldier as he proudly walked down the hall. It might be necessary to discredit him. He knew this soldier was not to be trusted. He waited to hear those all too familiar words.

The king will see you now.

The cardinal bowed his head after he entered the room. Your Majesty, I am here to report stolen property and my failure to exorcise the demons from a witch, who is also a whore, *una puta*. I will need more soldiers to complete my mission and regain my stolen property. He felt slighted because the king was now reading the second letter.

It's very rare when we get to hear both sides, said the king, when those two messengers are standing so far apart. Twelve have signed this letter, and my friends have signed the other. You planned to use your Inquisition to confiscate a tax and tribute paying winery. You have cheated in an honest lottery raising funds for a church. Using extorted money from that church, you have misused my soldiers and paid for the services of an unknown prostitute, beginning on a Sunday. You have further misused my soldiers when you ordered them to kill a small, innocent child on that very same Sunday. The king shook his head while the cardinal grimaced and continued to grovel.

Your reign in Spain is over. Tell your pope what you want, but I will have another cardinal. You will leave Spain and never return. Make haste and choose your time wisely, for in three days Cesaré will give your name to his friend, Micheletto; and we have all heard of him. The king watched the blood drain from the cardinal's face when he mentioned the name of that, known only to an unprivileged few, assassin.

. . .

Jane and the condesa were lying in bed, and Zeke as usual was lying at their feet. Her flood was almost over, and it had only been three days. Thanks to the condesa's skill and knowledge, a *godemichet* was never needed. Jane was examining Anna's navel.

You have a large red birthmark surrounding your navel.

The condesa smiled before bursting into laughter. We always kill the males who mount us, just like the black widow spider. No man mounts me and continues to live.

But he didn't mount you. Besides, you are my white widow.

Yes, but he tried. The count mounted me, but he paid for that pleasure with his life. The cardinal will pay … because he tried.

131

He will pay for his bad behavior and as one of God's false recipients. This is the worst kind of man, and God knows it.

God so loved the world He gave his only Son, so that man would have a perfect example. Consider the padre and compare him to the cardinal. The padre daily wrestles to be more like His Son in the midst of imperfect examples while the cardinal hypocritically and with malice subverts His teachings. Does a priest lose his respect for God as he further moves up in the order? Does his love for power, promotion, and politics replace his love for God? Let us hope this cardinal is the only bad example.

Tomorrow you will wield your new sword. Listen carefully to your uncles. Lessons are always more serious when testing mettle with metal. I will teach you as much as I can, but in a few years you will go to school in Barcelona ... dressed as a boy. The doctor and I have spoken, and he will take care of you. He has convinced me that you require tutors. Jane, there will be no backtalk because you are now a Barciníu. We will prepare you for this new role which will include pleasure but mostly duty.

We will ride through the trees to have breakfast with my brothers. Don't be surprised when my mother grabs you and sits you on her lap. She has been waiting to see you, and your uncles have for you their special present. Pretend to be surprised.

Tomorrow will begin your family education. That education will differ from your tutors. You will taste the vines and the soil in every section but mostly the grapes. You will know the land as well as your own hand. You will learn to cooper the barrels. You will learn to blow glass. You will ride with your uncles and learn how to market. You will learn to keep accounts of the winery's profits. Each winery will record its own accounts, but the production will be handled as one. Don't worry, little one. This could take years but will soon become fun.

Part Two

"... *a stone, a leaf, an unfound door; a stone, a leaf, a door. And of all the forgotten faces.*

Naked and alone we came into exile. In her dark womb we did not know our mother's face; from the prison of her flesh have we come into the unspeakable and incommunicable prison of this earth.

Which of us has known his brother? Which of us has looked into his father's heart? Which of us has not remained forever prison-pent? Which of us is not forever a stranger and alone?

O waste of lost, in the hot mazes, lost, among bright stars on this weary, unbright cinder, lost! Remembering speechlessly we seek the great forgotten language, the lost lane-end into heaven, a stone, a leaf, an unfound door. Where? When?

O lost, and by the wind grieved, ghost, come back again."

Look Homeward Angel, by Thomas Wolfe

Chapter Fifteen

Mendoza was sitting in his chair, smoking his pipe, and everything was missing. He so loved Mary but knew he had to let her go. Joaquin presented an excellent argument. She was still young and could have many children. He said that he could better provide for Mary than could the doctor.

It was the hardest thing the doctor ever did, but his first thoughts were of Mary. As a young man, he thought he would have forever to find a wife and soulmate. He thought he would find her, just around the corner. But when he did, she was in the wrong window.

The only woman he constantly found was just around every corner and in every window of time. He wondered if she had cursed him and if his only lot in life was that of her adversary. But then on the other hand that lot helped his fellow man.

He explained it to Mary on their way to the winery. He could not bear the guilt or the thought of usurping a radiant life or of keeping it in a cage like a songbird, even though it would break his heart. She held his hand, and with tears in her eyes said she would try to understand.

They cried together at her wedding when he gave her away. He would be content because her children would all carry the name, Barciníu. He had delivered Mary's first son, and the padre had christened him Fernando. It was the first time that Mendoza was a godfather.

Mendoza was carving pipes from five pieces of a white mineral found floating in *el Mar Negro*. Cesaré brought him five good pieces from his last trip to Turkey and suggested that he carve them into pipes. Mendoza set up the chess board and waited for Jane's arrival.

Four of five pipes were only roughly finished, but the artisan-supplied stems were a perfect fit to his handcrafted bowls. He was applying beeswax on his first pipe to that white mineral when he heard the sound of a horse, a solid dismount, and a knock on his door. The young lad burst in before Mendoza could get out of his chair.

When Jane removed her hat, he laughed at her freshly cut hair, but he was impressed by her leather backstrap and her beautiful sword. He continued to laugh. No way could she pass as a boy.

Jane! Do you have any idea how difficult it will be to make you appear as a boy?

The condesa said I should wear padding on my tummy and go to school as a cute, fat boy. She arched her back and stood in front of the doctor. Look! I'm not nearly as flat. I think it pleases the condesa, but my uncles don't even notice. They take turns teaching me how to handle my new Barciníu sword in battle. I would have arrived earlier, but now I am required to join in on family business discussions.

Mendoza bit his lip to hide his smile. And what were your family discussions?

The condesa wants to bottle our wine. She wants to slow its aging and sell it in smaller amounts. We would have to add a building with a furnace and hire a few more men. The furnace would be used by both wineries, and their men would work together during the harvest.

She wants all of her men to cooper and blow glass. She wants our regulars to pick extra seasonal workers when necessary for picking and crushing. Everyone has to be a carpenter, and that includes our family. The wineries will be managed separately but work together like sister and brothers in an emergency.

Mendoza smiled at the child trying to hide her pride and feelings of self worth. When Jane realized that she had not fooled him, she continued speaking.

That was our biggest family discussion. When the weather is fine, we usually hold them in the forest and have a picnic near the pond and watch and listen to that beautiful waterfall.

This time Jane did not try to hide her pride or feeling of self worth. Mendoza felt the warmth of her reflections and sharing but decided to hide it.

Stop talking and help my cook fix our dinner. Mendoza watched as Jane snorted through her nose and remove her sword and its backstrap before she went into the kitchen.

Jane always enjoyed chatting with adults after dinner, and she had not seen the doctor in months. She wanted to talk about Zeke, but knew that would not improve her social skills. The condesa told her to let the adults speak first. She remembered that the condesa and her brothers were laughing when they told her.

She looked around the room and waited for the doctor to speak. He was smoking one of his old wooden pipes and carving one from a white material that she had never seen. Because he was ignoring her, she would get her sword and polish it. When she got up, Mendoza told her to sit down.

I'll tell the condesa you showed adult patience during and after dinner. Jane, fetch the chessboard. The condesa wants you to learn how to play. I have something to tell you while we set up the chess pieces. The condesa and your uncles may not even know this. Do you remember the cardinal? Mendoza laughed when Jane clenched her fists and looked to where she had placed her sword.

The cardinal was found floating in his own blood in an old Roman bath that was part of a convent in Italy. The coroner said it appeared to be suicide. Jane, it's not polite to smile when you're hearing about another man's death even if you don't like him. What is even more distressing is that the church did not allow him to be buried in hallowed ground because suicide is a mortal sin. Jane! It's even more impolite to laugh.

I don't care. I can't wait to tell the condesa. I'm even going to tell Zeke. Oh, I'm not supposed to mention him. The condesa said I shouldn't always talk about my dog, but I already miss him. The condesa said Zeke would be happier at the winery and would interfere with my studies if he was with me.

I have very good news from the condesa. Our friend, the padre, is now a monsignor, but he wishes to be called Padre by his friends. Oh, I almost forgot to tell you. Mary is coming to visit you. Of course, she will bring Nando. That's what she calls him. And now, I have my very own first cousin.

Mendoza was smiling through moist eyes at Jane while he set up the chessboard. Chess has many moves. It is like the game of life. You have to anticipate your opponent's reactions. This piece, called a pawn, can move two squares on its first move but only one thereafter. It can only take a piece with a diagonal move. This is the queen. She has the moves of both a bishop and a rook. This piece is called the knight. He takes L shaped moves. He can move two squares in one direction and then one in another, or he can move one square in one direction and two in another. He always lands on an opposite color, and he can go around other pieces.

Jane interrupted the doctor. Where's the piece that has the moves of both a queen and a knight?

Jane, there is no piece having the moves of both a queen and a knight.

I thought you said that chess was like the game of life.

I did, but no chess piece has both those moves. They're only found in real life. You don't know how fortunate you are to have so many fine examples surrounding you.

The doctor smiled at his little friend. Jane, you have just learned your first lesson. You know the possible moves on a chessboard but not their probabilities. Your moves, and your opponents, as in real life or in chess, are covered by the laws of probability, mixed with the domino effect.

I think I understand the domino effect but not the difference between probability and possibility.

Mendoza smiled at Jane while packing his pipe. If I flip a coin, the probability of it landing on its head or its tail is one. The probability of it landing on its edge and balancing there is zero. Possibilities of events occurring when the probability is truly zero are known only to God. Those we call miracles. Mendoza wondered if Jane comprehended while lighting his pipe. Jane, it's your move.

Jane picked up the white queen and held it against one of the white knights. She smiled at Mendoza as she looked around the room. Her eyes were brightly shining. Her opening move was with the white queen's knight.

Mendoza's hand was on his face. His index finger was pointing up at the ceiling and his middle finger was on his upper lip, covering his mouth, and looking through questioning eyes. Jane, that's a very bold move for a beginner.

Jane removed her hand from the knight and squared her shoulders. The condesa said we of Barciníu will carry extra duties that may provide protection for others. Sometimes we will have to be bold. She was smiling but not at the doctor. When I grow up, I will become a knight … but not just any old knight. Her eyes smiled even more when she said, I will become the white queen's knight.

Mendoza smiled at the child studying the pieces. Her eyes never left the board. Jane, your moves are thoughtful and well planned. The condesa said she wanted me to teach you to play. Was she being honest with me?

The condesa doesn't know it, but Zeke and I watch her and Uncle Cesaré play. Doctor, I believe it's your move.

They traded moves back and forth until the game's conclusion. Mendoza was smoking his third bowl and pleased with his not too difficult victory. The game would be over in eleven more moves. However, he was astounded at Jane's thought process.

Jane pursed her mouth as he had seen before and held out her hand when only five moves remained. Before she spoke, she toppled her king.

Congratulations, Doctor, I hope you enjoyed the game.

It's time for you to go to bed. I'll come in and kiss you goodnight. Mendoza waited until Jane said she was ready.

You may kiss my forehead but not my lips. Only my uncles may kiss my lips, but they can't do it like the condesa.

Mendoza kissed her goodnight before he blew out the light. He left her door partly opened as he whispered, *Vaya con Dios*. He put away the chess pieces before he sat back in his old, comfortable chair. Mary would soon be there with her baby while her husband was away on business. She told her husband that she would be staying with Musetta and visiting the doctor to show him their baby. She was grateful to the doctor because her baby was born before its full term.

Mendoza picked up one of the five pieces of that white mineral Cesaré brought from his last trip to *el Mar Negro*. This one would be for the condesa and take the shape of a straight billiard. He would be at peace with Jane living in his house, commuting to the university, because the school's headmaster owed him a big favor. He did not know if it was his imagination or not, but if he did not make a sound, he thought he could hear the child quietly breathing. This was the first time since Mary left that his house was flooded with calm.

He blinked at the ceiling before closing his eyes and using his hand to wipe them. He could look forward to having Jane in his house for four or five more years. He removed his feet from his old ottoman as he examined the unfinished piece. He would take Jane to see the headmaster in the morning. There was much to discuss, but if their plans were kept simple they would work. His first rule would be that Jane lives with him. He knew her family would pay for her board and tuition.

The years would pass, but he would chronicle the Barciníu history. It would have small import to those who had lived it, but it might be of interest to Nando.

Mendoza tamped the tobacco in his pipe, rekindling until it was evenly glowing. He sat back in his most comfortable chair and placed his feet on his old ottoman. He examined the unfinished piece in his hand and then continued to carve.

Chapter Sixteen

Mendoza was smoking his pipe, but something was still missing. He did not mind being alone, but his conscience caused more pain than he could imagine. He felt that Joaquin had split him apart. The decision was his, and he would have to live by it. He hoped that little ray of sunshine would lighten his burden, but it would be unmanly to tell her why.

He had taken an oath but had overlooked that *do no harm to others* applied to himself, or that he would so soon need to internalize those now famous words, *physician heal thyself.*

His cook had arrived, and Jane was still soundly sleeping. He had watered and fed the horses and hooked up his carriage. Jane's clothes were folded neatly and on her dresser. Not one of them was a dress. He remembered her uncle's struggle when they, for Mary's and Joaquin's wedding, tried put her in a dress. She fought, bit, and kicked until she saw the condesa enter the room wearing a dress. She moved her lips from side to side and wrinkled her nose before she said, well … OK.

The wedding proceeded as planned. Jane would try to hide behind the condesa when the guests appeared at the reception and complimented the condesa's decorations and her choice of such a pretty, little, flower girl. Jane had tears in her eyes when she apologized to her uncle Joaquin for biting his hand. It was considered bad luck for a groom to be bandaged during his wedding. Joaquin picked her up and kissed her and said that nothing could spoil this day.

The padre performed the ceremony, and the sisters helped the cook. Musetta could not be there because she was in mourning and would not wear black to the wedding. The madam sat between Cesaré and Rodrigo, and the sisters positioned themselves between the guests. The madam informed Cesaré and the condesa that Jane would be welcome at Musetta's villa whenever the doctor had to leave town.

Wake up you sleepy head. It's time to enroll you in school.

Jane looked up and viewed her new surroundings. I don't want to go to school. I want to live with Zeke and the condesa.

Mendoza smiled before he spoke. Whom shall I tell first, your uncle Cesaré or the condesa? He watched her jump out of bed and remove her nightshirt. Her hips and breasts were just starting to form into those of a woman. She will be small but as exquisite as the condesa, he thought, but the color of her hair was honey blond.

Jane stretched and looked out the window as if he was not there before she started to put on her clothes. Mendoza stepped out and shut the door behind him, but this was not the first time he had seen her naked.

Jane was taking the dishes into the kitchen to help the cook. Mendoza said there was not enough time. The headmaster wants to see you before classes begin, and I will be there to bear witness as to how you are to behave. When Jane picked up her sword, the doctor told her to put it down.

How can I protect you without my Barciníu sword?

Mendoza laughed as he patted Jane's head. There are more ways to protect than using your sword. One is sacrifice, and you must be prepared for that. Your actions, as a boy, will go unchallenged, but be prepared, and don't get mad when your classmates call you pretty boy.

Just remember that you represent the Barciníu family, its honor, and its pride. Pride is not to be confused with something of which you are proud. Pride is what you had when you stood naked in your room. Unlike your sword, you will always carry it but should never wear it. Mendoza laughed when Jane twitched her nose and mouth from side to side.

I think I should wear more than my pride to school, she said looking away from Mendoza.

You should be grateful and enjoy your education, but your greatest joy will probably be that you will attend school dressed

142

as a boy. Before they got into his carriage, he told her to remember her sword. Mendoza was still laughing when he snapped the reins.

. . .

While delivering wine to the castle, the reason for their summons or why they were shown into a private room was a mystery to the condesa and to her brothers. The king was waiting when they arrived.

As you and your brothers already know, the French are invading our Habsburg territories in Northern France and Italy. What you may not know is that while most of our forces are committed in these territories, French soldiers are making successful raids in northern Spain. I may have to withdraw soldiers from our Habsburg territories, which would weaken those defenses.

If we had more soldiers, I would invade southern France and draw their forces from our Habsburg territories. It's been a long war, and your king will appreciate any irritation that you can give them. Obviously, there can be no documentation of this agreement, for both of our sakes, and I can no longer spare soldiers to give you safe passage when delivering your wine to the castle. I can only wish you safe passage back to Sant Sadurní.

Leaving the castle, Anna and her brothers were discussing the king's strategy and situation. Joaquin said it was nice of the king to take them into his confidence. The condesa shook her head in disgust before she retorted.

This was not an act of altruism. The king wants our support without his support or payment. If we should have any conflict with the French, it must be on Spanish soil. We are not soldiers, and if we enter their territory, the French could hunt us as spies. Our entry would be their reason to attack our winery.

Brothers, if you have any love for our Barciníu family, you will swear to remain on Spanish soil. I think we have a weak king. I much preferred his father.

. . .

Mendoza and Jane were in the office of the headmaster.

143

We all know why Jane is here, but this may be a surprise for the doctor. We have another disguised intruder, he said, and started laughing. Josephina is the daughter of the king but not the queen. He wants her to have a good education, so that he can present her at court. She and Jane could room together, and Jane would not have to commute. We don't have any single rooms because the architects did not anticipate royalty. Josephina's room is one of the few for only two people. Jane's accommodations would be completely paid by the king.

Mendoza wasted no time to interrupt the headmaster. Jane will be living with me. This has already been agreed to by the condesa. In the condesa's absence, I will teach Jane what she cannot learn in school. However, I will allow her to sleep in that room when I'm out of town. You should know that Jane is also welcome to live in the house of a nobleman in Barcelona. His widow would enjoy her company.

So you see, Headmaster, Jane has now three choices, but she will stay where the condesa tells her, and you must know that the condesa and I are close friends. Besides our own friendship, the nobleman's widow and the condesa have, for what shall remain unknown, a personal history.

Doctor Mendoza, I appreciate your protective instincts. I can see that you love her, but please consider the benefits for both of these children. Students will question why one child will have a double room to … himself. It would single out Josephina!

Headmaster, that was very cheeky of you to test my motives in front of Jane. I'll send your request to the condesa, and I will comply with her wishes, but first I want to see the child. Know that the condesa's and my concerns will only be for Jane.

Doctor, you have disarmed me completely. The benefits to them sharing are much more for Josephina's rather than Jane's. The child, raised to be a proper lady, finds boy's clothes disgusting and is afraid to leave her room. I selfishly wanted her to have a *sympathetic* roommate because it may be the only way I can satisfy the king. Let me repeat. The king will pay Jane's tuition, board, and lodging. May we, at least, let them meet each other?

The headmaster, Mendoza, and Jane entered a room to see a child lying on top of her bed and staring at the ceiling while weeping. Mendoza put his left hand to his forehead and shook his head. This won't work, he said. The headmaster has no knowledge of what Jane has endured. No way should anyone force Jane to assume responsibility for another. Mendoza was speechless when Jane walked over and sat on the child's bed.

Why are you afraid to wear *pantalones?* They're more comfortable than a dress, and you can sit down and spread your legs. But the best part is that you can wear boots and carry a sword. You can look any boy in the eye and scold him when he misbehaves. You will never walk in second place. You will forget the breach of being a woman, and your only concern will be the length of your reach.

Josephina stopped crying and held Jane's hands. Will you be my roommate?

Jane looked at Mendoza and then at the headmaster. That will be the decision of my condesa and the doctor's, but I think my answer should be, yes. I will teach you how to handle a sword and how to play chess. Jane covered her mouth and looked down at the floor. She was obviously embarrassed.

Mendoza laughed and then smiled at the headmaster. I'll send a courier note and ask the condesa for another sword. In the meantime, the child can use mine. Cesaré and his brothers will be coming to town, and I will unfold the whole story. Separately or together, they are more likely to say yes than the condesa. I'll be sending you some of Jane's clothes.

The headmaster walked out with the doctor. I thought I would be repaying a big favor, but I am in your debt more than ever. What does the condesa want Jane to study?

I want her to become a doctor, said Mendoza, but that would be unfair to Jane. She would never be accepted in that profession. She must find a profession where she can successfully masquerade as a man. Besides, the condesa will want to keep Jane with her. They seem to gather nourishment from each other.

The padre told me an interesting story. He thinks they can feel each other's thoughts or presence when they are in separate rooms. If the late cardinal had known this, he would have called it witchcraft, but the padre thinks they're soulmates. They would be Plato's split-apart, were they the same age.

. . .

The condesa was outside talking to her field hands. My brothers will be addressing their men, just as I am addressing you. A reliable source told us that the French have already invaded Spain. It's a tactical move to draw Spanish soldiers from France's northern borders, which means they could invade and loot our homes.

We cannot ask you to fight for us, but we want you to be able to protect yourselves. We will provide you with swords, muskets, and powder and teach you how to use them. Each of you will have his own horse. I have done my best to think of you as individuals, but I must remind you that united we stand, divided we fall. If ever we are in battle, it's all for one and one for all. The condesa spread her outstretched arms and looked up at the heavens. The sun reflected on her face, and her field hands tightened their circle around her.

. . .

Mendoza was sharing lunch with two brothers, who had presented him with a backstrap and a sword. This sword, Mendoza said, comes from Solingen. There is no better steel. How did it come to be in your possession?

Cesaré laughed with his brother, Rodrigo. We took this and others from dead French soldiers last year. They must have acquired them from German soldiers slain in battle. The condesa is grateful and is presenting it to Jane's chaperon. That's you, Cesaré said before asking the cook to bring more wine.

Mendoza made a *humph* through his nose and started laughing. Tell the condesa that I need no payment. I would do it for free if I could keep Jane with me, but the headmaster has presented me with another consideration. The king has a daughter, born a bastard, for which he wants a good education. The child has never masqueraded as a boy and will need Jane's help and protection. I wrestle with my conscience because consciously, I want to keep Jane with me.

Cesaré and Rodrigo smiled at each other. You share the same predicament as our sister. She knows her heart was split apart and requires a second opinion. Jane is always in our hearts, but we must first consider the needs of the child. At least, we are eating well. Mary does a fine job when she's not too busy with Nando, but our mother prefers Jane, her oldest granddaughter.

Our sister would come, but she does not even have the time to daily visit Mary or our mother. She would send Jane to season our mother's cooking, who always wanted Jane to dine with us. This became an amusing family argument. Jane asked the condesa if she should stay one night with our family.

The condesa said she could, but Zeke would remain with her that night. We had to bite our lips at Jane's predicament, but a solution was finally reached. Jane and our little sister would sleep in the same bed that night with our mother, and would cook breakfast for everyone in the morning. Jane hasn't a clue what she means to the family.

We must return to the winery to help our sister and brother. The men will want their sword-fighting lessons. We take turns training the men, who each have four instructors. They would have five if Jane were living at home. She would be good for the smaller men and teach them to rely on quickness. She and the condesa have perfected a roll from a standup that we can't even do.

Mendoza walked them to the front door and said, give my love to Mary and the condesa. He shut the door to his empty house and walked back to sit in his comfortable chair. He packed his pipe and kindled it while his cook cleared the dining room table.

Chapter Seventeen

Weeks had turned into months, and Mendoza was still unhappy. He should have had a daughter living in his house, supplying him with intelligent and amusing conversation. But here he was, trying to ignore his cook's banalities.

After returning from his rounds, Mendoza would sit in his favorite chair, close his eyes, and pretend to be sleeping. During that time, he would think about Jane and remember their conversations. It was much more than that; Jane could play chess. He had students in the past but none like her. He had that titillation of knowing he could turn an *ingénue* into a master who could surpass him. He awoke to the knock on his door. The young lad was impatiently waiting.

Doctor Mendoza, the headmaster wishes to see you. He said it's very important. He wants to speak with you about Juan. Can I tell him you're coming?

Mendoza just yawned in the lad's face. Tell him I'll be there after my breakfast. Mendoza lit his pipe in disgust before he left his house. That bastard has robbed me of four wonderful years. What could the headmaster want now, he asked himself on the way to the school. He tied his horse to the hitching post. The headmaster was waiting.

Doctor, it's been some time since I have seen you. Please come into my office, and let me serve you with wonderful coffee. I must speak to you about … and he whispered … Jane. The headmaster shut his door and continued to whisper.

Josephina, I mean José, checked out two textbooks from our library about geometry and trigonometry for Jane, … I mean Juan. She's, I mean he's, designing a castle. I've never seen one like it. The arrow loops are triangular.

Mendoza could not keep from laughing. Headmaster, don't freak-out because the girl shows interest in math. Her tutors will be proud, and her interests will aide the school in its deception.

The headmaster signaled the doctor to be quiet. Doctor, I am far more familiar with students than you. Very few of our boys show interest in math. Those who excel love it for its own sake, but Juan is interested in math as a tool. She ... I mean he ... has trigonometric notes on her drawings. I mean his drawings. I think the right choice for ... Juan ... and the school is for her, I mean him, to study architecture.

Mendoza was amused at the headmaster's fumbling and misuse of pronouns. Headmaster, do you now still think that you owe me two favors? He did not wait for an answer. I'll send a note to the condesa, and you can proceed with your plans for Juan. They may be just what the doctor ordered.

Mendoza kept his pipe in his pouch while he packed it. He would never spill tobacco on anyone's floor. At home he would pick up the spilled tobacco and put it back into his pouch. He walked over and selected a thin piece of wood from the flower vase on the mantle, kindled it in the fireplace, and sat down after the bowl's contents were evenly glowing. He knew that losing Jane to the school was the right thing to do even if it was irritating.

The headmaster could sense Mendoza's displeasure and decided to change the subject. Doctor, the discovery of those girls' identity could threaten my position, but we may be looking at the future of student enrollment. Those girls have excellent reports from their professors, and they carry the responsibility of their identity. They carry their burden, not me. If that were only my greatest problem.

The mundane is our most frequent irritation. Our oldest and largest student, the son of Don Diego, is a bully and a scholastic nightmare. He thinks that force is the only way he can gain recognition. So far, he has not picked on the girls, but I anticipate facing that problem. I will be having that conversation with his father about his son, who has not fallen far from the tree. Both feel that loudness gives them credibility.

Mendoza was amused that two issues which should be dismissed as trivial pursuits in reality were absolute milestones in academia. The headmaster was in a quandary concerning his actions over a stupid, adolescent bully and two intelligent girls willing to masquerade as boys in order to get an education.

Headmaster, consider the clues you have learned concerning Jane. While they cannot be kept secret, you must avoid their promulgation. You have seen the trees. Don't overlook their importance to the forest. Except for her analytical ability, she is an *ingénue* finding wonder, excitement, and a mentality concerning things we lost, forgot, or never knew.

The condesa and her brothers taught Jane all they knew, but it was only what they knew. I persuaded the condesa to hire special tutors, and it was I who recommended and selected them. When her tutor told me that Jane's gifts included geometry and trigonometry, I told the condesa that the study of mathematics could be a means to partition her mind and scar-over those awful memories that need forgetting. It was a great sacrifice for the condesa when she sent Jane to university.

Jane's mind has protected itself with these childlike partitions because, Headmaster, her mind truly burns that brightly. You can never acknowledge those *boys* who did not open the door for girls attending university. However, those bastard girls, masquerading as boys, will leave their footprints. You and I will never forget this historical event which will be lost in history.

Mendoza then sat back, took out his tobacco pouch, and tried to keep from laughing. He could not help but smile at the puzzled headmaster and his dilemma over trivialities.

Now, Headmaster, where is that wonderful coffee?

Chapter Eighteen

The condesa's and Joaquin's mother was watching her daughter and youngest son train the field hands for battle. She was sitting on her veranda and knitting a blanket for Nando. Jane's was already neatly folded and the name Barciníu, beautifully embroidered. She did not like the thought of war, but at least it kept her sons from drinking.

Mary was in the parlor nursing her baby. She also recoiled at the thought of war, especially when it involved her husband and his brothers. She was mad at the condesa for even thinking of becoming involved. When she was done nursing, she came out and sat next to her mother-in-law.

The condesa addressed the men while Joaquin inspected them. Because your horse is your best friend and protector in battle, you should be his protector and friend. You have all learned to handle your horses, but now you have to handle them using your sword in battle.

When two mounted soldiers face each other, who are equal swordsmen in battle, the finer horseman will win. If you face a better swordsman, you will strike his horse, and he will do the same. There is no honor in war or battle, and in order to save your life you will sacrifice your best friend even if you have to use him as a shield. But remember now that you are on foot you have lost your advantage. I repeat, she yelled. Sacrificing your horse is your last resort. Joaquin will show you where to strike your opponent's horse and how to protect your best friend.

The condesa smiled at the men and then mounted her horse. We have another advantage, and I hope it will inspire you in battle. They are the intruders, and they know it. You are defending your homes and the lives you love. Their inspiration is the joy of money, murder, and plunder. Yours is the holy war, and God knows it. He will not be looking for sportsmanship but rather for the efficiency of your killing in battle.

151

Joaquin, send out those three men.

Joaquin addressed the men. These three armored men will attack the condesa and her horse. They will surround her before they attack.

The condesa waited while three surrounded her before she jumped, rolled from her saddle, and slammed the broadside of her sword against all three horses. When their horses reared, she jumped back in her saddle. The horse's reigns never left her hand. By the time the men's horses were settled, she had slammed her sword against all three men.

Joaquin was laughing with pride over his sister's skill. These same three armored men will attack the condesa and her horse. This will be a frontal assault.

The condesa waited for their approach before she reared her horse and rode it on its hind legs between their standing horses, with her horse's front hooves striking two of the men. She turned her horse around to strike the other man on his back and pull him from his saddle.

Remember what we told you about the better horseman. You will find armor too clumsy in battle, but I wanted to strike you men without any harm. This will be your practice today and the rest of the week. Next week, we will show you a better attack against a fine horseman, and my brothers and I will show you how a good horseman attacks using his horse without any sword.

Joaquin shook his head with pride for his sister. He dropped on one knee as did the other men. It's one for all … and all for one.

The condesa could not help but smile at the men. Joaquin will show you these maneuvers again. His style is for larger men. I must return to the house. After your practice is over, she said while laughing, it's back to work in the fields. Still mounted on her horse, she leaned down and whispered to her brother.

There's trouble in Barcelona.

Joaquin faced the men. Those in armor will help put armor on three more others. I'll face those six largest men. He was interrupted by one of the men.

We would like to see you face the condesa.

Joaquin laughed as he faced them. I would not because I would surely lose. My little sister possesses an uncommon, almost lightning quickness. We wanted you to see it because it may work well for the smaller, faster man. But the only person who has truly mastered her style was Jane because she is even quicker than the condesa.

Half of the men, the condesa's field hands, followed Joaquin to the condesa's vineyard. They were not looking forward to farming but felt a comradery for each other and her brother's men, who remained to work their own fields. They looked questionably at each other when they crossed the stream below the pond created by that waterfall. Joaquin had stopped, gotten off his horse, and had given the sign of the cross. He waived goodbye to the condesa's men before he entered the house.

Little sister, what is troubling you?

The condesa was pacing in the living room. I have only one reason to feel this nervous, and it's in Barcelona. My instinct is to mother and hover over Jane, but I don't want to embarrass her. I'll dispatch a note to the doctor and ask him to look in on her if Cesaré and Rodrigo are not still visiting Musetta in Barcelona.

I'll spend the night with you and your family. I will cook and plan dinner for your brothers' return from Barcelona. Mary can rest, and my cook can take the night off and read her old love letters. At this point, I will need family around me and ample occupation.

Juan and José were studying for their final examinations. Juan was helping José with geometry, and José was helping Juan with French.

Oh, José, I'll never be as good as you are with French.

Oh, Juan, you would be if your mother were French.

Both girls were laughing and started to wrestle. Jane signaled Josephina to stop wrestling and suggested they go the sword room. We'll practice French while we fence. Josie, you have really gotten a lot better.

The girls put on protective clothing and selected their foils. Josephina started to laugh when they saluted and faced each other.

En garde, you cute, fat, little boy.

Before they could cross foils, Gabriel, the biggest and oldest boy in school, hit Josephina from behind, knocking her to the floor.

Fencing is for little girls. Too bad you can't fight like a man.

After kicking Gabriel in his groin, Juan confronted him. He was groaning, on his knees, and looking up when he felt Juan's foil against his throat. Juan then slapped his face.

Too bad you can't fight like a man. You have insulted me and my friend. The choice of weapons is mine, and I choose the sword instead of a foil. Your choice will be first blood or to the death. Get your sword and meet me in the courtyard. I'll be there in one long minute.

Gabriel watched Juan help José to his feet. He hated them for being honor students who ignored him. This would be his chance to dishonor them. He walked outside and called his friends. He wanted them to witness his triumph.

Mendoza was happy to have intelligent companions for lunch. His cook was a pleasant, superstitious, ignorant person who could only talk about her underwhelming grandchildren. He was almost bragging about his carving when he handed Cesaré the unfinished piece. Cesaré and Rodrigo examined it together.

If you were not a doctor, you would make a fine pipe maker.

Their lunch was interrupted when Mendoza's cook entered the room. I just put Ulysses into his cage and removed this note. He behaved as if he were starving. She handed Mendoza the note.

Cesaré, this note is for you and your brother. I'll follow you in my carriage.

The headmaster was having that dreaded conversation with Gabriel's father. Don Diego, thank you for responding to my letter. This conversation concerns your son. Several of our student's parents have complained about Gabriel. I have examined those children myself and have found bruising. The boys have not complained because I think they are probably too afraid. Don Diego, this discussion should include your son.

Don Diego smiled with pride. I left him in the sword room because this should be settled between men. Boys will be boys, and men will be men. I was the toughest and best swordsman if you can remember. I wouldn't worry about it. Headmaster, just consider the tradition my family has with this school. Besides, I am more concerned with my son's grades. He will need a tutor, which I will pay for.

The headmaster was looking out of his office window. He remembered the stories he heard since childhood that caused him to disliked the man in his office. Don Diego, I was not here when you were here as a student. That was my father. At this moment, I am needed in the courtyard.

The boys had formed a circle in the courtyard surrounding two swordsmen. The oldest and biggest was facing the youngest and smallest. Juan saluted Gabriel, her opponent, while Gabriel looked at Juan with scorn.

I will not dignify you with a salute, but I will wear your ears around my neck. This is what a real man fights with, and in the air Gabriel circled his sword.

Gabriel circling his sword above his head thought Juan would run, and he would win by default until he heard those words, *en garde*. He was confused when he saw Juan turn his back and face the surrounding circle.

The trouble you all had with Gabriel is that you forgot to face him. He will only strike if he sees your back. That was your only mistake. From now until semester's end, we will call him Gabriella.

Gabriel ran holding his sword and swung with all of his might. He stumbled when he saw his sword slice through air as Juan tucked and rolled behind him. He felt that smooth slice of polished steel behind his knees as he fell upon them. He put his hand to the side of his bleeding head to see Juan triumphantly holding his ear. He felt the kick of a boot in his face, knocking

155

him to the ground. He felt the sword against his throat and heard those mocking soft-spoken words, first blood or to the death.

Don Diego looked out of the window after the headmaster left, to see his son sword-fighting. He was smiling with pride until he saw his son on his knees with a blade at his throat. He grabbed his sword and ran from the headmaster's office.

Don Diego ran with his sword in his hand towards his son's victor and opponent as soon as he reached the courtyard.

I'll decorate my saddle with your head, he yelled.

He felt the boot in his face before he fell to the ground. He picked himself up and grabbed his sword and saw the horseman dismount. He was looking into the eyes of Cesaré Barciníu. The blood ran from his face when he heard those soft-spoken words, first blood or to the death.

Don Diego sheathed his sword. I would fight you but I must first see about my son.

The doctor stood in front of Don Diego. Put your son into my carriage if you want to save his legs, and follow me to the mortuary where I will have a table and the all instruments I need. The mortician will assist me, but without me he will assist you. There's not a moment to waste. Just be prepared for my payment.

Mendoza stood before Jane while Don Diego put his son into the doctor's carriage. Jane, I haven't a moment to lose, he whispered as loud as he possible could. Jane! Give me that boy's ear.

He tried to hide his amusement as Jane twitched her nose and mouth from side to side. She deliberately turned her back to him as she reached back over her shoulder and delicately with thumb and index finger handed the doctor Gabriel's bloody ear. He could not see her face, but he knew that she was smiling.

Cesaré rode next to the doctor's carriage. I'll wait until it's convenient for you to take your satisfaction.

Don Diego was too sad to feel humiliation. If I face you, my son will not have a father. Please accept our apology and my obligation to your family. Cesaré, without response, turned his horse and rode back to the school.

Mendoza laid the boy facedown on the table. Tie his hands and plug your ears. I must suture those muscles and tendons before they separate. Don Diego held his son's arms, and the mortician held his legs. The doctor paid no attention to either one while Don Diego prayed for his son.

Oh Lord, please have mercy for the boisterous cowards.

Jane stopped running after Cesaré when she saw him returning. She held up her arms and jumped as her uncle grabbed her by her pants and set her on his lap. He had a stern look on his face, but she had a big smile for him and twitched her nose on her face. Her eyes were brightly shining.

Cesaré looked straight ahead without smiling while riding back to the school. Jane could not see his face, but her back could feel his belly shake. Cesaré whispered as he set Jane down in the courtyard. If we were alone, I'd pull your pants down and spank your bare bottom. I just might tell the condesa that you've become a bully and are picking on the boys.

Go ahead she said when he let go of her hand. She twitched her nose when she saw her uncle's eyes. She saw him byte his lip to keep from smiling. Jane looked up and bit her lip, just as Cesaré had done. Go ahead, she said. I want them to know that you're my uncle.

Cesaré turned his horse and rode next his brother. The boys gathered around Juan and José, and they were cheering. Jane ran up the front steps to see Cesaré and Rodrigo, riding away and shaking their heads while laughing.

Don Diego paid little attention to the mortician when he heard him say that was the best surgery he had ever seen.

The doctor said that was all he could do, but his son should not walk or straighten his legs for months, … even when he shits. Now hold him down while I sew his ear back on his head.

The headmaster was waiting when Jane rejoined Josephina in the middle of the circle. He raised his hands, signaling everyone to be quiet.

Boys, the entertainment is over, and it's time to return to your classes. He placed his hands on Juan's and José's breasts to keep the girls from leaving. He waited until the boys disappeared through the doors before he looked directly at Jane. The doctor informs me that you are proficient at chess. Jane looked up at him and nodded.

He swung his hands over their heads and slapped them on their bottoms. Now girls, get back to your class. He watched them scamper up the steps before he turned his eyes to face the heavens. He tried to keep from laughing.

Oh Lord, what am I to do with the king's feminine daughter and a tomboy swordswoman, proficient at math and chess … in an all boys' school?

Chapter Nineteen

Exams were finally over, and the girls could not be happier with their results. Jane would be returning to study engineering and building. Josephina would be returning to study literature and music. Some of her classmates thought she was a very feminine boy, but they accepted her new name, Josie, as a nickname for José. Besides, they knew that Juan was her friend and protector.

Josie was arguing with Jane in their room. Why can't you practice here for the chess tournament, so our last few days will be together? It will be lonely here, and I will be afraid without you.

Jane twitched her nose and smiled at her roommate. Josie, I need to play the doctor. No one is better than he. You can stay at his house with me. He will surely not mind, and we can help him with his practice. Josie, I have to play against someone better, far better than me.

The doctor was pleased to have both girls in his house even if for only a few days, and the headmaster had delivered them. He thought a man could only stand so much quiet. Those girls were so much different from each other, but in between their laughter there was quiet and understanding chatter. He was smoking in his comfortable chair, his feet were on his ottoman, and nothing was missing. Mendoza continued his carving.

Jane answered the knock on the door. She was looking at a frightened man, who obviously worked with his hands. His clothes were tattered, and she could smell his frightened sweat.

Doctor Mendoza, the baby's not coming!

Mendoza stretched while getting out of his chair. I told you to keep your hands clean.

Doctor Mendoza, I was afraid to touch her, even though she was screaming.

Girls, get my bag while I harness my horse. He smiled at the frightened man. Get the water to boiling. I know the way to your house. I want to see you cleaning your hands when I arrive, and that includes your fingers.

Jane was holding Josie's hand, but her head was resting against the doctor. Josie said she thought she would be in the way, and perhaps she should stay outside in the carriage. The doctor said he would need their help. He might need their clean little hands.

Jane, we might have to turn this baby.

Josie looked at Jane and said she thought she would be afraid. I've never seen a baby delivered, and this sounds complicated.

Jane smiled at the doctor before she looked at Josie. Josie, just do what the doctor tells you. There will be no time to be afraid. I've only done this once before when I was staying with the doctor. He's the finest doctor in Spain, … not just Barcelona.

Mendoza tied his horse to the hitching rail and without delay went inside. Jane carried his medical bag. She stopped at the door and looked back at her frightened friend. Josie, get down from that carriage and get your butt inside. Don't think about yourself but only the part you're playing. All we have to do is what the doctor tells us. After it's over, delivering a child will not be unknown to you.

The doctor examined the man's hands. Wash them again and scrape your nails. Rinse them again, and don't wipe them. Fill the tub with hot water, then wash and rinse again. Mendoza got down on his knees as soon as the tub was full.

Lower her into the hot water, but keep your hands beneath her, and lift her when she shits. I want this baby to come out clean.

The man knelt on his wife's right, next to Josie while Mendoza knelt on her left. Jane was on her knees between the woman's legs, and Mendoza was feeling that pregnant woman's tummy.

Jane, move to her right and use your left hand after I have rotated the baby. Insert your left hand into her womb and help me deliver this baby. Josie was watching Jane's hand, which was now out of sight. She saw the baby's head and the doctor pushing on a pregnant tummy that suddenly got smaller.

160

Jane stood and handed Josie the baby. Slap his butt, and make sure it's a good one. I have to help the doctor with the baby's navel and clean the mother.

Josie listened to the doctor as he instructed the man. Lift her from that shitty water and throw it outside. Wash the tub and then bring it inside. We'll use the rest of this unused hot water.

Josie watched Jane and the doctor clean the mother and then help her into bed. She could not control the tears from running down her face. It was the first time she was part of a miracle, and the baby's cries had announced it. She heard the sound of her name when Jane called it for the second time.

Josie! It's time to give the baby to his mother. She felt the baby lifted from her arms and saw it placed with his mother. Tears were still running down her face while Jane and the doctor were laughing. She saw the man on his knees thanking the doctor, but she was surprised at the doctor's answer.

Don't worry about the money. You will pay me when you can. Never kneel before a doctor because he is performing his oath. I'll send my girls with food, and you shall pay attention to both. Jane and Josie will tell you where to clean. Do you have someone to help with your wife?

The doctor looked away and blinked his eyes when the man said, no. I'll drop by from time to time when I'm not attending to other patients. Now you have to take care of your wife and son because I have to go home to help a dear, little friend.

After the girls climbed into the carriage, the doctor told Jane that he remembered the man. He was a broth of a lad, fighting on the front. I remember him because he had that same fear in his eyes when he banged on my door. We all change as we grow older, but that look of fear never changes and is unique to each man. It was a long night, but I knew I had saved his leg and life when she left. You can always remember a man by that peculiar fear in his eyes.

Why didn't you remind him? Jane asked.

The man is worried sick … about his wife. Besides, he has no reason to remember me.

161

The three sat in the same places, but Jane was holding the reins and sitting as close to the doctor as she possibly could. Josie was admiring Jane, who only paid attention the horse. She leaned forward and looked at the doctor. I will never forget this day. My father said you always received a well deserved payment, and you were the best doctor in Spain. I just saw you deliver a baby, without charging any fee.

Mendoza's smile broke into a chuckle. Will you keep this conversion in confidence? He continued after Josie nodded her head. I gouge the rich whenever I can, so that I may attend to the poor. It's an addition that I've made to my Hippocratic Oath. It requires a great deal of money from the rich to buy instruments and food … and to care for the poor.

Josie smiled as she looked ahead. This conversation does not require confidence because I overheard my father telling the queen that it's your way of giving back to the poor. I can tell that he holds you in reverence when he speaks your name.

Jane let the doctor off before she drove his horse and carriage into his stable. We will unharness him, rub him down, and feed him. The doctor has to relax and prepare for a very long chess game. You can help his cook prepare food for a man who has only one friend. After that, would you be willing to play for us on your recorder?

Josie was playing her recorder before Jane and the doctor started their game. She was the king's daughter but treated like one of the doctor's servants. She excused herself for blowing a false note. It was so difficult to keep from smiling. She recalled the events of that morning and shook her head. Will I ever stop learning from my little, best friend.

She watched the doctor and Jane set up the pieces. He tamped and kindled his pipe. Jane, you have always taken white with its first move. Will you have that same choice?

Jane shook her head without taking her eyes from the chess board. The winner of the toss has the first choice.

Mendoza tamped his pipe and relit it, using the same kindle. I, in my mind, have made the toss, and you have just lost. Rotate the chess board. Jane joined him with his smug little smile. She did not have to suggest it. She twitched her nose while waiting for his first move. He paused before he made it.

Jane, I love the way you twitch your nose and smile, but it could be considered *a tell*. Try not to smile while he's making his moves, but don't let that concentration distract you. Remember the moves that make him gloat. He may try them again.

Jane had a question for Mendoza. I've never seen you gloat, so why would he?

The doctor smiled and continued to puff on his pipe. Because, my little friend, he is a child and hasn't learned to not gloat over a game. Chess is merely a pleasant distraction. Jane, it's your move.

Josie watched the pieces moving back and forth while Jane covered her mouth. Josie was not sure if she should speak, but she had a further suggestion. Doctor, I don't know if this important or not, but sometimes Jane's eyes light up like candles, without any smile.

Mendoza was pensive and then nodded his head. He pointed his index finger at Josie. You're absolutely right. I've overlooked those candles that always warm my heart. He turned his eyes to face his little friend.

Jane, keep your eyes down while making your move, and study the board. Observe his face and eyes when he makes his. Josie was right. Your eyes are your biggest *tell*. Mendoza sat back and puffed on his pipe while Josie picked up her recorder and continued to play. Josie stopped playing when she saw Jane not smiling or twitching her nose and mouth.

Mendoza reloaded his pipe. I've been waiting for the day when I could stress you. What are you thinking about?

Jane's eyes never left the board. I'm thinking about eleven.

Mendoza had tears in his eyes but not because his pipe was glowing. Jane, when you're this far into the game, you should consider the sacrifice. I'll give you a hint. It's your favorite piece. They watched Jane study the board and then move her knight. Her eyes were brightly shining when she said, check.

Mendoza nodded his head. And now I have to take your knight in order to protect my king. After his protective move, he said, Jane, do you now see it? Jane was twitching her mouth from side to side.

In a dozen more moves, I'll castle to protect my king. Do you wish to continue the game?

Mendoza wiped his eyes while attempting to hide his pride. That will not be necessary. He held out his hand. I officially declare this game to be a draw, and this is the first time I have enjoyed one. You girls deliver that family's food while I put away the chess pieces. Return as soon as you can, because I, too, am hungry.

Josie turned back to look at the doctor before they left his house. Oh, my sweet little Jane, I could feel his love and his pride for you. All over me I still feel warm, and I think he is still smiling.

Jane smiled while harnessing Mendoza's horse. I have many that so love me, and on our way to deliver that poor man's food, I will tell you where I came from. She snapped the reins with Josie's arms all around her. She smiled at Josie when she heard her say … you will always be my best friend.

The next day, the girls jumped from Mendoza's carriage. He handed them their bags. I will check on the new mother and her husband. I want to see if you two did a good job. He looked up the steps, winked, nodded, and then snapped the reins.

Josie looked at Jane with apparent shock on her face when she felt Jane slap her bottom. I think you're far too familiar for a boy. They laughed on their way up the steps. The headmaster was waiting.

He put his hands on their shoulders. Girls, I mean boys, go to your room, and prepare for dinner. News travels fast to the headmaster. The doctor has taught you what does not, except in theology, exist in a university. I will be glad when you both have graduated. I will be so tired from sticking my neck out. But you should know that I am very proud of you girls. Jane, I mean Juan, how do you feel about the tournament?

He straightened up and smiled when he saw Jane look up at him and wink. Now, boys, it's off with you. He walked across campus to the faculty room. He wanted to place several small, illegal wagers with professors who believed the odds were in their favor.

After lunch, the hall was packed with tournament players. Josie was in the first round to lose, but she had played the school's chess champion. He showed no mercy.

Josie waited with the other first round losers. She was happy because her friend was still in the game. She felt less lonely when the second and third round losers joined her. She watched them place their bets as she walked among them. She covered her mouth and said, I'm putting my money on Juan. She recorded their names on her tablet and twitched her nose from side to side. Her eyes were brightly shining.

There was a hush when the forth round losers joined them. Josie said she had enough money for only one more bet and wrote the boy's name on her tablet.

Jane and the school's champion stretched before they sat down. He won the toss and rotated the board, taking the white side. Jane covered her mouth and lowered her eyes after each of her moves. She looked into his eyes while he made his.

Jane laughed and said it's only a game when his mood became serious. She twitched her nose and winked as she looked back at her friend and at the headmaster. Her eyes were brightly shining.

She turned back to face her opponent. I would offer you a draw had you shown some mercy to my friend. Make your move. You only have five left.

She stood up after he toppled his king. She held out her hand and said it was a pretty good game. I thought this would be a far more difficult competition. She walked away when he would not shake hers. She laughed when she joined the others. They heard him slug the chess board with his clenched hand.

Jane stood with her classmates, and those betting winners were cheering. Josie was collecting her bets by reminding the boys of

Juan's victory in battle. The headmaster had an announcement to make.

Let's have a round of applause for our finalists. Our school has a new chess champion, who will be returning. We should all remember that this game is played only for sport and entertainment. He looked away while Josie collected the rest of her winnings. He told himself that it was only just a little, harmless betting. Besides, he would be taking his wife out, with his winnings, for a well deserved sumptuous diner.

The girls were in their room, and Josie wanted Jane to take her share. Jane asked Josie what she would have done if she had lost. Josie only laughed.

My father said that the doctor is the finest chess player in Spain. Do you really think I would give consideration to a very old boy after seeing you play the best … to a draw?

After the girls returned to their room, Josie started pushing Jane with her palms outstretched. Both girls were laughing. What started as a pushing contest, turned into a pillow fight. What started as a pillow fight turned into wrestling in bed and continued on the floor. Anyone down the hall could hear their riotous laughter. Besides, this was not the only pillow fight in those rooms along the halls. Some would be graduating, and some would be returning. There was no sorrow in their laughter, and all were looking forward to their summer vacations.

Chapter Twenty

Mendoza was sitting in his comfortable chair, and only Mary was missing. He was smoking his favorite pipe and carving a new one. He had trashed all of his *cañuelas*. He would never again put up with that rank taste of weed, but that brought him no satisfaction. He would only have the girls for a precious few more days. The condesa wanted them returned.

Making his rounds was so much more pleasant with their company. The days were getting warmer, and the nights were getting shorter. The girls were doing his cook's shopping and going on some of his rounds. He ordered a new stethoscope with the leftover household funds. He approved of its larger bell and its shorter shank. It would be a fine addition to his collection.

He looked forward to his evenings at home and to the girls' antics, in spite of his cook's bickering. They would wait until his cook left for the day and then invade her kitchen. He would be smoking his pipe and listening to their conversation. Their banter interrupted only when they tasted, added herbs and spices. They would sit together and talk about the day's events. Jane and Josie were pleased to tell the doctor that the baby they turned was healthy, strong, and well. His father had named his son Fernando.

Josie wanted to play chess with Jane, who was twitching her nose at the doctor.

Josie! Jane is not ready to teach. I don't want her playing beginners. She thinks in twelve consecutive moves but has only just arrived there. Play against me, because I have been on this plateau for many years. Jane has a chance to arrive at another. I would send her to France if we were not at war.

Their king has a champion who lives for nothing else. I played him years ago at the invitation of his king. I was not pleased with that outcome for sporting reasons because the king's champion, from the beginning, played for the draw. I think Jane can beat him. This war can not last forever. From now on, I won't be enjoying wine while I play Jane.

The next morning, Jane handed Mendoza a note delivered by his pigeon. She said she had taken it from Hector, who was now feeding and drinking water. The doctor winced while Jane read the note.

It's only five words, doctor. King believes Josie already here.

Pack your bags, girls. We'll leave as soon as my cook arrives.

The girls were smiling at Mendoza. He had that sheepish look of a boy who had been caught stealing candy. He knew the Barciníu brothers could not fetch the girls because their presence was the winery's security. He remembered to bring his travel pipe that had a short stem and shank. He handed Jane the reins before he loaded it.

Doctor, why are you loading your pipe?

He laughed knowing that she was right. Perhaps we will find fire along the way, or I just might have to wait until we arrive at the madam's brothel. He put his pipe into his pocket and took back the reins.

Josie felt suddenly nervous. She looked back and forth at them with eyes larger than saucers. Did you say brothel?

Jane looked at her while twitching her nose. Josie, I told you we were going to have a really good time.

Mendoza reached up and messed with Jane's hair. Josie, don't let this rascal fool you. Our stop will be a short one. One of my duties as a doctor is to examine the madam's girls. You will be spending a few weeks with the condesa's and Jane's family. They will allow you some time to appreciate their humor, but be prepared for the absurd. That is their humor as well as it is mine. Josie closed her mouth when she saw Jane's smile, then altogether they started laughing.

The doctor parked his carriage behind the brothel and ushered the girls inside. Josie felt apprehensive until she saw the madam. She was a handsome and well-dressed woman. They sat in the madam's parlor while the doctor inspected her girls. The madam served them hot chocolate and biscuits before the doctor returned.

168

Josie thought she should wait until the doctor and the madam had tasted their wine until she saw Jane without hesitation spread her biscuit with marmalade. She was not sure why the doctor and madam were laughing until she noticed Jane's face.

Jane, she giggled, you have a chocolate-marmalade mustache!

. . .

Jane suddenly stopped talking on their way to the winery. She was looking up the road and listening. Josie thought she could hear the sound of a dog barking. She watched Jane jump from the carriage before it completely stopped. Her little friend was running as fast as she could, and then she dropped to her knees. A dog was standing on his hind legs, surrounding her head with his paws, and licking her face.

Josie watched Jane climb back into the carriage, followed by a jumping dog. There was so little room, and the dog was licking everyone's face except the doctor's, who pushed the dog away. In between his licking, she could hear the dog singing to his long lost friend. She thought she saw a halo surrounding their heads and shared the quiet joy from the whispers of her little friend.

I'm almost home.

The doctor steered his carriage and parked next to another. Josie saw three men and two women standing on a covered veranda. Another woman, the most striking she had ever seen, was running towards the doctor's carriage. She watched Jane jump into the arms of her condesa, to embrace each hug and kiss, and then to be carried up the steps to the veranda.

Josie could only hear Jane, now so suddenly hidden by that circle of three men and three women. She watched Jane, body arched and with arms outstretched, as each brother tossed her to another while the condesa approached her and the doctor. From the carriage, they shared the joy from their laughter.

We can't wait to spank your bare bottom.

Josie, with head bowed and eyes closed, listened to those delightful squeals while Jane was flying in that circle of love and laughter, and wondered if she, like Jane, would possibly find her own personal paradise.

Please forgive our poor manners, because we haven't seen her for as long as you have been with her, the condesa said laughing. Jane will show you to your room after she stops flying between uncles and brothers. But first, let me introduce you to the Barcíniu family.

Jane and Josie were having a quiet discussion. We have to tell the king that you had your own private room. He would think you were mistreated. Besides, Zeke, the condesa, and I always sleep together. Sleeping with her and Zeke always renews me. How about I come and kiss you good night? I'll hold you until you fall asleep. Will that be OK?

Jane and Josie washed before dinner. Oh Jane, I am so happy for you. I wish I had half as much of the love that surrounds you. Jane put her arms all around Josie. At least she tried to.

Josie, remember that you're a Habsburg without a Habsburg jaw. Your father has made special arrangements for you. He must love you even if the queen does not. Your time is just beginning. I can certainly feel it. Just remember where I came from.

Josie was surprised to see four sisters, a padre, and the madam when they entered the dining room, but Jane was not. Jane introduced Josie to them and led her towards the kitchen. The stern look from the cook blocked their entrance.

This is my kitchen she said as she turned them around and slapped their bottoms. It will be my decision who I allow in this night. Jane looked back and saw the cook smile and shake her head before turning away.

The doctor was carving the turkey. He said it was the finest *Black* he had ever seen. He stood at the center of the table with Mary sitting at his side, nursing her baby. The sisters were helping the cook serve, and Jane was looking at the condesa.

When did we start raising turkeys?

We don't. Your uncles shot this turkey in the forest after Zeke found and pointed it. We will raise them if you like it, the condesa said laughing, but you will have to promise not to make them your friends.

Their mother had an announcement to make, in spite of every one's laughter. She stood with the help of her sons and read from the parchment of paper. Her eyes shifted back and forth between Jane and the letter.

Jane, you are the only Barciníu who does not have a birthday. Whether you never knew it, forgot it, or lost it in the forest is of no matter. This letter, drafted by my daughter, officially transfers my birthday to you. From this day forward you shall celebrate your birthday on the nineteenth day of October. This document will help you remember it as well as of your grandmother.

Her sons helped her sit as they kissed and helped her with her handkerchief. The youngest of the sisters and the cook went into the kitchen when they heard the condesa tap her glass with her spoon. All eyes were on Jane when that sister and cook reentered the room. Jane crawled onto the condesa's lap as she blinked her eyes at the plate they carried. A large bowl of mixed fruit and table grapes were a common sight on the table, but this was the first time Jane had seen a chocolate cake.

Jane was sprawled on the condesa's lap. She liked to lie across it, spread her arms out, and look at her friends, who were upside down. She smiled at the condesa.

I miss my birthmark.

The condesa was looking into the fire, smoking and holding her pipe in one hand while the other was resting and rubbing on Jane's tummy, just under her shirt. She looked down at Jane and told her to check her neck in the morning. She reminded her that Josie was sitting alone. Zeke followed when Jane got down and walked over to get down on the floor with Josie. Mary was singing and strumming her vihuela.

Josie was surprised that she knew all of those Irish songs and whispered it to her schoolmate. Jane smiled and whispered back.

I know you have your recorder. Have you ever played in a duet? I'd really love to hear you.

The sisters sat among the smoking brothers and silently watched the padre and Mendoza play chess. Mama and the madam sat next to each other and traded back and forth, Mary's baby.

The doors and windows were open, a gentle breeze carried their smoke from the room, and the cook was silently reading her precious old love letters.

Cesaré stood and made an announcement. Mama is tired and needs to sleep in her own bed. We must leave before it gets too dark. He whispered in his sister's ear before they left.

Don't over-feed Homer.

The king and queen were having breakfast and sharing that same worn out argument. The king wanted Josie home, and the queen said she was not her daughter. What infuriated her mostly was that Josie, his illegitimate living issue, was healthy. Their only living issue, Margaret Theresa, was not. She almost choked on her forced smile when the king suggested she spend more time in his bed. He had conferred with his generals and was writing on a small piece of paper.

She watched the king ring for one of his servants and hand him the note. Dispatch this immediately.

. . .

Jane, Josie, and Zeke were outside, playing. The condesa, the doctor, the madam, and the padre were discussing the last meeting the family had with the king. The men were lighting their pipes when Jane ran in, followed by Zeke and Josie.

Condesa, this is the nicest parchment I've ever seen. It's almost too good to wrap around Helen's feet. She handed the condesa the note the cook had taken from the pigeon.

Jane, fetch our swords and have one of the men saddle our horses. Doctor, I want you, the madam, the padre, and the sisters to wait here for our return. Keep Josie with you. If we do not return within two hours, release my brother's pigeon. Tell my cook to release Homer. They watched the condesa grab the crossbows and quivers and then run from the house.

From the covered veranda, they watched the condesa talking to her men. They watched the condesa and Jane mount and steer their horses northwest and slap the reins. Jane turned in her saddle, waved and threw everyone a kiss.

They had been riding for almost an hour when they saw two mounted French soldiers riding on Spanish soil. The French soldiers charged with their sabers drawn. There was no communication between Jane and the condesa as their arrows shot home. Jane and the condesa helped each other lift and tie the dead soldiers onto those French horses. They knew there would be precious little time.

Four horses galloped back to the winery. Jane had killed her first man. The condesa dismounted and pointed at Jane and then towards the men. Jane rode past the house and dismounted in front of them. She told them to hide the two dead French soldiers as well as their horses.

The condesa went directly into the house. The doctor, the padre, and the madam had examined the note and returned it to the cook. Her cook was holding the note she had taken from the pigeon. I can't remember his name. I hope it's not important, but here is the note I gave Jane. I don't know if you had time to read it, because you ran out so fast.

The condesa said the pigeon's name was Helen, and she had already read the note. Tell me that you released Homer, my brother's pigeon, instead of Helen.

The cook was pleased to say she watched Homer fly directly south until he was out of sight and that Helen was feeding. The condesa smiled and patted her cook's shoulder.

The king's message warned me about the French crossing our borders, but he had the gall to demand Josie's safe return. Go fetch both of his pigeons while I write these duplicate notes.

Jane ran into the house to look for Josie. She found her sitting with the madam. Josie! Are you OK?

Josie said the madam was actually the source of her calm. Don't worry Jane, I'm really OK.

The condesa wrapped the notes around the pigeon's legs and released them. She walked out to face her men. French soldiers are on their way, and I have dispatched three pigeons.

One of her men asked the condesa how she knew.

Jane and I killed two of their scouts. The rest should be right behind them. She smoothed an area on the ground with her hand and held a stick in the other. She drew two lines representing the forest and the area west of the house. My brothers will come from the forest, but they will stay to the left, hiding in these trees. She paused when she heard the madam's interruption.

Give me those French muskets. With a proper loader I can handle all four. The doctor and the padre will be the loaders because they have taken an oath … to do no harm to others.

If I had known this, she thought while taking the muskets into the house, I would have brought my dueling pistols. She checked each musket's sight against the rod she placed it its barrel and cleaned and reloaded each one.

The condesa advised her men that her brothers would attack from the south side, and they should hide in the bushes and behind the trees on the north side of the road. The madam will be firing muskets and our cannons into the center. She wants to shoot only the French, so stay out of cannon's way. Jane and I will be riding with you in battle. With my brothers and their men, we and the madam number thirty. We will have the advantage of surprise and flanking.

Remember your training and fight together and for each other, she said while throwing the stick away. We fight for our homes, our children, and everything we love. After she circled her men around her, she told them to eat but to drink water instead of wine. Walk away partially full but not thirsty. It's one for all and all for one. She walked into the house and told the doctor and the padre to step outside and uncover the cannons.

Mama was rocking the baby on the veranda, and Mary was sleeping. She watched a pigeon circle the house and then perch on the hitching post. She recognized Homer and let him into his cage. There was no note. She waved her arms at her sons, who were training their men for battle. The men were resting after finishing their lunch. One of the men told Cesaré and his brothers that he saw their mother waving.

174

Joaquin, see what Mama wants. It may be about your son. Cesaré watched Joaquin ride to the house and kiss his mother while remaining in his saddle. He saw his brother rear his horse, circle his sword, and thrust it in the direction of the forest.

Mendoza and the padre uncovered the cannons. The madam was aware of their plight. She watched the padre give the sign of the cross before she went back into the house and called Josie.

Three columns of five rode into the forest, the overhead branches shedding patches of black and light on their determined faces. They nodded with recognition for each other. Not only were they soldiers together, but from this day forward they would be brothers in battle. Their swords reflected red, yellow, and green from the sun and its shining between leaves. A single column of fifteen rode through the stream below the pond and its waterfall. The horse's hooves muddied the colors of mist rising and reflecting red, yellow, and green. Today would test their mettle. Their bodies may prove red on the field of battle … but never yellow. There was not a forest animal in sight. Each had escaped the terror of horse's thunder. Cesaré told them to hide at the north edge of the forest.

The condesa, Jane, and her men were hiding on the north side of the road leading to the winery. The condesa told Jane to ride over to the north edge of the forest and talk to her brothers. She told Jane that she could see Cesaré waving. Tell my brothers, now your uncles, about the cannons and their projectile's direction. I'll wave if you have a clear return. She watched while Jane galloped Charlie through the vineyards.

The madam was talking to the doctor and the padre. I know you two have taken an oath, but consider whom you are protecting. It's either the lives you love or those you don't. It cannot be both. We will need you to lift the chained cannon shot, to ignore the horror, and together work as a team.

Josie, we must light the cannons and remember to light them precisely together. She watched the padre give the sign of the cross.

In nomine Patris et Filii et Spiritus Sancti. Amen.

The condesa lay in the middle of the road with her ear against the ground. She stood up from that sound of silence, waved at Jane, and then waited. She saw Jane lean down to hug and kiss all three brothers while they turned her horse around and slapped him on his bottom. She watched Jane galloping through the vineyards and then helped her hide Charlie.

The two women lay on the side of the road among the concealed men. With their swords drawn and their crossbows in front of them, they held each other's hand.

If we must die ... then let it be together.

Chapter Twenty One

A small regiment of apprehensive French soldiers was approaching Sant Sadurní d'Anoia. Their captain was angry because his king had deployed them as a decoy to draw Spanish soldiers away from Hapsburg territories. The king should have sent him to the north of France to invade those territories, but here they were, hungry, low on food, and pillaging innocent homes and wineries. Their mission was to slaughter as many as they could, even women and children. They had confiscated a wine cart to carry their plunder.

Their captain was looking at a quiet road with a large house beyond it. He could see the fork in the road leading to it. He wondered why he could hear no birds on such a beautiful day. After he waved his men forward, he heard the shrill sound of chained cannon shot whistling through the air. He watched in consternation as he saw ten of his men and their horses cut to pieces.

Arrows were flying at his men from his left, and horsemen were charging his right. Those horsemen stayed to his right while another chained cannon shot chopped more of his men, who were fighting from the middle. He could barely see his men in that field covered with smoke from more cannon and musket shot. He could hear the screams from his men fighting in the center and attacked from every side. The smoke had only started to clear but not the smell. He could hardly see, but at least his remaining men were hand-to-hand fighting.

More of his men fell from arrows, and those archers on his left were now attacking. He had never seen peasants so well trained or so well armed. Those unhorsed rolled on the ground, and from the other side hacked his men and their horses. He watched them being swung and remounted by arms from larger men. Those men, whether on foot or mounted, fought with their backs protected.

He had no time for admiration for those slaughtering his men. When adding pillaging to slaughtering were his general's orders.

He yelled retreat, but only two of his soldiers were still mounted. He would have to hack his way in order to follow them, but one of those, remaining, small, well-trained, men blocked his way. He easily dismounted him, drew, and cocked his musket, only to see his shot intercepted by a larger man jumping from his saddle.

He turned his horse to follow his soldiers only to see the face of Cesaré. He successfully blocked that left handed swing to feel a dagger thrust and then twist in his middle. He heard the cacophony and felt his belly ripped open and the pain when thrown to the ground.

That was my brother!

He was on his knees when he saw that fatal swing. His eyes could see the stump of his bloody neck when his head rolled around. The last thought of his severed head, before day turned into night, was that he would have been better off had he been deployed to the Habsburg territories.

Cesaré helped Jane onto her horse. Jane, take my musket and kill those deserting men. He leaned back as she turned her horse around and yelled at him.

Keep your musket. I have my sword, my bow, and my quiver. May God save our brother, she said as she slapped the reins.

Cesaré saw Mendoza, running on the uneven ground. The doctor paid no attention to cannon or musket shot but only to keep from falling over dead French soldiers. Cesaré dismounted and in his arms held his wounded brother. He felt the hand of the doctor on his shoulder and listened to his orders.

Stay with your men while I attend to your brother.

Cesaré watched the doctor carry his brother in his arms like a baby into the condesa's house. He had forgotten the breadth and the size of the man, but it all returned when he saw him carry Joaquin across that bloodied-in-battle field of fallen men.

Cesaré, the condesa, Rodrigo, and twenty-four men walked between a regiment of fallen French soldiers. They all harkened

178

to Cesaré's final orders. Whether you have doubt or not, use your swords and lay open their throats.

Where is Jane, he heard his sister's yell?

I sent her after those deserting French soldiers. She told me to stay with my men. Little sister, she is truly a Barciníu.

Jane, in full pursuit, handled her bow and reins in one hand while she drew an arrow from its quiver with the other. She waited until Charlie was airborne before she let go the string and then drew another. She passed the horse without a rider before she drew back the string. She heard its twang and watched the arrow leave the bow sideways to be straightened by its fletching.

Jane captured the fleeing horse without a rider. She returned holding its reins and dismounted to examine the nearly dead soldier. She cut the arrow from his back and turned him over. She raised her sword and then without hesitation laid open his throat. Sir, you're on Spanish soil, and my name is Jane Barciníu.

Jane rode back to the house passing the field hands, who were following Cesaré's orders. Tears were running down her face as she counted twenty-four tired and heavily breathing men. They all acknowledged her when she raised her sword and circled it in the air. Twenty-four men and one almost still a child yelled together. It's all for one and one for all.

Jane hitched Charlie and ran into the house. Joaquin was lying on the kitchen table. She did not understand the doctor's words that he desperately whispered over his shoulder as he finished his stitching.

Please go away.

Blood was still dripping from the kitchen table. The condesa was crying, and her two brothers were holding Joaquin's arms. The condesa handed Jane the bloody shot, and they cried in each other's arms. He was proud to have saved your life.

. . .

The king was pacing in his courtyard. He was not used to waiting. He decided to seek out Victorio, recently promoted to captain. It was a beautiful day, one that should encourage peace, but this was the best time of year for advancing soldiers and cannon. Nevertheless, he found wonder and enrichment in the cloudless sky and the two pigeons circling in the courtyard.

Victorio came running. Sire, I couldn't unravel the note without reading it. The winery near Sant Sadurní d'Anoia is under siege. What are your orders?

Take twenty men and save my daughter. Do not return without her, even if it's only with her dead body. He went into the castle to face another argument with his queen.

The sisters were on their knees, praying. Josie and the madam were cleaning the soot from each other's face. The doctor turned to face the padre. He is now in your hands, my old friend, but I think I have lost to that woman I call *Aquella Señora* again.

You don't know that, the padre said. You have preformed brilliantly, and Joaquin is still breathing. I am so proud of you.

Mendoza did not look at the padre. He scanned the room from side to side before he faced his friend. With tears in his eyes, his voice cracked when he answered him.

Padre! She's still here.

The brothers, the doctor, and the padre carried Joaquin up to the room next to the condesa's and Jane's. The padre gave the Last Rites as they laid him onto that bed. He stayed with Joaquin while the others climbed down the stairs.

In nomine Patris et Filii et Spiritus Sancti. Amen.

There was so much work to do. With the cook's supervision, the sisters were cleaning the kitchen. The two brothers were outside with the field hands. They were looking at all the French bodies when Cesaré addressed those men.

We'll have to get rid of these bodies. We will do it in the morning. The cook is preparing food for you all. He paused before further addressing the men. The only man we may have lost is our brother.

Cesaré found himself facing two men. One was from his winery and the other was from his sister's.

Sir, we are the two captains chosen by the men in case you were lost in battle. We, the least likely to fall, would have fought

180

for and reported to the condesa. We have decided to sleep tonight in the stables in case more French soldiers return.

Cesaré saluted them with his sword. My brother and I will eat and sleep in these stables with you brave and gallant men. This day, you have become more than soldiers. We and the condesa were proud to fight among you, and so was Jane.

The next morning, the cook was supervising the sisters. The padre and the doctor were solemnly thanking Cesaré and Rodrigo for the use of their beds. Josie and the madam had slept together, and the condesa, Jane, and Zeke had slept with Joaquin to keep him warm.

Jane awoke with her head resting on Anna's outstretched hand. Her condesa was staring at the ceiling, and the bed was wet from her weeping.

Jane, my brother, who is also your uncle, is now lying cold between us. I tried to keep him from reaching out to *La Muerte*, but he only smiled at me. He must have thought I was Mary when he looked at me and spoke his final words.

God bless you, my sweet Mary. Thank you for these last two years, but you must know that I always knew.

Jane reached over her dead uncle's chest, taking the condesa's hand. I want Cesaré to take this shot and melt it into a cross. I will wear it for the rest of my life.

They covered Joaquin's face and came down to breakfast. The condesa walked directly outside and then into the stables. She was thanking the men while Cesaré and Rodrigo ran into the house to kiss their brother and then walk back to that battlefield with its smell of piss and shit, and, of course, blood and sweat.

Field hands encircled that family of four who walked among and thanked them for their courage with tears dripping from their faces. The condesa ripped away her clothes and stood crying among them. It's one for all and all for one; and we have only lost one.

Pile their bodies away from the house, and be prepared for putrefaction. After you cover them with lime, go home and kiss your wives and children. We will decide what we will do with their bodies.

Cesaré and his brother watched their sister bare her breasts and walk among the men to hug and kiss them. They were concerned for their sister's honor until they saw each man drop to one of his knees and salute her.

It's one for all and all for one.

Chapter Twenty Two

The condesa saw a coach and mounted horses approaching while telling the men that the dirty part of their job had just begun. The field hands were nervous because their horses and swords were in the stables. She had thankful tears in her eyes when the approaching soldiers waved and circled their flag. She recognized Victorio leading his men.

They're Spanish, she cried while wiping her eyes.

Condesa, we brought these two dead French soldiers in your wine cart. Our scout returned to us when he saw them lying on the road.

The condesa was not surprised when she saw the king's coach. I see that your king will not take no for an answer. Josie is perfectly safe, but we must attend to our own brother's dead body.

Victorio dismounted and kissed her hand. The only signs of French soldiers are lying in your field. Condesa, tell us what you want us to do.

Pile their rotting bodies onto that wine cart. It doesn't belong to me. Use the king's coach if their bodies number too many, and take one of their horses. Take their bodies away from the winery. If time permits, leave them within French soil. Strip and further mutilate their bodies. Take their uniforms and heads back to the castle. Remember to hide their tracks leading to the winery and those that you leave on French soil.

Let it be known that savagery and carnage await French soldiers on Spanish soil. The French king will be wiser to deploy his soldiers to the Habsburg territories where Spanish peasants do not fight to the death to protect their women and children.

Victorio, she said attempting a smile, for you this will be a puzzling day. We will bury our brother on Barciníu soil. His wife and mother already know.

You may find it difficult to get Josie to sit in the king's coach. You will face the predicament of seating Josie on a horse for her entire return home or letting her keep the company of dead French soldiers for half of the day and in a blood-soaked carriage for the rest of the way, … or you may leave her here as my guest. Keep the wine cart for me if no one claims it.

The tragedy of war disrupts all good plans, even our brother's burial. We must prepare for our own tragic day. We have the carpenters for his coffin. My brother will be buried with his sword and mementoes from his family. This is the time when tears and justice surrender to postponement. Our cook will feed your men, and our padre will bless them.

The condesa, her remaining two brothers, and Jane were trying to console two still crying, hysterical women. The doctor was outside preparing Joaquin's dead body while hearing the sounds of hammers thumping in syncopation. He loved Joaquin, but his main concern was the bereavement of his sweet Mary. He turned to face the heavens with tears in his eyes and clenched his hand before he shook it.

Why did you have to take him?

Mary ran to his arms when Mendoza stepped inside. He held her and remembered their last carriage ride as she whispered.

My mother and I will be in mourning for one year if she has that long. I've learned to love her. But when our mourning time is over, I will return to you if you still want me.

Mendoza could not stop the tears of joy and sorrow running from his face or hearing the crying sounds of Mary's baby.

The family, Mendoza, the padre, and the sisters circled themselves as field hands lowered Joaquin into his final resting place. Each one in turn said how and why they would miss him. They listened to the padre's final words: ashes to ashes and dust to dust.

In nomine Patris et Filii et Spiritus Sancti. Amen.

Field hands were waiting when four returned. Victorio and his soldiers had already gone. The condesa and Jane walked among them saluting with their swords and receiving returned salutes from them.

Brand your saddles with our family crest before you return to your homes. Sant Sadurní must know that together and for each other we carry Barciníu protection. It's one for all and all for one.

Jane walked impatiently behind the padre and the doctor. She was relieved to see the madam and Josie still consoling each other. They had handled the cannons well, and the madam had reestablished her reputation. The madam was teaching Josie how to clean a musket as Jane approached.

When you return to your father, if God allows it, you will have your own sword. Uncle Cesaré took it from the French captain and said that you should use it. Tomorrow, you will begin a different training. I'll teach you the sword, and the condesa will teach you to ride. You will help me teach reading and writing to our field hands' children, and then we will work together with their fathers in the vineyards.

The padre and Mendoza played chess after dinner. The condesa and the madam were still sitting at the dining room table. The sisters were relaxing after cleaning the dishes, and Jane and Josie were lying on the floor with Zeke. Jane straightened her head and looked at the chess board after the doctor made his move.

Doctor Mendoza, are you sure you want to … She was interrupted by the doctor.

Jane, you were not invited.

Jane and Josie continued to lie with Zeke. Josie said she thought the doctor was rude. Jane said all she wanted to do was tell the doctor that he was making a bad move. Jane was sitting on the floor when the doctor looked down at her and, out of the corner of his eye, winked.

The padre was startled when Mendoza extended his hand. The doctor said he had to sacrifice his queen in order to protect his king. The game would be over in five more moves. The astonished padre asked if they could still play those moves.

After the final move, the doctor toppled his king, reached out, extended his hand, and offered his congratulations. The padre,

185

straightened by excitement, hesitated before he told the sisters to stop clapping. He winced as he realized that he would have to ask God's forgiveness for his false pride. This would cost him an additional three Hail Marys. Mendoza was smiling.

The condesa entered the room and said it was time for bed. She told Jane to kiss the doctor, and Josie offered to share her bed with the madam. Mendoza reached out both arms and signaled the girls to sit on his knees. He whispered in Jane's ear while each kissed him. My dear fragile friend, the padre, should carry a memory more pleasant than that of fallen men. This will not be your kind of game for several more years. For you, I have in mind another.

The next morning and after their breakfast, the sisters were sitting in two carriages. The padre and the fat nun would ride with the doctor, and three sisters would ride with the madam. Mendoza spoke softly to the condesa as he held her.

Please tell Mary that if she is ever in Barcelona to bring Nando. Tell her I wanted to see her before I left, but I thought she would want to begin her mourning. Please pay my respects to Mama, Cesaré, and Rodrigo.

Jane and Josie were in front of the barn waiting for the field hand's children, who wanted to read and write better. They waved at Mendoza and the padre.

Josie, I don't think you should tell the king everything you did this summer. You may tell him that you taught school and learned to ride a horse. You might even say that you helped deliver a baby. But you should forget to tell him that you helped kill a regiment of French soldiers, can wield a sword, fire a cannon, and slept with a prostitute.

The padre had little concern why Josie and Jane, while in each other's arms, were openly laughing. His main concern was to get back to his church and record another historical event. He had beaten the doctor at chess in the summer of fifty-nine.

Chapter Twenty Three

The girls were sharing tearful goodbyes. Victorio had arrived with a royal coach to collect Josie and deliver an unclaimed wine cart. He was inside the house and spoke to the condesa about what he thought could be distressing news.

Condesa, although I only recently heard of this, it happened last year. A fellow soldier and acquaintance of mine fell during the Battle of the Dunes. I never paid attention to his family name until I read it in the report. He was the count's older brother. Primogenitor is never a concern to soldiers because most of us are younger brothers. He didn't like the business of running the winery and had chosen the life of a soldier.

The condesa was not smiling. How many know of this?

I don't think there are many, and I'm afraid I blurred his name when I read it, Victorio said smiling. Condesa, I have further news from the king.

He took me into his confidence when I returned with that regiment of dead French soldiers. The king swore me and my men to secrecy and said to bury them without any record. He knew Louis XIV would be suspicious and hopefully superstitious about losing an entire regiment of soldiers without any trace.

The king said there will be no history, only mystery for why a French regiment vanished from sight. The king smiled at me and said there is only one explanation to tell the French king. He would tell the French king that an entire regiment of French soldiers deserted when they saw the banshee of Sant Sadurní d'Anoia. The king was laughing when he said Louis XIV could believe him or think he had a secret weapon.

Condesa, the king realizes the sacrifice you and your brothers made for Spain. He knows that you were his secret weapon, and there is no name the king will respect more than Barciniú. He sent me to do this for him, because he can not. This I do for my king but mostly for myself.

Victorio knelt on his knee and kissed the condesa's hand before he stood and smiled at her. The king will be signing the Treaty of Pyrenees. The fighting has already suspended. That's why I came with just enough men to handle a royal carriage and deliver this wine cart.

Victorio, you're a good friend, and let's keep this between us.

Before they stepped into the king's carriage, Jane presented Josie her new sword. Now that you know how to use it, we have decided to let you keep it. Cesaré and Rodrigo made the backstrap, and I stamped it with the Barciníu crest. I hope it will help you remember this summer, and bring it with you when you return to school. You may be the king's daughter, but to me you are my brave, Barciníu soldier.

Oh Jane, this will be my fondest possession, and I am proud to be your soldier. I am happy that you and Zeke will be riding with me, she said while laughing, but I would be even happier had you not brought Charlie. Have you ever ridden in a royal carriage?

Josie admired her sword while Jane looked at the warm, cloudless sky. Josie knew her little friend would not be impressed with trappings that provided no function. Zeke also looked out but not at the sky.

Zeke and I planned to ride with you for a long time, but the condesa just released two pigeons. You can see them flying. This could be about our family business, Jane said while holding Josie's hand. I can ride with you for one more kilometer, but then I'll have to ride back on Charlie. Josie was upset because Jane was watching pigeons flying. She was not paying attention to her, and neither was Zeke.

The condesa was pacing in the kitchen when Jane returned. Jane, this does not concern you, but I just released two pigeons. They're for my brothers and the doctor, who I'll be expecting for dinner. Don't be concerned if we do not invite you to this family discussion. I want you and Zeke to go and play in the forest. At this moment I have to consider the effects on our brave field hands and do my own soul searching. Don't forget to take a clean rag to dry with.

Keeping a safe distance from Charlie, Zeke followed Jane into the forest. He watched her while she examined a tree and removed her clothes. She looked at him and said ... look, they're almost gone. For every scar I put on that tree, it put one on me. Zeke was puzzled but happy and excited to follow Jane's crawl and to sneak behind that water-falling wall.

Cesaré and Rodrigo rode up while Jane and Zeke were still swimming. They and their men had built a dam to harness the river and expand the pond created from that falling river. They watched Jane smile when she and Zeke climbed out from her now larger swimming hole. She stretched and held up her arms while Cesaré scooped her into his.

Cesaré laughed and watched with pride as this exquisite, little *ingénue* careened and outstretched herself across his lap, looking at her tree, who she turned upside down, while at the same time jutting her chin to showoff her refreshed birthmark.

What d'ya think, Uncle Cesaré; am I becoming a woman?

He handed her to his brother. What d'ya think, Rodrigo, is she becoming a woman? Both men were laughing as Rodrigo lowered her to the ground.

We think you're off to a good beginning, and we already love your cute, little butt that has taken the shape of a pumpkin. It's the perfect shape for spanking.

Cesaré and Rodrigo were still laughing after Jane paraded and dried herself before putting on her clothes. Cesaré's mood suddenly changed when Jane checked Charlie's reins. He waited until he had his brother's attention. If any man touches or even looks at her, he dies!

Rodrigo smiled and nodded his head. If only Joaquin could have been here to have seen this day, the *ingénue* for which he gave his life and the cross she never takes off.

The condesa was waiting and ushered them inside as soon as they arrived. Jane, go into the kitchen and bring back wine. She told them what she learned from Victorio after Jane left the room. She also told them that she was expecting the doctor.

Jane and Zeke were playing tug of war on the floor when they heard the knock on the door. Mendoza entered before Jane could answer. She simply got up and filled his glass with wine. She pursed her lips from side to side when the condesa told her to go to her room. The condesa said she wanted to talk about Jane behind her back. Their first topic was whether Jane could participate or not.

The doctor was the first to answer. You may think of Jane as an *ingénue,* and so she may be, but that little girl is the chess champion in her university. Jane is not easily trapped. We should allow her in this discussion because she could face questions about this transition. He waited while the condesa called Jane, who was trying to listen from her door.

Jane, get Zeke and your cute little butt down here. We have to talk about something far more important than Zeke's royal carriage ride.

Jane moved her chair slightly away from the condesa and placed her hands on the table. She sat as straight as she could and looked directly ahead. Out of the corners of her eyes and in syncopation she moved nose and mouth from side to side without smiling, but her eyes were brightly shining.

The doctor, more familiar with the laws of primogeniture, was the first to speak. As a doctor, he had signed many death certificates and was familiar with family squabbles.

Jane, for your benefit and possibly for your bothers, I will give a recount of *primogenitura* in our country and in others. Simply stated, the eldest son is the only heir of his father's estate. The condesa was right to call me. Her husband was never the count but only a pretender. The winery was not his when he died, and Anna was, at that time, not the condesa.

Title to the winery and the older brother's title automatically passed to his younger brother last year, who was already dead. Both titles will pass to Anna if there is no contesting. But under her supervision the winery has become a source of noticeable income, a plum to any scavenger, including some cardinals. You have no idea the abundance of family squabbles I have witnessed after signing death certificates. Vultures will not descend if they believe there is neither meat on the table nor on the bone.

Mendoza could not keep himself from laughing. I am the only man for this job, he said to Anna and her brothers. He looked directly at the condesa, and said this will cost you. You will keep your promise and let Jane live with me during her final year at the university.

There is no time for me to dine with you on this night. I will dine with the padre where he records and keeps records of marriages and deaths. Tomorrow, I will return to Barcelona and call in an unpaid favor. Jane, Josie, and I, without any payment, turned a baby in the womb of the wife of the apprentice to our local stone mason. The doctor stood and authoritatively said, Condesa, you were married in fifty-nine.

He laughed as he walked towards the door. To protect the lives of so many and do no harm to others with some little scribbling of ink on parchment, he considered part of his Hippocratic Oath. The worst part would be that he would lose another game of chess, but only if he had to. They all could hear the doctor laughing as he got into his carriage.

Jane pursed her nose and lips from side to side. She had that feeling of self-importance of one now included in family secrets. She giggled as she climbed onto the condesa's lap and stretched out her chin.

Mendoza parked his carriage in the church stable. He was welcomed by the padre and the sisters. After dinner, he and the padre played their usual game of chess, but that was not the only game the doctor had in mind. Padre, while you ponder your next move, I must make important but simple corrections to the Barciníu family records without your presence. Do I have your permission?

The padre leaned back in his chair and closed his eyes. Doctor, my dearest and oldest friend, you never asked of me this favor. It must be very important. You and I are bound by our fight for life and our common foe. You have the advantage of knowing when you have won, but I never really know where *La Muerte* takes

191

them. I can only pray for their souls. As they stood, the padre placed his hand on Mendoza's shoulder. Fernando, let me help you. Any changes made should be in my hand, and you do not have let me win.

. . .

Mendoza's first order of the day after breakfast was to visit his namesake. He was pleased to examine a strong, healthy baby. The father was apologetic for having saved so little to pay for the doctor's services. Mendoza suggested they take a ride to the local graveyard.

They were standing inside that smelly crypt when the doctor said to change that seven to a nine and then to forget it. You can also forget my payment.

The apprentice's wife was singing and rocking her little Fernando when her husband stepped inside. Well, that didn't take very long. It's time for you to clean up for dinner. Did you extend our best wishes to the doctor?

I did, my dear wife, but first I must put my tools away and resharpen my chisel. He thought that a poor apprentice to a headstone cutter could have no greater friend than this doctor.

The condesa, instead of Jane who was swimming with Zeke, was teaching reading and writing to her men. Some of you may know how and when the count died. It was not in a glorious manner. For his family's sake and for the sake of this winery, remember that he died in battle, the same day as my brother. She smiled as she watched them walk into the vineyard and listened to their chanting.

It's one for all and all for one.

Chapter Twenty Four

Mendoza was sitting in his most comfortable chair and smoking his latest creation. He wondered if something was missing, even though he had Mary and Nando. He remembered the family squabble after that year of mourning. Mama was upset and did not want to lose Mary or Nando. Mary said this was the time to speak for herself.

Mama, your sons will soon marry, and I would be the odd woman out because I will have no husband to fend for me. The doctor still loves me, and I will be the mistress of my own house. He is a brave, gentle man, who will take care of me. Besides, there will be less confusion in this house with three instead of four women.

The brothers were laughing. We will miss your quick, logical mind, and your singing, but you must remember that you will always be welcome, and this is also your home. We only ask that Nando carries the name Barciníu even if the doctor adopts him.

Mary rested her head on Mendoza's shoulder while holding her baby on that long winding road back to Barcelona. Oh Fernando, I cared for Joaquin, but he was not my soulmate. I was always suspicious of fate, but something I don't understand intervened so that I could come home and resume my life with you. She was laughing when she removed her head from his shoulder because it was the second time she had seen the doctor, as big as he was, with tears in his eyes.

. . .

The girls had finished their third year, but the headmaster had not yet delivered them. Mendoza had grown more ambitious because he was carving two pipes from those white mineral lumps Cesaré had given him. These pipes must be exactly alike because each brother would compare his against the other's.

They would take the shape of a stylized horn befitting each of those huntsmen. They were perfected and polished to the point

193

where Mendoza could not tell the difference between them. He set one in the jig he had built for their drying. He was patiently brushing the other with hot, liquid beeswax when he heard the knock on his door. He was not surprised to see the headmaster.

We pulled it off again. Jane is captain of the fencing team and president of the chess club. Josie sings in the choir and plays her recorder in the orchestra. She and three of the boys are writing chamber music. The choirmaster said she could sing castrato as long as her voice maintained that lovely falsetto, and we both know that could take a while, he said and stopped laughing.

He pulled Mendoza to his side and whispered. Not even our professors can stare these girls down. They're afraid of nothing when they're together. Now it's time for me to get back to the university and prepare for this year's graduation.

Mendoza abhorred smugness, but he could not stop smiling at the thought of having three women in his house, and there would be absolutely no confusion. He and Jane would play chess while Mary and Josie would sing with the accompaniment of a vihuela and a recorder. The girls would accompany him when he visited his patients. He would keep those girls as long as he could and purposely wait until the condesa dispatched his second pigeon.

. . .

Mary said she could not go with them to Sant Sadurní because morning sickness was absolutely intolerable on a carriage. She laughed when Mendoza said he thought it was a reason to stay. She reminded him that he was a doctor, not a foolish husband, and he had no reason to delay their return.

It was a happy time, a time of peace, with the treaty of Pyrenees respected for almost two years. Mendoza was pleased to see his old friend, the padre, and the sisters. He was amused at Jane's predicament, who thought bridesmaids should not have to wear a dress. The condesa would not considerer them wearing pants.

Jane was decisive and resolute with anyone other than her family, but with them, and that included Mendoza and Mary, she was childlike and trusting. But they all agreed the best part was that Mama would see her sons marry.

The doctor was not there to see a royal carriage take the girls to the castle for those weeks before school started. He was not there to see the incident as the girls were leaving Sant Sadurní. He read the letter to his wife, Mary, written in the condesa's hand. She had recounted it from Victorio's story.

Jane demanded that the carriage stop when she saw three boys picking on a frightened little girl. She unsheathed her sword as she got out of the carriage and then slapped the biggest boy on his butt with its flat side. She disarmed all three and held her sword against the biggest boy's throat. This girl has Barciníu protection, she said. Victorio said he thought he heard the girls laughing all the way to the castle.

. . .

Cesaré and Rodrigo were delivering wine to the castle when they saw Victorio running towards them. He could not wait to tell them about the girl's antics. After sword fighting with him and his soldiers, the girls would ride into town on two of the king's finest horses.

The queen was furious to learn of their skirmishes in town with the sons of local shop owners and demanded the king return them to school. The king enjoyed their company, but his first priority was to his queen during her difficult pregnancy. The brothers could not wait to tell their sister Victorio's story.

. . .

Mendoza was grumbling on his way to the school, even though he had the comfort of a royal carriage, but the king had summoned him. The girls had only recently returned from their vacation at the castle. He did not like taking them from their studies even if for a few weeks only.

He understood the king's concerns, and for this he might need Jane. He knew that Josie would not remain in school without her, and to add to his displeasure he had to leave his sweet Mary. He managed a smile when she kissed him and helped him with his coat.

Don't be such an old grump, Fernando, I'm just starting to show, and our cook will be here to help me.

The girls were ready when he arrived and as expected were dressed as boys. They got into the carriage while the driver secured Josie's trunk. The girls had packed their clothes together, and the headmaster had supplied them with their studies for those weeks. There was nothing for him to do but listen to banter and laughter on that long ride to the castle.

Mendoza knew it would be cruel to scold the king, who had been plagued with so much misery. Philip had seven children by Elisabeth, his first wife, only one being a son, Balthasar Charles, who died at age sixteen. Mariana, his niece and second wife, had borne him a living daughter. All others had died. The king was desperate to sire an heir to the throne.

The girls thought the doctor was looking out of the carriage window, but he was thinking with his eyes closed.

Someday incest will be forbidden, even among kings. It will be illegal and abandoned, and so will be bloodletting. He opened his eyes and smiled at the girls. I'm getting too old for these long journeys. You have turned a long boring ride into one that's entertaining. Perhaps I selfishly brought you along, but the baby could need turning. Little hands will work far better and will have less impact on the queen than mine.

They had an immediate audience with the king. Mendoza was analyzing that Habsburg jaw. Sire, we desperately need sleep and can do nothing until the queen breaks water. Let us hope that she lets us sleep until the morning and gives us time to eat.

Mendoza and the girls were having breakfast at a royal dining table. He sat between them so he could participate in their conversation. He was smoking his pipe and explaining its creation when a servant entered the room. The queen had broken her water.

The king was in the royal bed chamber when they arrived. Mendoza without hesitation said that he should take charge. Sire, I'll need two strong women with strong stomachs, and you should leave this room, and take the rest of these people with you. This is a bed, not a stage, and we may have to disrespect her.

I'm a doctor, and you should know that I'm not a Catholic when I deliver a child.

The king nodded and followed his entourage out of that royal bedroom allowing Mendoza to take control. The first thing Mendoza did was to address those two strong, older women.

You ladies are here to move the queen and clean up her shit. Josie, stand across form me as you did for little Fernando. Jane, I want you between her legs and prepared to use your arm and hand. Just think of your arm as a large male member while I ascertain the position of this baby.

Mendoza was guiding Josie's hands and using his own to caress the queen's pregnant tummy. He and the queen groaned together when he tried to rotate the baby.

Josie, there seems to be a blockage. Try to rotate the other way. The doctor told Jane to use her hand when he saw that it was working.

Jane, can you feel its head? Get your hand behind it if you can.

Doctor, I think my hand is holding an ear.

Well then, Mendoza said, let's rotate this little diver, and then you ladies will place the queen into that tub of hot water. The rest is up to the queen.

The doctor was on his knees when the queen shit, and he delivered her baby. He held it up by its feet and handed it to Josie.

Josie! Give him a slap on his butt, and as before make sure that it's a good one. Ladies, clean the queen and help her back into bed, and then get rid of this shitty water. Josie, clean the baby, and put him into his mother's arms after I cut the umbilical cord and Jane helps me sew his navel.

The king answered Mendoza's knock on the door and entered with his entourage. He saw three people washing their hands and the smallest paying particular attention to one of her arms. The doctor was soaked with shitty water but still smiling.

Rest, plenty of rest, and I'm not talking about myself or my girls. Let the queen eat anything she wants, but push milk and cheese. I don't know why, but they all want pickles. For one brief moment the king did not understand why Mendoza was laughing.

Sire, I think it's time for our dinner and to let your son finish his.

Mendoza smiled as he was leaving the room. He did not look back when he said that it was acceptable for men to cry during these times. Congratulations, Sire, you now have a son!

The girls were still standing near the queen's bed. Jane had never seen such elegance and wondered what part the canopy played. She also wondered why Josie had delayed.

Josie, you heard what the doctor said. We have to let the queen and her baby rest. Jane then smiled before she paid attention to the queen and helped her adjust her baby. She noticed that Josie was crying.

Josie, this is the time for laughing, not crying. Jane giggled and then whispered in the queen's ear. Her eyes were brightly shining at Josie, who was still crying. In the briefest of moments, Jane shed a tear for Josie. Perhaps it was because Josie helped deliver another baby, or perhaps it was because the queen was smiling at Josie and would not let go of her hand. Jane's thoughts shifted to the condesa and remembered that there were so many ways a woman's touch could open the door to paradise.

Four were having breakfast the next morning. Jane was pursing her nose and lips from side to side. This was the first time she had sat next to a king. Even Josie was impressed but not the doctor. Mendoza's hand was gentle when he placed it on Josie's.

I think you will see a difference in the queen. She is now the mother of the rightful heir to the throne and watched you helping without hesitation to remove yourself from possible consideration to succession. I think the queen, from her different situation, will look kindly on you. The king, sitting across from Josie, nodded and smiled but said nothing.

They said goodbye when their bags were delivered, packed with clean dry clothes. Mendoza was in a hurry but remembered to pack his pipe and on it balance an ember while getting into the carriage.

On their way out of town, they saw local children chasing and throwing stones at a frightened dog. Jane jumped out of that moving carriage, grabbed the dog, and brought it back inside. She said the young bitch looked just like Zeke but had a gentler face.

Jane and Josie sat next to each other, picking and discarding flees from the body of that frightened, undernourished dog. They giggled together after Jane said that Zeke would be absolutely delighted to make her acquaintance.

Josie asked Jane what she whispered in the queen's ear.

I miss my Zeke and my Charlie. I told the queen that Charles would be a really good name.

Mendoza could not help but smile or control his belly laughter. The long journey would be so much more pleasant with the girls. He thought to himself that the young prince was a product of incest and would probably be sickly. The king was not aging well, but Queen Mariana would make a strong and fair regent. He was concerned for the future of Spain, but that was not nearly as important as the next stop at a tavern where he could load his pipe and smoke it.

He knew Charles II was named after Charles I, who died so young, but the girls would tell everyone that the young prince was named after Jane's horse, Charlie. He was eager to get back to his sweet Mary, Nando, and his unborn child. He had successfully faced his adversary twice and with those girls' help had won. He twitched his nose from side to side, remembering his first carriage ride with a girl, dressed like a boy, and her dog.

He smiled at the *basura bastarda,* sitting across from him, whom he loved as if she were his own, perhaps even more. Jane had opened her heart to Zeke, another bastard borne from a *Pachón Navarro* who hunted her in the forest. And now she would open it to another bastard that she found on the road.

He smiled at the young bitch lying across two laps. The dog, lying on her back and sometime looking at the girls, would close her eyes during those heavy exhales. Nevertheless, he did not want it licking his face. He would have to share his king's carriage ride with a dog that looked as silly as Zeke. Jane was

199

right. That dog resembled Zeke enough to have come from the same litter.

Mendoza only shook his head when the girls asked him why he was smiling. They were too young to appreciate the outcome of incest. If he explained it, those girls, closer than most sisters, would argue and say that it did not apply to canines. Besides, Jane would say those two dogs could not have come from the same litter.

He knew that Zeke was the only survivor, but thanks to Jane there was another. He smiled at the irony. He was sharing a royal carriage with three of life's survivors, and all three including the dog were bastards. But even so, if those two dogs each had their portraits painted, they would look like the work, humor, and imagination of the same silly artist.

Mendoza would rest and relax amongst delightful chatter and keep his pipe glowing as long as he could between tavern stops on that long, winding journey back to Barcelona.

Chapter Twenty Five

Mendoza was sitting in his most comfortable chair and smoking his latest creation, and nothing was missing. He had lived his declining years with his soulmate. With the children away in university, Mary was constantly fussing over him. Nando was about to graduate, and Sophie had just enrolled. With Mary's help and creative sewing, Sophie would pass as a boy. This was also with the help of the headmaster's son and now his replacement.

The years had treated him and his family well, and much of this was because of the family Barciníu. Sophie and Nando spent many happy summers with that family. Mendoza wanted his children to appreciate the nobility of hard labor and recognize the value of a man from his efforts. They worked and played in the vineyards along with the Barciníu children.

It was Jane's and the condesa's decision that those children learn equestrian skills as well as the art of self defense. They played and practiced with swords and muskets with Cesaré's and Rodrigo's children, especially the boys, who thought it unfair that they could not marry Sophie, their cousin.

Cesaré and Rodrigo wanted to tell their sons that Sophie was not their cousin, but the condesa intervened. She said that Sophie should have all the love and respect of her brother, which should not depend on bloodline. She said that Jane was the perfect example. Jane concurred with what she heard, and her eyes were brightly shining.

It was Cesaré's decision that Nando carry Barciníu protection, but it was the condesa's decision that because Nando was their nephew and Sophie's half-brother, she also carries their protection. Moreover, because Mary was their mother, and the doctor, who had proved himself on the field of battle, cared for them all, the entire Mendoza family would have Barciníu protection.

This was all part of the Barciníu history that Mendoza had faithfully recorded. Nando had recopied all this in his neat hand, but when he entered the university, Sophie took over his duties. Her writing skill was elegant compared to his.

The most difficult part of that history was recording the passing of his lifelong friend. Mendoza was grateful for the condesa's note, carried by his pigeon. Come at once, it read, your friend is dying. Mary held his hand while Nando drove the carriage. On their way her husband complained about the new padre, who could not see past the first domino. With lips drawn between his teeth he looked away and blinked his eyes.

He'll never replace the Padre. His chess skills are nonexistent.

Mary adjusted the shawl around his shoulders and patted his hand. Don't let your friend see you weeping. He's going to a better place. Just let him know that you haven't forgiven him for besting you in the summer of fifty-nine.

That was the first time Mendoza needed his whole family around him. He held the padre's hand while holding his crucifix. He smiled at his friend who was smiling back for the last time. They did not understand their father's words on their way back to Barcelona.

I know she waits for no man. I don't know if she can, but perhaps she wanted me to be the one to close his eyes.

Mendoza would not visit the winery or the madam's brothel unless either had a dire need. Traveling had become such an ordeal. The madam had changed it back into a hotel that included special amenities. She would always visit Mary and him when she was in town, and she always stayed over.

Mary would tell the madam the news from Barcelona and some of the gossip, which she tried to keep to a minimum. The madam would talk about Sant Sadurní and all the new faces in town. She would talk about the goods sold in the new general store, but of course she preferred to shop in Barcelona. She would do this until she saw Mary growing impatient and then ask about her children.

Both women shared the news they had received from Madrid, Barcelona, and the winery. Jane was smiling when she told the madam that Cesaré's oldest daughter had enrolled in the university with Josie's only daughter, who a good cardinal had christened *Juana-José*.

With the love of the king and the guidance of the queen, Josie had married well. Her daughter and Cesaré's would be rooming with Sophie. Both women laughed at the thought of three girls dressed as boys and sharing each others' clothes.

Mendoza asked about the boys, and Mary responded while he closed his eyes and listened.

Oh Fernando, have you forgotten already? Those boys are now men. Cesaré and Ricardo are mostly retired. Their sons are running the winery, and they're happy to have their sister in university where she can't order them around. Even though she has the palate of the condesa and the training from both women, those boys prefer to be managed by their aunts. Mary turned her attention back to the madam.

The doctor was so pleased that the condesa kept her promise and let Jane live with us during her final year at the university. It was practical because Josie had graduated, which would leave Jane to live in a double room by herself.

I remember Jane climbing into bed with us after she rekindled the fire. Fernando was embarrassed to find her snuggled against him while I was nursing Sophie, but he soon looked forward to it. He said the condesa had given him another daughter. That was also true for me. Jane and I were like mother and daughter, but the condesa was her only soulmate.

She and the doctor would discuss disease and its treatment while playing chess. He reveled in mental stimulation and cared not from which it came. He said that mental acuity was only the luck of a lottery draw, and those blessed should not look down on those who were not.

Jane would pack his pipe and light it when he was ready for his second bowl. He had to wait many years after she left before Nando came of age. And then there was Sophie. I remember the doctor telling us that someday girls would not have to masquerade as boys to go a university. Education should ignore gender, especially when it came to the gifted. He was the first to know that Jane's mind burned that brightly.

I don't know if you know this, but the new buildings on both wineries are Jane's creations, and her designs are desired in other countries, not just France or Italy. But Jane prefers to work locally because she won't travel far without the condesa.

The madam leaned closer to Mary and whispered. Everyone knows it, but nobody cares. Then she placed her fingers over her mouth as she chuckled. Sometimes I lunch with them, and on warm days we picnic by the pond below the waterfall. It's complete mayhem to see them swimming with Zeke's and Lucy's descendents, who have absolutely no respect for his monument. I wouldn't be surprised if that is where the condesa and Jane plan to be buried.

Mary smiled as she looked at her husband, who was at the time dozing. She looked back at the madam and whispered. When I first met the doctor, I wanted to belong to him, but I didn't know he was my soulmate. My first clue that I was also his soulmate was when I first met Joaquin. I felt the presence the doctor said what we see he had felt many times. I didn't understand it then. I just thought it was an unseen friend.

Jane told me of the doctor's desperation to save Joaquin. The man who loved me spared no effort to save the life of the man who had taken his. I could feel her presence when he yelled at her for taking Joaquin, and in time I came to know his adversary. I think she took Joaquin for the doctor's sake. He is a great doctor, but he is a noble and a magnificent man. I have never known a man such as he, and Nando will follow in his father's footsteps.

Mary smiled at the madam before wiping her eyes. Because I have felt her presence outside and waiting, I have that same consideration and have sent a letter to our stonemason.

The doctor kept his promise to Cesaré when he adopted our son, who is the only brown-eyed Barciníu. But I have long been a Mendoza, even though the name has less prestige.

Most of my life that mattered has been with the doctor. To remember where I came from replaces the sorrow with love and kindness. I am a much respected woman in town as well as in my own home, but sometimes I feel guilty when I see Cesaré and Rodrigo because I can hardly remember Joaquin.

Someday, I may tell our son where he came from, and that the doctor left him his choice. But that will lead to a further consideration. Those Barciníu boys will be delighted to be reminded that because of different bloodline they are no longer Sophie's cousins and fight for her hand in marriage … and with the encouragement of their fathers.

When that time comes, I'll ask Fernando, but I know what he would say. He would tell Sophie that life-styling should be selfish but not harmful to others, something he neglected to do. He has no guilt when deciding what is best for me and our children. But now, my faithful old friend, let me brag again about my family.

Dinners were always open discussions between the four of us. Because we had a cook, who helped with other domestic chores, I had time for music and reading. I think I advanced my education studying the books of my children.

I became the doctor's bookkeeper, managed, and scheduled his agenda. And, of course, I as the doctor's wife was always engaged in polite conversation whenever in town.

Much of our conversations were the doctor's observations concerning his practice and his patients. He didn't dwell on it, but we all knew when he had lost to *La Muerte*. He would always let Nando recount his observations when he accompanied the doctor. Then it was time for Sophie and me to do our own recounting.

After that, all four engaged in discussions and observations concerning the choice of paradigms, and some of this was free association. The doctor liked to point out how important it was for a medical man, a man of science, to keep his paradigms scientific rather than political. He said that most political paradigms depended on a camouflage of science but often began with gossip. He said that one should lead the heard or follow it but not without a scientific paradigm. Mary waited until the madam stopped blushing before she continued speaking.

He would smoke his pipe after dinner. Nando would transfer the doctor's notes using his neat hand after he finished his homework while Sophie and I washed the dishes. It may seem boring, but it kept our family closely together. Nando could already pass as a doctor before he went to medical school.

Mendoza interrupted their conversation when he awoke. He had his own favorite story to tell. The ladies smiled at each other, because they had heard it before.

After the signing of the Treaty of the Pyrenees, the French king, Louis XIV, suggested a chess match between the two countries. The Spanish king, Philip IV, although not pleased over the treaty, agreed and offered to host the match. His first thought was of the doctor. Mendoza smiled at the ladies.

The doctor conferred with the king but collaborated with another. He told Jane that she was ready to play the French king's champion. He'll be defensive and play for the draw if he plays me, but he'll be aggressive with one on my students. We won't tell him that you're the only one. He smiled at the ladies again.

As hard as I tried, I could not get her to wear a dress, but I coached her as I did for the Madrid school's champion. She looked back at me and twitched her nose and mouth as she likes to do. Her eyes were brightly shining. I said nothing when I looked at the board and then returned to my seat. She would have him in thirteen more moves.

The French champion was furious. No man, he said, had ever beaten him. Jane was quick when she opened her blouse and then closed it before she answered him.

Sir, that's still very true.

Mendoza laughed so hard that he almost dropped the pipe he had just finished carving for Nando. Mary took it and placed it on the table next to the shingle her husband had made for Dr. Fernando Barciníu, another gift for their son. After resting his eyes on Mary, Mendoza turned to face the madam.

Although he enjoyed every carving and was proud of their results, this would be his final and favorite piece. The madam could see the love in Mary's eyes when she covered and kissed her husband. They watched the doctor lean back in his favorite chair and then close his eyes.

When the madam offered to help her put the doctor to bed, Mary said that he got heartburn if he lay down too early. He would join her in a few more hours. We will see you in the morning and together go to Nando's graduation where we will sit with those three special boys.

Mendoza awoke when he heard the knock on his door and with caution approached it. He looked back to see the old man slumped and covered in his favorite chair and then flung wide the door. He always wondered what his adversary looked like because he had been in her presence, without seeing her, so many times before. This was the first time he would see his adversary's face. Surprisingly, it was sympathetic and kind. He asked if he could see his sweet Mary for the last time.

You may, but this will not be your last time. Did you think your footprints, especially when you carried Joaquin, passed unnoted?

He walked in to kiss the hand and face of his sweet Mary, but his lips could not feel her. He was in another place, a place where he would not see her for the last time. Before he left their bedroom, he whispered and gave the sign of the cross.

Vaya con Dios.

What surprised the doctor mostly was that his adversary could talk. Perhaps it was talk or perhaps it was thought, but every question the doctor had was immediately answered. They could soar over the town like eagles or fly together in the streets like lovebirds.

Arm in arm they soared through the town until Mendoza found himself in the stonecutter's workshop to see him with chisel and mallet in hand. His son was sitting across from his father and watching him wiping his eyes while reading the letter and engraving its words on the headstone.

Father, you should let me cut this stone. I can do them as well as you.

No, my son, this one I must do by myself. And you should never forget the man who delivered you and fed your mother and father when he had not two coins to rub together.

Mendoza wept while reading the letter.

What is wrong with wrong, is right.
Must days-end always lose its sight
And too few candles last the night?

If some lives could live forever,
Where true friendships never sever
And some dead rise up never.

Could that but end the plight?

Good night dear heart, sleep tight.
Sleep tight dear heart, good night.
Yours was a beautiful light.

If only he had been younger, he would have had more time with Mary. He was not soaring above the city again. He was walking in another place. He was standing in the center of that forest with the waterfall where autumn covered the ground with leaves of every color, and the sun shone through the trees where red touches green and then becomes bright yellow. The ground embraced the river, and leaves covered the pond in which he could swim or walk upon.

He looked around, but she had gone. He dropped to his knees when he saw Zeke running straight towards him. Zeke jumped over his own statue and stood on his legs to hold Mendoza's head with his paws while licking his face. Mendoza made no attempt to stop him. He felt the hand upon his shoulder and stood to see his old friend, the padre, laughing at first and then smiling at him.

Arm in arm they walked while Zeke ran and circled around them. Mendoza knew his old friend would show him the way. He asked why his adversary had gone, and the padre slowly shook his head before he answered.

La Muerte is merely a transporter, but she rarely enjoys it.

Mendoza used his hand to wipe his eyes because she had done more for him. While they were souring and before escorting him to his final dimension, she had taken the form of Mary and his mother when they were much younger, and each had hugged and kissed him. With the wave of her hand and when she turned him around, he saw everyone he loved and cared for, including Joaquin, applauding and cheering.

Well done!

He looked around, noticed that Zeke was gone, and asked the padre about him. He was not surprised at the padre's answer.

Zeke chooses to wait for Jane and the condesa.

Mendoza was smiling because it was she who had solved his mystery. It was her decision who she looked like and whether she smiled or not. She was far more than just a transporter and no longer his adversary. He regretted that she left before he could properly thank her … because *Aquella Señora* had waited until Mendoza had finished his carving.

Epitaphs and Epilogues

It is true that we find history in fiction, but it is equally true to find fiction in history. Moreover, the spelling and pronouncing of surnames change from man to man as he tells his story.

The term *cañuela* is a Spanish name for reed. It actually was one of the earliest forms of smoking. Packed with tobacco and smoked like a cigar, it sounds absolutely dreadful.

The first long-stemmed clay pipes were made at Broseley in Shropshire as early as 1575, but it was not until the eighteenth century that the bowls were bent forward and had an attached spur to serve as a handle in place of a flat bottom. Some had stems more than sixteen inches long and hung in taverns. They rented for one English penny, including the tobacco. The hygienic smoker would snap off the last inch of the stem before inserting it into his mouth. Called the churchwarden, it is still sold to this day.

The first use of the term *OK* occurred more than a century after this story's history. The author's favorite account of its origination, and perhaps the oldest, comes from Andrew Jackson misspelling *all correct* when he initialized acceptable bills from Congress as Oll Korrect.

A complex magnesium silicate, the typical chemical formula for which is $Mg_4Si_6O_{15}(OH)$, was first recorded for the use in making pipes around 1723 and quickly became prized as the perfect material for providing a cool, dry, flavorful smoke. Because of its porous nature, meerschaum, a German name for sea foam, draws moisture and tobacco tar into the stone.

Meerschaum became a premium substitute for clay pipes and remains prized to this day, according to Wikipedia. Bowls of this material were also inserted into a gourd for which the Spanish name is *calabaza*. Conan Doyle's Sherlock Holmes smoked a calabash.

It is likely that the author's dog, whom he named Zeke, descended from the German Bird Dog, which is related to the Old Spanish Pointer, the *Pachón Navarro,* introduced into Germany in the seventeenth century. It is also likely that various German hounds and tracking dogs, as well as the English Pointer and the Arkwright Pointer, also contributed to its development. It is impossible to identify all of the dogs that went into its creation because the first studbook was not created until 1870. The American Kennel Club in the year 1930 officially recognized the breed as the German Shorthaired Pointer.

In 1891, Robert Louis Stevenson learned that the 12-year-old daughter of Henry Clay Ide — then U. S. Commissioner to Samoa, where Stevenson lived — was unhappy that her birthday fell on Christmas Day. Stevenson immediately hatched a charming plan and sent a letter and a legal document to the family: a document in which he transferred the rites to his own birthday to young Annie H. Ide.

The vihuela is a guitar-shaped instrument from fifteenth and sixteenth century Spain, Portugal and Italy, usually with five or six doubled strings.

In Greek mythology we find that Zeus with Mnemosyne had nine daughters, muses, each a goddess and a source of inspiration to creative artists, and in the book of Ruth 1:16, perhaps the most beautiful declaration of love between two women.

La Celestina, a popular book published in1499, contained this passage. *On the advice of a corrupt servant, Sempronio, Calisto seeks the help of Celestina, a former prostitute, and now an active pimp, witch, and virgin-mender.*

Cesaré Borgia, the son of Pope Alexander VI and brother to Lucrezia, was well known and feared for his resoluteness, wit, intelligence, and bravery. In *The Prince,* he was Machiavelli's hero. In *The Borgias,* Cesaré had a devoted friend named Micheletto, a well known assassin who was present at the death of Cardinal Versucci. Cesaré's prowess and appetite was well known, and although his story ended in 1507 at the age of thirty-two, his name, and bloodline were probably passed down by grateful mothers.

Bingo, still played every Saturday in Italy, traces its history back to 1530 to an Italian lottery called *Lo Giuoco del Lotto D'Italia*. From Italy the game was introduced to France in the late 1770s, where it was called *Le Lotto*, a game played among wealthy Frenchmen. It was first known as *Buena* but a winner mistakenly called out Bingo. Cards contain no duplicate numbers, and the game is played with seventy five balls instead of dice.

As you Like It, by William Shakespeare, written in 1599, was printed in 1623. *All the world's a stage, and all the men and women merely players. They have their exits and their entrances, and one man in his time plays many parts: Act II scene VII.*

In the late 1580s, English raids against Spanish commerce, and Queen Elizabeth's support of the Dutch rebels in the Spanish Netherlands, led King Philip II of Spain to plan the conquest of England. Pope Sixtus V gave his blessing to what he called *The Enterprise of England*, which he hoped would bring the Protestant isle back into the fold of Rome.

The giant Spanish invasion fleet was complete by 1587, but Sir Francis Drake's daring raid on the Armada's supplies in the port of Cadiz delayed the Armada's departure until May 1588. This gave England time to build warships and, with the help of foul weather, defeat the Spanish Armada in August, 1588. Spain never fully recovered.

Anna Codorníu married Miguel Raventós in 1659, uniting their families, each with a long wine tradition. Jaume Codorníu founded the winery in Sant Sadurní d'Anoia, Spain, in the year 1551. Years later, in 1872, Joseph Raventós produced cava for the first time in Spain using the *Traditional Method* and established a completely new industry in the Alt Penedès region. It is labeled Anna de Codorníu. That winery is the oldest family business in Spain and to this day still bears her name.

The Drumroll

She looked out the window before the train pulled to a stop. There were no reasons why anyone should be there. She had boarded in the city where there were many reasons for being there. There wasn't a clue why anyone should be in this God forsaken place. The other question she had was how anyone could get here. It must be a leftover whistle stop from the days when people traveled on horses. The platform— made from old, rotting, wooden boards— which anyone in his right mind would be afraid to stand on, was a clue.

She wondered if he would sit across from her when that only passenger came aboard because when it came to turning men's heads she thought she walked on water. She was not surprised when the young man sat across from her, but she was surprised that he had only a backpack and a snowboard. Where was his travel bag?

He set his backpack and snowboard on the adjacent seat before he sat down. He was looking at an attractive face whose eyes were looking into an imagined mirror instead of him. It's going to be a fine day; it looks like snow. Will you be going to the end of the line and staying at the hotel?

She was surprised again, because he hadn't checked her out before speaking. In fact, he asked politely without any eye contact. Perhaps he was just another fag, or, on the other hand, he could be smooth and calculating. The first thing she noticed was his parka. It was old and showed many repairs. The next thing she noticed was his face. It was trying to smile, but his eyes did not. Perhaps they couldn't.

This is the first time I've noticed this train stop, she said. How does anyone get here?

Have you ever been at the edge of a forest and wondered how and why you got there? Sometimes we have to take a wilderness walk to realize who we are and how we got there. That's how I got here. I took a long walk.

She wondered what he was thinking about.

He was thinking of Marylou, even though many years had passed. He would always be grateful to her because his first sexual encounter was with the girl he loved. He reveled in the majesty and mystery of another and never for a moment thought about himself or another when he was with her. He remembered the letter he wrote after she broke his heart.

Remember the time when invincibility prevailed
and the sophomore so impressed with what he
knew. I was nineteen and knew everything when I
took you to your Prom.

We house-sited your aunt's home and swam
nude in her pool with you laughing as I back
stroked with my periscope up. We stopped
laughing in the shallow end when we were set for
salient running.

After you dumped me for the fireman, I tried to
hate you, but I could only see you laughing with
your hair surrounding your face in water. I studied
so hard that year, but I never stopped loving you.

I guess I never knew you because I thought you
were someone else, and so soon you left me. Who
was he and who am I? Reaching back into that
night when you became another, I was so
reminded that I also was someone else. Why
weren't you?

He laughed at himself for being sophomoric, but he had not the scar tissue then to be analytic. She and the fireman probably had a good laugh after reading his letter. He remembered the many he dated after Marylou dumped him, but none ever stood him on his head. He defined love as one hundred percent appreciation, one hundred percent of the time. And, of course, they would have to, if only figuratively, stand him on his head.

Another lament was Margie. Although he loved her, he could not say it unless he was ready to accept responsibility, and he could not be responsible without a college degree. He should have asked her to wait, but he could not impact her life without a promise he could definitely keep. If he should fail, he would have to support her on the salary of a gas station attendant. He tried to find her after he graduated, but by then she was gone, probably back to St. Bonifacius. Those last two years centered on nothing but surfing and grades.

She noticed the smile on his face, but she knew it was not for her. It was irritating to go unnoticed by someone who obviously had no appreciation for beautiful women. She decided to practice her social skills until the next stop where her friends would come on board. They had all pursued her on campus, but now she could pay attention to those who had graduated with a remunerative degree. Her own, in sociology, was merely a ticket to a government job, but it was also the way to meet the right people.

What was your major in college?

He smiled knowing her question could be innocent or a contrived putdown. My post graduate degree is in economics and statistics. My undergraduate was in industrial management. I was an economist for one glorious year until they transferred me into programming because I was the only one who could program my economic models. That's when I became just another DICK degree, voting for more government and what benefited me. But I never switched to become a liberal.

That was not the answer she wanted to hear. She preferred admiration to confrontation. Well, I majored in sociology. It required intelligence, and I was always liberal. Do you think that I am just another DICK degree?

Not if you become a sociologist, but you will be if you become just another socialist, and I apologize if I have irritated you. On the other hand, I am not a dedicated individual cajoling knowledge, and students majoring in economics, other than mathematics, had the lowest grade point average in my school. It's was not an easy major. I'm not saying that mathematics and economics are the only departments with smart students.

I only know of two measures for intelligence. One is the IQ test, and the other is financial success. Of course, those who have failed financially dismiss financial success as a test of

216

intelligence. I've known many with a high paper score, who collapse when facing something new. I realize that we use history when reacting to something new, but a good mind can extrapolate from what was never historically true.

She was pleased because he had finally taken notice of her. You must think of yourself as a brain.

We all have a brain. The question is how well it works. I think what most call the brain is sectioned into memory, regurgitation, and thinking. Memory and regurgitation may expand and minimize the thinking section, which is extremely complex. The thinking section is what some call the mind, but most are impressed by memory and regurgitation and call that the mind.

The thinking mind can section itself by expanding or contracting depending on forces or their lack. One of the sections is common and another is abstract. It is sad when the best part of the abstract must give way to the poorest of the common, but is equally sad when the best part of the common must yield to the poorest of the abstract.

She laughed at him. You sound like you're still in school and writing a term paper.

I don't mean to appear as if I'm still in school. I suppose I do, but I try to keep my thoughts condensed so I can apply them to myself. How often have I been guilty of reaching a decision based on debris rather than the relevant.

I hope I answered your question. Perhaps you can answer one of mine? What did you study in Sociology?

She was pleased with the chance to put this windbag in his place. Sociologists aren't as focused on why individuals do the things they do, but rather how they fit into larger patterns. The science of sociology examines structures within societies and the interplay of people within those structures. She thought that would shut him up, but it didn't.

Would that include the study of money, price, value, and power? When I speak of value, I'm using the common definition rather than an economic one. I wouldn't ruffle the feathers of a famous economist like John R. Hicks, because price determines value in an economic world, but there are so many instances when it does not.

When we read in the papers that some old, disheveled codger died leaving millions to whomever, we may wonder what value money had for him. How many of us take perpetual solace in an enviable bank account? Wilde wrote that *a cynic is a man who knows the price of everything, and the value of nothing.* I hope a contented person learns to value what he has and not think of money as a delineating factor of status. In short, that old codger's monetary holdings did not define him to himself.

If it's not the money that gives daily self satisfaction, what does? What is an alternative or substitute for money? Could it be power? In order to know, I would have to have a friend who was an honest politician. I never found one.

Why does one fight for unremunerated power? The answer is, that those who do have found real value and the thrill of power. I know it's extremely addictive, but I don't know why. Have you ever known a politician who admits to the joy of power? How many will admit to the value of money and deny that value of power? Power, earned or inherited, in the private sector was achieved, but it took propaganda in the public sector. Status, realized with money in the private sector, does not come close to the power achieved in the public sector. Between the two sectors, playing *King of the Hill,* status is the common denominator. The public sector too often augments its own status by reducing it in the private sector. The public sector can reduce and even annihilate the private sector and fail the country, but if, and for only a brief period of time, they all had status. The growth of government is the inevitable destruction of the Renaissance man. If we could plot destruction against growth, they would have a perfect correlation.

Man is the result of genes that successfully faced the environment in primitive times. He has successfully cultivated his environment and confortized it to fit those needs. It is with regret that those genes survived with the desire for power, procreation, control, love, protection, sacrifice, and domination.

He owes his greatness and misfortune to their success. The enlightened man analyses each and reacts without their control. He looks into the abyss, and it looks back. It is here that he may see the beauty and horror of each. The self seeking sees only one side, and the enlightened ponders perhaps too long. This imbalance allows success of the self seeking who will control man's fate and destroy the Renaissance man.

If this is your idea of flirting, it's not working, she thought to herself. One of the things we studied was transactional analysis and the games people play. My favorite was— Me Tarzan, You Jane— and the roles of gender. Are you playing it now?

Oh God, I hope not. It's a game I haven't seen played since high school. I never had to outgrow it because even then, it made me sick. It's always fun to play the game, —Me Tarzan, You Jane—, until Jane tests Tarzan's ability to perform. Me Tarzan, You Jane is not about gender. It's about subordination. Tarzan is the master, the professor, and the commander, and he always talks about or alludes to himself. Jane is the disciple, the pupil, and the subordinate. She will try to convince others of Tarzan's abilities as a good disciple should, and if successful, they, at least in her own mind, will not cast her as just another Jane.

Jane can ask for performance while Tarzan beats on his chest, continues his tease, and casts his fishing line. Tarzan can comply with Jane's request, or he can continue the tease. If he continues the tease, Jane should ask what is his essence and what needs does he serve? That will explain who he is, but it will not explain why. That is a question Tarzan probably can't or would not want to answer.

The better question is for Jane. Does she seek another Tarzan, or does she stay on the line. That will explain her essence and what needs she serves. I will have contempt for Jane if she stays on the line, but I will wish her well if she seeks another Tarzan who performs and does not feed on the tease.

On the other hand, Jane may learn to beat on her own chest. She can say OK, and spit out the bait leaving Tarzan to fish in a fished-out pond. Tarzan will have to find another Jane or other

Janes to provide him with disciples and that sought after drumroll.

However, as long as Jane stays on the line Tarzan will feed on her until there's nothing left. When that happens, Tarzan will simply look for another Jane, perhaps one providing him with a better drumroll.

This was the first time that snowboarder intrigued her. But what if Jane wants to stay on the line?

It may be appealing at first, but Jane will wake up in a few years and with a few kids. She'll have to stay on the line or look for another Tarzan, who does not beat on his chest. All this, Jane could have avoided if her first choice had been a Tarzan who did not cast any lines. Remember, the best of Tarzans perform without beating on their chest.

She thought to herself that this guy won't shut up, so she might as well play along. You remind me of my grandfather, a republican, who won't even vote for a republican because he's not conservative enough.

That's all well and good, he said, but you should ask your grandfather if he believes the political pendulum in our country, with its diverse demography, will swing from left to right without going through the middle. He, on the far right, is as deluded as those on the far left, terrified by the complexities required of the middle.

The politics of conformity belongs to the extremes. The least conformity is in the middle where they weigh those complexities of each side. Consider the simplest form of entertainment such as your choice of reading. Do you read what you want, or do you read from another's selection? In school, we read what our professors selected, and I am not complaining about that. What I am complaining about is our lack of choice after we graduate.

Take the most nondirected form of reading. Our choice in fiction is in millions, but our selection is from less than a thousand authors. Publishers only accept submissions form literary agents, who are not looking for good stories. They are looking for a blockbuster and a piece of the signing bonus. They look for books that will sell themselves, namely the author's name and previous success.

What is amusing is that most of those agents have degrees in creative writing. They went to school and learned the rules and formula for creative writing. They adhere to those rules when they select a submission.

The alternative is self publishing, and those authors number in the millions. The choice is overwhelming. The successful have their own websites and support group promotions. Their marketing is minuscule compared to traditional publication. So remember that what you read is limited to the choice from another's selection.

He smiled as he cast his eyes out the window. I just realized that what we read is a choice from another's selection. In that sense we are the Janes, and the promoters are the Tarzans. Those contributing to the book's traditional promotion are also the Janes. They are the Tarzans promoting from the rules they learned as Janes. Literature is only one of the examples, although it may be one of the most important because it is the foundation of education. There are so many others to consider. We laugh over the question, which came first, the chicken of the egg? The more important question and perhaps the most important is which came first, Tarzan or Jane?

Well, that was all very interesting, she said, but we're coming to the next stop, and I will be joining my friends. She wondered if he had tasted life to the extent that it made him sick and asked if he had any female friends.

You know, he said, I don't think I do. I always wondered when Mina cut off Dracula's head, destroying the last of his kind, if she found true love with Jonathan. Perhaps it's too common place when a women metaphorically cuts off her lover's head and ends him and the last of his kind.

Why couldn't she have just cut off his balls like the rest of her kind and proudly joined the sisterhood? My friend, another Mina, found true love when she met Mention. He had survived chemotherapy from colon cancer and could no longer get it up.

To add to his quintessence of desirability, he displayed that he was too shy to talk and had no opinions of his own. She was twittering like a school girl when she told me of her true love. Even though a nurse, she was delighted that she didn't have to exert herself with his castration. I wished her well and that she would enjoy the dance. She loved to do dirty dancing. She learned it on a cruise.

She watched him stand up and smile.

Those of us in the fight to stay young simply, not yet exhausted by life, find some nobility in that fight even if it's a losing one. I guess any good cause doomed to failure must be noble and embraced. You know people I have loved have done well and those I've hated have done poorly. I know God isn't impressed with me, but maybe he is with who I am?

Do you think God cares about you?

Of course not, but I hope he may care how and why I became who I am. Heaven is not forever. It's those last brief few moments that flash before us. Those who have done well will find peace. That leads to another question. Do the corrupt think they have done well? Will they find an entrance into heaven? Perhaps they will crawl on their belly as they did in life. I hope there is a creator, who will sort them out, because I am tired of living with them.

You won't have to move. Your next stop will be my last stop.

She watched him put on his backpack and pick up his board. His last words, *Vaya con Dios,* irritated her. She watched him standing near the door and then step out before her friends came aboard. She hoped he would see her friends hitting on her, and realize the chance he had lost. It did not occur to her that she had talked to a Tarzan who did not talk about himself. She stood up and waved at her friends, so they could not miss her.

It was quiet outside, and she watched him buckle his boots and then strap them into their bindings. He rolled forward and stood up as his board changed from a skid into a carve. She watched him crouch and then carve over the cornice and drop out of sight. In a matter of seconds, she could see him carving and S-tracking down the mountain. All she could see was snow and trees and a body growing smaller without a destination.

She was happy when her friends surrounded her with their appreciation and their laughter. She didn't even have to smile to be the center of their attention. She looked outside, but his body had become the size of a seed; and then it was gone. The train moved forward perhaps with a syncopated sound as it moved down the track, but surrounding raucous laughter hid the sound of that clickety–clack. She shook her head and wondered why she paid him any attention before joining her friends and their laughter.

Riding down that mountain, he remembered Morse, his father's friend, who was proud of his part Cherokee blood. Years ago when he was a boy, his father would take him to Yosemite during deer season. His father took his 306 and his son carried his 22. At the age of fourteen, he was the gun bearer. There were no buildings then, only forest. Hunters, in consideration for each other, made their camp miles apart.

That year, Morse, it might have been Morris but he pronounced it Morse, went with them. They were heating coffee in a pit he had dug out with the wood and tender the gun bearer gathered.

Morse asked him if he had ever heard the dawn break. He remembered shaking his head and looking at his father with that skeptical look. It's only in the eyes, his father said, but you can tell when a man is lying. That was the fondest memory he had of his father, and his gun bearer kept it with him.

I'm not kidding, Morse said. You can really hear it. Want me to prove it? As a boy he remembered nodding his head. I'll get you up very early, Morse said.

The next morning around 4:00 am Morse shook his sleeping bag and said to follow him if he wanted to hear the dawn break. They hiked fifty yards from camp before Morse found the right spot. They were crouched when Morse looked him in the eye and whispered. You have to be quiet and not make a sound if you want to hear the quiet. He remembered closing his eyes and listening to the sound of his heartbeat.

223

It wasn't long until he heard a very soft roar, maybe a very faint drumroll, which got loader until it was unshakable. The dew was dripping from the leaves, and the birds were airing their wings. It wasn't a break or a crack but rather a slow and quiet drumroll. He looked at Morse and nodded. He would always remember when he and that part-Cherokee-blood listened to the sound of the dawn break.

They didn't get any deer that year, but he got a rabbit. He believed everything Morse said from that day on. Yosemite is now a tourist trap and hard to find parking. He knew he would never go back and take the chance of losing that memory of the gun bearer's dawn break.

Another memory that flashed across his mind was whirlpools. When the sun was too hot, he as a child would jump into the water and let that small whirlpool wash away the beach sand. He came out from the water feeling clean again. He had encountered other whirlpools in life. They were not at the beach or in water, and they always left you feeling dirty. Those were the ones to be careful of because they, as part of that populated ocean, would take you down and keep you there without warning. It was only the luck of the draw if you avoided them.

But outside in the cold and during that last transition, he turned to the last black page of his final dimension. He rolled his board onto its inside edge and continued a perfect carve while listening to that final drumroll.

About the Author

    I have included my two short stories, Not All Together and The Drumroll, with A Physician's Footprint for those who only read paper.
    I have also added two articles I wrote for coastsider.com, an online newspaper, and another for a ski club news letter.

He that troubleth his own house

My mountain bike was my Christmas present to myself. It took several months before my legs could handle the streets of Montara. Part of that time was training my dogs, Fred and Jackie, to heel to the bike.

I soon tried the trails in the Montara Mountains, and there was one that I couldn't get up, well at least peddle up. I must have tried a hundred times. It was impossible, and my wife said to give it up. It's not worth the trouble, she said.

Known to be obsessive, I asked myself if I was bringing trouble to my own house. If so, it was definitely a mole hill.

And then, one day, I saw two guys peddle up, without touching ground. I had made it up that hill many times by pushing my bike. Watching those guys, gave me hope and ammunition. I tried again and made it without touching ground on the forth try. Pace is everything as I found out, and the vendetta had begun!

At the end of the season when the trails became streams and the ground had turned into mud, I had made the hill forty eight times. I told myself that when my career count reached one hundred, I would peddle up on that one hundredth and first time, whip it out, pee on that hill and say, we're even friend. That would be my *beaner*.

By next April the mud had turned hard. The soft dirt was gone, but the silica remained. The ruts were deeper and more slippery than ever, but what the hell, I still had fifty three more to go.

I finished last week with an even fifty. With a three day rest I made the hill today, three for three, bringing my career total to one hundred and one.

After that last assent, with Fred and Jackie at my side, I got off my bike, stood on that hill, whipped it out, and realized that I, in that proverbial wind, had peed on my leg.

Heroes are listed Alphabetically

It was December third when I got the tree up, the lights and the top ornaments. Di could do the rest. There were still a couple of hours remaining that day, and Fred and Jackie needed the run.

It was too cool for shorts. As I got dressed, Fred and Jackie figured out what was happening and started to whine.

Tethered as always, the three of us went up Farallone to the P.O.S.T where I unhooked them. We headed for the grammar school and then turned left, then right at the bench, and then left on Old San Pedro Road.

There's a path to the top of that mountain leading to the old road, where five posts block cars from entrance to the park.

The kids, Fred and Jackie, love that assent because I have to push my bike up to reach the top and those eucalyptus trees. During that time, Fred and Jackie investigate everything. We all drank water at the top. The path leading down is steepest at the top but rocky and less slippery than the second part.

Even though I've done that path forty times, I always stop to take a breath before that decent and wait for the kids to catch up. I always check to see that my feet are squarely on the pedals before releasing the brakes.

My next vision or sight was the sky, with no memory in between that time when my feet rested on the pedals. I was in real pain and flat on my back. I couldn't get up by myself. Oddly enough, my bike was inline with me and laying on its left side.

I was able to dig in my heels and push myself up where I could reach my bike's front wheel and pull it over and parallel to me and then use as a crutch it to get up.

Using my brakes and bike, I used them to get down to a shallower trail. I knew my wife didn't know the park and would never be able to find me. I called Hug, and he was still in his office.

Because he disliked his name Hugo, his friends called him Hug. As soon as he answered, I said, Hug, I took a bad one and don't think I can get home. Can you come and get me?

Maybe we need the paramedics, and it might be better if you called them, he said.

As the phone slid out of my hand I said, Hug, I just made my last call and pitched forward on the trail.

In the arms of a Texas woman

I could see and feel Fred and Jackie licking my face. I've never seen them this scared, probably because I was shaking. I must have passed out because my next recollection was Diane holding me in her arms and wrapping me with her sweatshirt.

Hug, his daughter Victoria, and Di were also there with the ranger, endlessly asking me so many stupid questions.

I awoke again, feeling my body placed onto a gurney and prayed they wouldn't slip or drop me. I awoke in the ambulance.

By the way, Hug and Diane met in the first grade in Houston and were buddies until his family changed school districts when he was in the fifth grade. They met again, reuniting their friendship at Rice University.

Resurrection

During the next thirty-five days at Stanford, Kaiser, and the Pacifica Rehab center, more people have seen me naked than in my entire life, excluding my high school gym class. It was at Kaiser that I learned what happens to rejected airline food.

Hug came to visit me at Pacifica after my bedpan stage. I had lost sixteen pounds and received four units of blood, with my neck, scapula, sternum, ribs, and pelvis fractured by my fall. My punctured lung had already healed by itself.

During the first two weeks, pain avoidance was my constant obsession. I was terrified at the thought of catching a cold. Coughing would have killed me. Besides my wife, Di, I had visits from Hug and my family, including Jeff and Henry. During Hug's visits, I asked him to give me an account of what he did to save my life.

228

Hug's Account

He realized the urgency, shut his office, and hailed Ana, his neighbor, to drive him home where he told his wife and daughter to get on their running shoes. We have to find Cam.

They drove to the top of Old San Pedro Road and each ran a trail. As Hug ran the trail, he saw Fred and Jackie out of the corner of his eye. Fred was standing over me. Whether it was protection or curiosity on my dog's part, I'll never really know.

Hug had called Di and told her how to get there. Victoria was running to the Ranger's house when she met her lifelong friend, Lauren, who relayed that message to the ranger by ridding her bike. I awoke to see them standing over me. Di took the kids and Victoria rode my bike home.

The stanchion tube dinted the crossbar when it smashed against it. Hug later told me that my cell phone lost signal twenty-five feet east of where he found me. That would be where I first fell.

Some Came Running

It was at the Pacifica Rehab center that I was able to reflect on their heroism rather than my own pain. I think I only once saved a life. I was nine years old, at a public pool, when I saw a kid vertically flaying and gasping for air.

I couldn't swim either, so I held on the pool gutter's edge and stretched out my body, so he could grab my foot and pull himself in. There was not one word shared between us. At that age I didn't give a damn about his life, but I sure do about mine, and if I thank them any more it would probably embarrass them. But one can neither set aside the human heart nor the human touch. That was the first time I realized that we are all connected.

I can only relate to the reader that heroes live in every town and can be found alphabetically, and suffice it to say, that on that day, some came running.

Tell 'em they're Beautiful.

Some years ago I was sitting in a Mammoth Shuttle and noticed a skier coming aboard. I saw the gloved left hand holding two pairs of poles and the other clutching the hand rail. One pair was regular and the other had mini skies instead of baskets. The right hand dropped to lift a metal braced leg up the first step. Dropping the poles, the right hand clasped the other handrail and the left hand dropped to pull the other metal braced left leg up the step. The next step was reached as methodically as the first. Holding the vertical bar the skier swung around and sat across from me, picking up the poles.

The skier, dressed in black with a black helmet and visor, took a deep breath, and then she took off her helmet. Her long auburn hair dropped down her back. Her face was tanned, weathered, and well chiseled. Out of eyes which noticed nobody, she looked as if she did not care to rise. Not from the dark side, but the force was definitely with her.

There are times when we are all heroes, and that day she was mine. God, you're beautiful, I wanted to say. Was it caution, prudence, or lack of heart that kept me from telling her how beautiful she was? She was certainly not lacking for heart. My shuttle stop came first, and I got off without saying a word. I never saw her again. She never heard the praise.

I don't fully understand why, but that question has remained with me these many years, and I still observe the seat where she sat when I'm on the Mammoth shuttle.

It could happen to you. Some day you may encounter one of those heroines of heart; so whether you see it as courage or not, be warned my lot, and tell 'em they're beautiful...while you have the chance.

Made in the USA
San Bernardino, CA
12 June 2018